Shadows

of

Humanity

J. Armand

Table of Contents

"Those who cling to life die, and those who defy death live."

— Uesugi Kenshin

Prologue

"I'll be gone a couple days, so try not to wreck the city again. Think you can handle that?"

"It wasn't my fault a parasitic mutant horde nearly wiped out New York City." I defended myself even though I was used to taking crap from him by now.

"That's not how I remember it," he smirked.

"Let me borrow your sunglasses."

"Not a chance. I don't want your grubby hands touching my stuff."

"Come on! What if I need to use my powers around people?"

"Wear a bag over your head if you're worried about scaring people."

"You're an asshole. What do you need sunglasses for, anyway? You haven't even seen the sun in over a hundred years."

"They complete the look." He smiled in approval at his own reflection, brushing his blond hair out of his face.

"Trust me, you don't need sunglasses to look like a complete tool." Using my powers, I moved his sunglasses through the air and settled them on my face. "There, no hands."

"Now I can't wear those anymore; you've tainted them."

"Bye, Noah."

"I hope you realize you owe me a new pair!"

It had been awhile since I last walked the hectic streets of Manhattan. I had just returned from two years of isolation on a mountain in Japan, which made Times Square an even more jarring experience than I remembered. Throngs of tourists, glaring billboard lights, and the deafening sound of traffic filled the air. This was going to take some getting used to again. Despite suffering from extreme culture shock, it felt good to be back in civilization.

Three years ago, I left my sheltered lifestyle in Boston to start a modeling career in New York. I hadn't even gotten my foot in the door when everything went off the rails and I was hurled into a dark world I never knew existed. Mythical things that went bump in the night all turned out to be real. Demons, phantoms, and most of all the undead waged an endless war behind the veil of humanity's ignorance.

That war between three rival undead covens had claimed the lives of my adoptive parents when vying clans attempted to kidnap me. Why were those groups of all-powerful undead so interested in a shy twenty-year-old boy from the Boston suburbs?

Power.

Everybody wants it, few people have it, and those who don't, fear it. It's addictive, it's seductive, and it's volatile in any form it takes. I was born with a gift that first manifested itself when I was a teenager: telekinesis, the ability to move objects with my mind. I didn't always consider it a gift. At first I was scared. I thought I was some kind of freak or a monster. I tried forgetting about it and living like a "normal" person. That wasn't easy once I had attracted the attention of the covens who wanted me enslaved as a soldier in their war.

And my power was how I met Noah.

The pinnacle of masculinity, the apex of athleticism, the epitome of male physical perfection, Noah had the speed and power of a lightning bolt and was even more awe-inspiring to watch in action. He only had one major downfall: his personality. Noah's narcissism was so suffocating you couldn't help but breathe a sigh of relief every time he stopped talking. He had the muscles, skills, and swagger to make anyone weak in the knees and any man seriously doubt his self-confidence, and he *never* missed an opportunity to talk about it.

Buried deep underneath that serious character flaw remained a heart still capable of remorse, deny it though he may. Noah is a member of the illustrious Archios, a coven of undead known for their beauty, allure, and the manipulative games they play with both mortals and undead. But Noah is the black sheep of his people. He has no interest in politics and mind games, and his roguish no-nonsense approach to handling situations often gets him scoffed at. Still, when the shit hits the fan, it's him they all run to for protection. And whether he wants to or not, it is his duty to uphold that service even when it would mean his death.

Noah was sent by his progenitor and coven leader, Aurelia de Saint-Pierre, to stop the other two covens from kidnapping me for their own use. I didn't know it then, but behind her angelic face and charming words, Aurelia's intentions were just as sinister as the rest.

As a human, Noah had fallen for the same facade, so much so that over a hundred years ago he left his family and everything he loved behind in the Wild West to be with her. Seduced by her beauty, he swore his eternal loyalty, and so she granted him the gift of immortality and the curse of vampirism along with it. His love was unrequited. Aurelia never intended him as anything more than a slave to be thrown in the face of danger and deal with her enemies so she didn't have to. Over the years Noah became bitter, but was helpless to take control of his own fate. Aurelia was many times more powerful than even he could ever hope to be and her will was undeniable.

He took pity on me as he watched me become tangled in the same web Aurelia had trapped him in over a hundred years ago. Together we fought back the hordes of mutants created by the hideous Carpathian coven and a demon summoned by the diabolical Strigoi. Not only were my parents a needless casualty of the war, but Noah lost the one person in the world he trusted.

Her name was Vivian. Beautiful, kind, and also Aurelia's progeny, Vivian loved Noah as he did her, but neither of them spoke of it until it was too late for fear of their emotions being used as leverage against them. The final battle to save Manhattan from the Carpathians claimed her, but her death motivated Noah to break his shackles before he was lost, too.

Noah never spoke of his triumph over his former master or just how she met her downfall, and he never discussed Vivian either, choosing to honor her memory in silence. He traveled with me to Japan, where he had once trained to become the killing machine he is today. Before Vivian perished she let me know that Noah respected me after I'd spared him from the Carpathians, even though I knew he had orders to kill me. That was the only definitive clue I had to what Noah really thought of me and why he was going out of his way to teach me survival in the supernatural world. Many times he was harsher than the enemies we had encountered together and his trials often crossed the line of suicidal, even for someone who was as difficult to kill as I was.

Whatever his reasoning was for taking me under his wing, I was grateful to be on his good side, no matter how small that side might be. My life would never be like it had once been; I would never go back to college or pursue a modeling career. Even having human friends was a risk, with one supernatural or the next always interfering in my affairs. If I was to have any chance of survival on my own, I would need to learn how to use my powers to their full potential.

After the loss of my parents, who meant the world to me, it was impossible to focus on simple tasks, let alone vigorous training. Surprisingly, for someone who led such a violent existence, Noah was quite balanced and centered. His Zen-like philosophies, several of which he had tattooed on his body in *kanji*, helped teach me ways of coping with the loss of loved ones and the stress of the new life I was thrust into. They seemed almost cliché at times, and the message behind them frustratingly obvious; but it is often what is right under our noses that is hardest, and most important, to see. He constantly emphasized the importance of trust, and although we had a past checkered with deceit, I felt he had redeemed himself in his own way.

Now, after we'd spent two years at an abandoned Buddhist monk encampment, Noah decided it was time to return to civilization. He said he had business to take care of and that was fine by me. It gave me a chance to reconnect with an old friend.

Chapter One

"Lyle!" I pounded on the door of the apartment where I had stayed before leaving for Japan. "Open up! Search warrant!"

"What's all the noise? Do you have any idea what hour it is? People are trying to sleep here!"

"Yeah, it's 7 PM ..." I responded to the voice coming from the apartment door across the hall before remembering our elderly neighbors. "Oh. Hi, Estelle."

"Dorian? Is that Dorian? What are you doing back here?" Estelle was everything I thought she would be within the first minute of talking to her: whimsical, just senile enough to be cute, and just nosy enough to be helpful. I never knew my grandparents — they passed away before I was adopted — but I would have wanted them to be just like Estelle and Jacob.

"It's me, Estelle."

"What are you making so much noise for? And why are you wearing sunglasses? You're too young to be getting the cataracts."

"I'm here to visit Lyle. Do you know if he left for work?"

Estelle and her husband, Jacob, were huge fans of Lyle due to his being a police officer. They thought living across from a cop was prime real estate and acted like he ran the city.

Their admiration for him was deserved, but it wasn't just his badge that made him a hero. I met Lyle when he was still a rookie on the force, which unfortunately for him was also the same time a mutant plague swept across Manhattan. To make matters worse, most of Lyle's co-workers were under the hypnotic control of those responsible for the plague. With only a handgun and an unwavering sense of courage, Lyle survived the apocalyptic event and helped save millions of lives, including my own.

"Why, he moved last year, dear."

"Moved?" Lyle loved New York City and the NYPD as much as he loved women. I couldn't see him going far. I didn't have a cell phone or any way to contact Lyle. We had also parted ways on a bad note.

"Yes. Are you feeling all right?" Estelle stepped out from her apartment to whisper to me in the hall. "You aren't involved with drugs, are you? Is that why you left? Is that why you're wearing those glasses? Are you high right now?"

"Estelle, no! I was studying abroad. We just lost touch. I'm going to check the precinct to see if he's on duty. It was good seeing you." I kept backing away as I got myself out of the conversation and headed back down to the street.

It was the last week in November and already dark outside. This was always my favorite time of the year: I loved breathing in the crisp air, dry leaves crunching under my feet, and the mounting anticipation for the holidays. But fall hasn't been that way in some time. I haven't celebrated a holiday in two years, and the last time I did was with Lyle's family in Ohio. He refused to leave me behind to spend my first holiday alone since my parents' death. At the time I hated him for dragging me into an awkward situation, but I was grateful for all the effort his family put into making me feel welcomed.

I walked briskly up Lexington Avenue toward Lyle's precinct on East 102nd Street. It was getting colder out as the moon came into view and all I had on were a T-shirt and jogging pants acquired at the airport in Osaka. I debated hopping on the 6 train, but the only money I had was a twenty-dollar bill.

It's funny how much something matters just because the people around you have it. When Noah brought me to the Ōmine mountain range in Nara, Japan, I didn't know quite what to expect. He wasn't big on easing me into anything, and since we first met his methods had always been a tad unorthodox.

The moment we arrived, Noah stripped me of my cell phone and wallet, leaving me with only the clothes on my back. He told me not to leave the area under any circumstances and not to be noticeable or disruptive. The concept of respect was a gray area with him, but I could tell he held this place and its inhabitants in the high regard.

The mountains there are well-known for their rich culture and ties to the occult. Ascetic hermits known as the *Yamabushi* have lived there for many generations and are believed to have supernatural powers and spiritual clarity. Noah had trained with them over a century ago, but he had something different in mind for my pilgrimage.

He left me in the middle of nowhere overnight without a clue of what I should be doing. My first thought was to try and find him, but after another day passed I realized he didn't want to be found. It was my stomach that put me on the right track. I was getting delirious with hunger by the end of the second day and I had no idea if I could die of starvation.

A ritual was cast to save me when I became infected by the same parasite that was mutating the citizens of Manhattan. As an unexpected side effect I was thought to have achieved some level of immortality, but the limits of that theory were never fully tested. I had recovered from fatal wounds in seconds and my hair and nails stopped growing unless I cut them, but wasn't sure if I still needed to breathe or eat.

Days turned into weeks waiting for Noah on that mountain. After one sad attempt at making a meal out of a rabbit, I decided to stick to berries and fish I found in a stream. I didn't want to kill. The bloodlust and apathy toward life that had built up inside me when facing the disaster in New York had begun to recede. I started to like being alone on the mountain; it was serene and I had no worries other than finding food. I actually started feeling human again, even if I was living like an animal.

I lost track of time after the first two weeks and came to appreciate the simplicity of having nothing. Now, after two years, things like money felt unnecessary. Sure, I *wanted* it, but I didn't *need* it. Money and material goods were supposed to make life easier, more comfortable. Looking back at my life before Japan, it seems like those things are less of a luxury and more the result of social anxiety. You won't die if you don't have the highest-paying job on the block. The world won't end if you don't get that flat-screen TV.

I felt the crumpled bill in my pocket as I passed another subway stop. Is coveting this piece of paper worth all the stress it brings? Probably not. Still, I'm not against trading it for some coffee.

A few more blocks through Spanish Harlem and I'd be at the precinct. Everything here had such a different vibe from the rest of Manhattan. The buildings were all drab grays and browns; the only real color anywhere was the graffiti. Manhattan was so lively and full of lights, with unique storefronts and skyscrapers, yet this part of the city somehow felt tired. Lyle loved working here, though. According to him, this area had come a long way since he was a kid, and I think he liked feeling that he was helping make a difference.

A group of guys standing around in front of a bodega got my attention. One of them looked at me as I walked by and I could tell right away there was something different about him. Unspoken words hung between us in the brief seconds that our eyes met. I wondered if the people he was with knew about him — if he even knew about himself. He looked just like the rest of them on the outside; baggy clothes, skull cap, tattoos on his face. But what he was on the inside would drastically change people's opinion about him.

He was supernatural, like me. I didn't know what kind exactly, but I could see it in his eyes. The eyes are always a dead giveaway when you know what you're looking for — when you're one of them. Other supernaturals I'd met had told me that in the past, supernaturals lived among humans openly; it's where most fairytales and legends came from. They were even worshipped as gods by some. Now, humanity greatly outnumbers supernatural beings and technology outclasses most of our powers.

Like lepers, we're forced to keep our true nature a secret to avoid persecution. I didn't know what was happening to me when I found out I had powers and there was no one I could ask. I can only imagine how many more of us are out there feeling lost and confused, scared of what they are and what people will think. I was fortunate to have run into Lyle years ago. He just seemed to accept everything, unlike how most people in society think.

I was worried about what kind of reception I'd get when I saw him. The last time we saw each other we had an argument about what I was doing with my life. I wanted to be human and lead a normal life, but after losing my parents and being hunted like an animal I started to suffer from post-traumatic stress disorder. It was hard getting used to daily life again, even with Lyle's help. I was constantly paranoid, especially once the sun went down. It scared me that anyone I got close to, friend or otherwise, would be in danger just because of their association with me.

The only thing that had given me some amount of solace was taking things into my own hands and preemptively looking for trouble to deal with. Lyle was in on my vigilantism for a time and it earned him a lot of street cred as the lone officer who stopped a record number of crimes each night thanks to my help. People started getting suspicious after a while and Lyle wanted out. He argued that I wasn't stopping crime for the right reasons. According to him, I was just venting my anger and frustration on criminals and not doing it to help clean up the city. I didn't see why my intent made a difference. But to him I was walking a fine line, in danger of becoming just as bad as those who manipulated things behind the scenes for their personal games. He wanted me to get a job and play human. Although part of me wanted to start a career, make friends, and find love, that desire felt like a reminder of things I could never have for long. Things got heated so one night I decided to leave, and then Noah approached me about going to Japan.

I never got to say goodbye or even let Lyle know I was leaving. After I cooled down I tried to convince myself he was better off without me. But now that the precinct was in sight I had a knot in my stomach that got worse with every step. Everything should have been fine, though ...

Chapter Two

"Quit? What do you mean, he quit? Lyle would never quit."

"Well, he did. Left the force a little over a year ago," the silver-haired officer behind the front desk answered. "Surprised us all. Kid showed real promise, too. Just came in one day and said it wasn't for him anymore."

"Did he say what he wanted to do instead?" That knot in my stomach was about to burst. I had just lost my best friend — my only friend — for good because of a stupid argument.

"Nope, sorry. Listen, I can't spend time chit-chatting." The officer's attention shifted to some of his co-workers, who had just walked in. "Hey,

Hernandez. You used to hang out with that Turner kid, right? This guy is asking about him."

I remembered Hernandez. I had never heard anyone use his first name, but he was always part of the group when I went out with Lyle and his cop buddies. We used to go down to a sports bar in Times Square to watch the game whenever the Yankees played. Between the two of them there wasn't a single woman that walked by who didn't get attention.

"Hey, man. Dorian, right? Long time. How you been?" Hernandez's friendly greeting was a good sign. At least Lyle hadn't told his friends I was involved in drugs.

"I'm all right. I'd be better if I knew where Lyle went. I just got back in town and found out he moved and quit."

"I don't know, man. I tried to call him after he handed in his badge, but he got cagey. Didn't really seem like he wanted to talk and by the next day his phone wasn't in service anymore. The boys are saying he peaked too early. Probably burnt himself out and didn't know where else to go once he was on top. It happens."

"Do you know if he moved before he quit? He's not at the old apartment we shared."

"It had to be right after he quit. Some of the guys went to visit after work, but he was gone. Neighbor said he moved the same day. You could try asking his old partner. I thought quitting and moving must have been on his mind a while for him to have a new place lined up so quick."

"The schoolboy?" I asked. After Lyle was promoted to sergeant he was given a rookie to train who looked like he was still in high school.

"Yeah, man. He's a big shot now, just got a promotion and transferred down to the East Village. Turner had the golden touch when he was showing him the ropes I guess. He ain't so little anymore. He's bigger than you!"

"Ouch." That hurt. I'd be turning twenty-four in March and still looked like a boyish, fresh-faced, barely twenty-year-old. Thanks, immortality. Couldn't I have stopped aging around twenty-five at least? Maybe by then I'd be able to grow some facial hair. "Thanks, Hernandez."

"Stay safe. If you get hold of Turner tell him to look me up."

There had to be more to this. Lyle would never have quit the NYPD or bailed on his friends like that. Lyle took so much pride in being on the force. His father had been a cop and had died on the job. All Lyle talked about was how he wanted to make his father proud.

A homeless woman on the sidewalk was hugging a small cat for warmth. I bent down and handed her the twenty from my pocket. They needed it a lot more than I did. She blessed my soul a multitude of times as I walked away, but it didn't help take my mind off what might have happened to Lyle. Did he "peak too early" because of all the action we had been through? Maybe he was in trouble. What if someone was after me again and got to him first, like Noah had warned me about?

Heading downtown to speak with his former partner wouldn't get me anywhere. If this had anything to do with the supernatural it would be covered up too well. His mom had moved to Dayton, Ohio to be with her sisters when I was still living here. Noah would be back by tomorrow night, so I couldn't leave the city to go searching in a completely different state.

I took a seat on a park bench and closed my eyes to contemplate my options. It was nice and quiet for the moment. I wanted to let myself drift off to sleep, but I was too on guard in my new surroundings. My paranoia had nothing to do with the neighborhood itself; I hadn't slept more than a few hours at a time in years, and almost never without experiencing night terrors the first year abroad. Dreams of monsters and of my dead parents constantly plagued me. It didn't help that a few weeks after I had finally achieved some sense of calm in Japan, Noah decided to shake things up by attacking me in my sleep.

It wasn't like the funny or obnoxious pranks that college kids love to play on each other. Noah full-on attacked me. He had stabbed his *wakizashi* through the palm of my hand.

"You can't leave yourself open, especially not when sleeping. That's when people are expecting you to drop your guard," he told me. I never knew when he was going to strike again.

Sometimes days or weeks went by until I'd get ambushed, but each time was worse than the one before. I had been beaten, stabbed, poisoned, and even thrown from a cliff while blindfolded. It didn't take long for me to start sleeping with one eye open. I'd take catnaps throughout the day instead of trying to settle in and give Noah another opportunity.

Of course Noah couldn't just give me my beating and leave; he had to be smug about it, too. That was what really motivated me even further. Noah was too damn fast and stealthy to give off any indication he was closing in. After a while he started ambushing me when I was awake just to rub it in.

Even though I healed in a matter of seconds, I still felt the pain as a stinging reminder that he was taunting me. So, I got creative. I set a trap, if you could call it that. I hid in a crevasse and covered myself over with leaves to be less conspicuous while I pretended to sleep. I knew it would be too tempting for him to resist foiling my pathetic attempt at camouflage. Within the hour he struck.

I took a blade to the forearm, but before he could get away I used my telekinetic power to wrest the sword from his hand and fly off with it. He grabbed me by the ankle before I could get more than a few feet off the ground, but I kept going up and took him with me.

"Give me back the sword or I'll tear your leg off, you little shit!" He threatened as we cleared the trees below. Noah was always expecting me to just roll over whenever things got dangerous, but I had already been through so much I wasn't sure how else to prove I was ready for the next step.

"Go ahead! I'll still have your sword and it's a long way down." I didn't doubt he could survive the fall, but the fact that I showed him he wasn't untouchable was more than enough for me. I could swear I saw a faint smile of approval right before he let go and disappeared into the clouds, but he never admitted to it. When I woke up on my own, Noah's sword was gone from my hands and I still had all of my appendages intact. For a very short time after that I slept well and had blissful dreams of flying free.

I stopped myself from dozing off on the park bench and headed to Central Park. I had no money and nowhere to stay; the park was the most obvious place to hide out, not to mention the closest thing to the nature that I was used to. Less than a block from the park, I could feel something wrong in the air.

Noah had been teaching me to pay attention to what I *couldn't* see when looking for danger. The real threats out there weren't just going to walk right up and announce themselves. Since I couldn't use my powers without seeing the target I was no better off than any other human in the dark. Noah had the brilliant idea of temporarily removing my eyes by replacing them with rocks so they wouldn't regrow, but I talked him into just using a blindfold by promising I wouldn't cheat.

Noah and I went over the basic martial arts techniques that we had practiced earlier, but this time without my vision. Of course, it wouldn't have been a fair fight even if I could see and he didn't use his superhuman speed; Noah could bench press a small car with ease and had more combat experience under his belt than every martial arts grandmaster combined. Sparring with him was meant to train me how to use my telekinesis to anticipate and block incoming hits that my body wasn't fast enough to react to and my eyes couldn't see. I lived that way for a year, even searching and hunting for food through the use of my other senses, and periodically attempting to thwart ambushes from Noah. Eventually, my powers helped me develop a sixth sense, something like telekinetic sonar. I could project my telekinesis to radiate around me at very low power and feel the objects it came into contact with.

And that was exactly how I knew I was being followed into the park.

The intrusive sights, sounds, and smells of the city weren't too much for me to pick up on the invisible stalker lurking a few feet behind. It wasn't Noah testing me, or anyone nearly as talented as him, because they wouldn't be keeping such a close distance between us. That was bad news for them. Without the element of surprise on their side, I was leading them on a leash into a trap. I wanted to spring my trap far from any innocent bystanders, and I didn't want to risk the slightest chance of being caught.

We were deep in the park when I could hear the very faint sound of the breeze moving around the invisible figure behind me. Whoever my stalker was, they were a real amateur. I brought them to a dark, secluded spot not far from the Alice in Wonderland statues and turned to face my second shadow.

I smiled at the empty air before me and took my sunglasses off so whoever was there could see my eyes change as I pinned my stalker against a tree.

"I'd say nice try, but that's being too generous." Wow! I'd been around Noah for so long I was starting to sound like him. A bearded middle-aged man in a tattered brown hoodie covered with stains stared back at me. He didn't seem bothered as the whites of my eyes turned black, leaving only the gray ring from my natural color.

"Relax! I'm just here to deliver a message." There they were: the elongated canine teeth when he spoke. "Your grandpa wants you to visit."

"Is that supposed to be some sort of joke? My grandparents are dead."

Noah had instructed me not to get involved with any supernaturals during my time in New York. The consequences were never good, according to him, but he didn't trust anybody. It was sad to me that we couldn't trust our own kind, especially since supernaturals were such a minority, but at least I had Noah on my side.

"This guy is dead too, I mean like me, you know." The bearded man pointed to his teeth. An undead grandfather of mine? Only one person came to mind and he certainly wasn't what I would consider family.

"What does he want?" I released the man from my telekinetic grip. "Grampy," as people called him, wasn't bad for an undead bloodsucker. In fact, his insight was startlingly accurate in ways, although his eccentric demeanor made him difficult to take seriously. I wasn't about to look down on him for his strange antics, though. He had tried to warn me about the crisis in Manhattan before it happened. If he was getting in touch again, it was probably to be helpful.

"I don't know. I'm just a fang-for-hire. He didn't tell me anything except to give you that message."

"Take me to him then," I ordered.

"You gonna pay?"

"That depends. What'll they call you if I take the fangs out of your fangs-for-hire?"

"All right! Relax already. Damn. He's squatting in a burnt-down apartment building in the projects. Head up to West 138th — it's not far from the hospital." The mercenary wouldn't stop twitching and scratching his arms and face while he talked. I didn't think the undead could tweak out, but this guy was in serious need of a fix.

"What's wrong with you? You need blood?"

"Not unless you got some stuff to go with it." He was looking around, even more paranoid than before.

"Stuff? What the hell are you talking about?"

"You know, stuff. Snow, blow, crack ..."

"I wasn't offering you my blood, and for the second time tonight: I'm not on drugs. How does that even work if you're undead?"

He looked at me like I was stupid. As if this was in the brochure when I found out about the supernatural. "Drinking from users passes on some of the high."

"Great. Well, enjoy yourself." The end of that grimy conversation was the perfect segue into a visit with Grampy.

Grampy's building was just what I expected: a filthy, hollowed-out shell of what was once part of a low-incoming housing project. What I didn't expect was for it to be filled with other neck-biters in addition to him. They all looked like homeless men and women of varying ages. None of them gave me more than a passing glance as I let myself in. It was nice feeling accepted by them, knowing none of us had to hide our identities. These vagrant undead were called the Outsiders for their lack of affiliation with any of the three major covens or their signature traits.

The whole place was covered in dust, most of the windows were broken or blacked out, and the rooms were decorated with arrangements of musty mixed-and-matched furniture that must have been recovered from the trash. It wasn't the nicest place, but it was home, I guess. Some teenagers in hoodies and leather jackets were sitting around an old TV playing ... video games? This was unusual. I hadn't expected to see the immortal undead partake in something so youthful for entertainment.

"Hey, do any of you know where Grampy is?"

One of the kids waiting for his turn to play pointed upstairs, never taking his eyes off the screen. His face was made up to look like a skull with black and white face paint. Obviously, blending in wasn't his first priority, but then again maybe the irony behind his self-expression was disguise enough.

A room on the second floor stood out from the rest. The door was open a crack, enough for me to notice the sea of pink inside. It looked like someone had covered the room in bubble gum from floor to ceiling. Everything was painted pink, including the furniture. There was a pink wooden pony for a child to ride on, a queen-size bed with pink sheets and a pink comforter with cartoon princesses on them, a dollhouse in the shape of a fairytale castle, and a large pink toy box filled with dolls. The only thing of a different color was a massive flat-screen TV playing some black-and-white monster movie. The little girl watching it from a pink beanbag chair was dressed in a pink ballerina tutu and clutched a black stuffed cat made out of socks with two buttons for eyes. She was probably the cleanest thing in the whole building; her hair was perfectly combed and her clothes were spotless. She took notice of my bewilderment in the hallway and ran over to hiss at me and slam the door shut.

"Nice to see you again too, Emilia," I said to the closed door.

"Ahoy, there! You came!" An old man's voice greeted me cheerfully. I couldn't see anyone and my powers weren't picking up any hidden people around.

"Where are you, Grampy?"

A broken chair next to some garbage jiggled and then transformed into the nutjob I was here for.

"I was takin' a nap," he stated casually and shuffled over to me.

"You can turn into a chair? What kind of power is that?"

"All smoke and mirrors, my boy! No point in being invisible if I got kids runnin' 'round that can feel me out. Better to give ya something to see and overlook instead! Mhm!"

"How did you know I could do that? Nobody was around except Noah when I learned."

"'Cuz you just told me, silly."

"That's not an acceptable answer." I tried to keep a straight face and stare him down, but the strange old man was too amusing to stay serious around for long.

"But an answer nonetheless! Now, what did you bring your Grampy?"

"Bring you? I didn't bring you anything. You sent for me; I came. I didn't think this was a dinner invitation, seeing as I don't share your acquired taste."

"Terrible guest, just terrible. And I see you're still blindly following your elders, if not respecting them! I was hoping you'd bring drapes. I need new drapes for the penthouse suite."

"Did you invite me here just to show off your housekeeping skills?" I knew there was more to him than his ramblings by now, but he had a way of very rapidly eroding my patience.

"'Course not. There's a storm comin' though. You're welcome to stay if ya need a place out of the rain." His hospitality was disarming. Part of me was touched by his offer because I knew it was genuine, but I was still weary of dealing with his kind. "Or maybe it was a fire?"

"I'll be fine. I don't mind the rain."

"Oh ho ho! So you're a tough guy now, huh? Go on a little trip and you're not the quivering pup from Boston anymore?"

"I was trained by the best." It was a little hurtful to be called a "quivering pup." I thought I had held my own the last time I was here.

"You mean that Archios? Pffah! He's just a kid playing with toy swords. You want real training, try living for yourself!"

Grampy was really pushing it now. Noah might have been an arrogant prick, but there's no way anyone could deny he was the best out there. Even though it shouldn't have, it still pissed me off to hear someone speak ill of him. "You wouldn't say that to his face and I don't want you saying it to mine, either."

"You could always try to find the sergeant." Grampy didn't seem at all bothered by my aggressive defense of an Archios.

"Find him? What do you know? Where is he?"

"Don't know, honest! But I could make it my business to know, if you do somethin' for little old me first."

"Uh-huh. And you look down on the Archios for being manipulative? What is it you need?"

"I'm askin' for a favor. A big one, I know. But you were trained by the best and all that, so I figure it should be a snap." He gave me a wide toothy grin from behind a foul-smelling bushy gray beard that was caked in god knew what. "There's somethin' strange about. Just showed up tonight and started killing us off. Thought you might know 'bout it since you just got here too. I'm 'fraid they might find us here and ... Well, I just couldn't bear to see my little darling get hurt."

"Little darling? You mean Emilia? The girl you kidnapped?" Technically he rescued her, but I was feeling a bit spiteful from his comment about Noah.

"I've been taking in wayward souls longer than you've been alive, boy! I didn't kidnap nobody and you know that! Her keepers would have tossed her for dead when they found out she got the disease. I saved her by turning her, but now I might not be able to save her again. We're not fighters and the hired fangs just won't cut it. But you — you took down an Ancient and ya got that big ol' friend of yours."

"Fine." I agreed even though I knew I'd regret it. "Where is this happening?"

"All over. Can't keep track of 'em and nobody who survived got a good look. That's all I know. Just make 'em stop, any way you know how."

I wouldn't be surprised if Noah set this up as a test by throwing Grampy a few bucks. I was going to chase shadows around the city only to find out they were Noah. Noah's involvement would explain how Grampy knew I was back in the city so fast, but I couldn't see Noah putting up with him long enough to strike a deal.

"Yeah, okay, I'm on it. Just find me info on Lyle by tomorrow night and we're even."

"Hoo-hoo! Couldn't be happier!" He waddled off down the hall and shouted back to me just before turning into a room. "Just don't get yerself jumpin' at every shadow now! Remember, the dark is our friend! Would serve ya well to get acquainted with it nice and intimate-like."

On my way out I looked with some amusement at the Outsiders tending to their home. Someone was decorating a dingy room with "Coming Soon" and "Under Construction" signs taken from various stores. Another was feeding bread to some rats in a pen that he had decorated with those tiny umbrellas you put in drinks. I was happy that they had found something to enjoy and call their own. Grampy was right about learning to survive, though. They might have shelter, but they couldn't really defend themselves. They weren't in any real danger at the moment, but it felt good that I had gotten strong enough for them to rely on me.

Using the shadows behind the building as cover, I flew up top to scope out the area from the roof. "Hey." I gave an unkempt Outsider woman tending to some pigeons a grin. It wouldn't be too difficult to remain undetected in Harlem, but once I got further downtown I'd have to be extra careful going from rooftop to rooftop.

If I knew Noah, he wouldn't make this easy on me. He'd want me in the busiest, most distracting place possible so he could jump down and ridicule me for not paying close enough attention. The best place for that would have to be Times Square. He'd be able to see me coming from blocks away, so I wanted to be as high up as possible to have any sort of chance at spotting him.

I could tell when I was getting closer to Times Square by the bright lights and pungent smell of pretzels and exhaust fumes. I wasn't sure what made that so prevalent in my mind, but I had had a strong scent memory ever since passing my first street vendor in the city.

Looking for Noah was a lot trickier than I had anticipated. The traffic alone was making me dizzy as I tried to scan for anything out of the ordinary, and the buildings were too high to see the ground accurately from above. I'd have to try something else. *He can't think I'd be able to find him like this*, I thought.

I landed in an alley right as someone dashed away into the darkness. I followed, hoping it wasn't a human that I had just scared the life out of. The alley led to an empty dead end with no fire escape or windows. I couldn't sense anyone around. Whoever I was following had to be Noah or at least someone fast enough to get away without me noticing. There were almost no supernaturals at Noah's level and after training with him I knew his style pretty well. This had to be Noah.

I went back to the roof to see if he had run up the wall. There was no sight of him, but I knew he wouldn't go too far. He'd want to stay in the area to keep taunting me. Staying out of sight wasn't easy here with all the lights. There was an abundance of bars, clubs, and restaurants around. I noticed a figure run out the back exit of a nightclub and start fiddling with a manhole cover on a side street. It wasn't Noah, and I couldn't picture an Archios getting its hands dirty, but it certainly had me curious.

Down on the street the figure — a man in suit with a terrified look on his face — turned to me as I landed, pausing before entering the manhole. I'd been wrong about the Archios getting their hands dirty. The Archios were notorious for being the best at blending in with mortals; they had infiltrated the government, the media, and many major companies. This guy was practically impossible to differentiate from a human except for the Archios' signature aesthetic of being a little *too* perfect.

"Wha —" I didn't get to finish asking what was wrong. The man was stabbed through the chest from behind and crumbled into ash. I didn't get a good look at who did it, but I knew it was Noah from the quick glimpse I got of his blade before he was gone again.

"Noah, what the hell?!" I couldn't abide by him killing random people just to test me, even if they weren't human. I dumped the man's suit in the sewer and replaced the cover to get rid of any evidence. I knew Noah liked to show off, but he was normally good about hiding his tracks and was against needless and sloppy killing. He was really pulling out all the stops. I knew if I didn't take care of that little detail he'd get me for it later.

A fit of loud screams came from back at the plaza in Times Square. The screaming spread into a full-blown riot and soon people filled the side street where I stood. Some people stopped along the way to take pictures and video with their phones. There was no way I'd be able to find a hiding place to fly away from now. I waded through the crowd to see the first responders trying to calm the situation. Beyond them in the now-empty plaza was ... absolutely nothing. I tried listening to what people were saying, but everyone was frantic.

"He cut his head right off!"

"I saw it!" Two friends shouted at each other over the screams. The police were fighting the tide, trying to calm everybody down.

"It was just a hoax, people! Nothing to be afraid of. Just another street magician trying to go viral," a policewoman yelled over the uproar. I would have been inclined to believe her assessment if it weren't for the pile of clothes blowing against the barricade of the plaza.

Was Noah really getting that reckless? Or was his arrogance just getting the best of him? I had to stay focused despite all the confusion, and it was a good thing I did. I spotted Noah's shadow up on one of the billboards overlooking the crowd. There wasn't an easy way to get up there without going around the block first.

I was sprinting down the sidewalk to find somewhere I could fly from when a man in a trucker's hat and red parka pushed past me. He came up behind a couple holding hands and shoved one of them to the ground.

"Fags!" The man in the hat jeered and spit at the guys before running off.

That word alone made my skin crawl. I put on my sunglasses and kept my eyes on him as he ran. I would have loved to send him into traffic.

Instead, the man in the hat had his own fateful encounter with the pavement when he mysteriously lost his footing, slammed into a street sign, and fell back onto a row of motorcycles. I thought karma could use a little telekinetic help. I heard swearing coming from the group of bikers who had just watched their rides get knocked over. I looked back to see them surround the bigot, who was cowering under them as the couple he had assaulted walked past with a smile.

I made it up and around to where I'd seen Noah on the billboard, but of course there was no sign of him anywhere. It was going to be sunrise soon and I was getting tired. This game of tag would have to end. I wondered where he would hide for the day. He had never given any indication of where he went to sleep or feed when we were in Japan. Maybe he still didn't trust me enough to leave himself vulnerable. Tonight was turning out to be a complete failure. Taking Grampy up on a place to stay might not be a bad idea. At least I could check in to see if he'd found out anything about Lyle.

The pigeon lady wasn't on the roof when I returned. The sun would be up in an hour, so she could have been inside. However, something was off. Everything was so quiet. The door was open, but I couldn't hear any sounds coming from inside.

Ashes and piles of worn clothes lined the side of the stairwell as I made my way down. One of the teenagers' hoodies was caught on the broken glass of a window and the others were strewn about in the ashes. The lights were still on in the building. The killer was either sloppy or didn't feel the need to cut the power.

"Grampy? Emilia? Anybody?!" I ran downstairs, wishing I had stayed there from the start. Someone really was hunting the Outsiders, but if that was the case, why go after the Archios downtown, too? Emilia's door was open, but there was no sign of her anywhere. I checked around the room for any signs of her hiding. My heart sank when I found ashes coming from under a closet door. There wasn't anyone left and it was making me angrier by the second. These guys played video games and kept rats and pigeons as pets. They were innocent and didn't deserve to be hunted. Emilia was just a little girl, an actual little girl, no more than maybe eight years old.

I searched the rest of the apartments on the floor in vain. I came across a locked door and knocked, hoping for some sign of life — or unlife.

Nothing.

This place was cleared out. I forced the lock and let myself in to take a look around. The room was set up like a very dirty makeshift office. I checked out the desk, which was made out of two beat-up garbage cans with a door resting across them. There were stacks of paper everywhere. Some of them were especially colorful — crayon and marker pictures drawn by Emilia. Most of them depicted her and Grampy together and were titled "Grampy and Me" or "My Grampy." They looked happy. Other pictures were of the rest of the Outsiders she lived with; I could tell by the hoodies and pointy teeth. Those pictures were titled "My Minions." The man with the rats and woman with her pigeons were in a few pictures too; those were titled "My Friends."

Seeing this was just making me feel worse, but there was another paper that looked interesting. It was an old medical form that had been badly water damaged and stuck to some sort of certification. Most of the writing was illegible. From what I could make out, someone named "Octavio Jules" was certified to practice psychiatric medicine. All that was left of the address was Amsterdam, New York. The paper was dated 1893. Could that have been one of the Outsiders? It seemed like a pretty strange thing for them to collect at random, but then again they were all a bit strange to start with.

I took a look around the room again. A fake Christmas tree in a pot, a torn-up couch near the desk, a broken tape recorder and lamp next to a big cushioned chair — was this an attempt at recreating a psychiatrist's office? There was a picture without a frame nailed to the wall behind the couch. It was a sepia photo of a prestigious-looking bearded man in a suit and top hat. Judging by the quality of the photo, it appeared to be from the turn of the twentieth century.

The man in the photo seemed familiar somehow. He almost looked like Grampy. I pulled the picture off the wall and flipped it over. The back had the name Octavio on the back and the start of a date, "July 20th, 19 —" The rest of the date was covered by a stain. The more I stared at the photo, the more I could see it being Grampy.

"What happened to you, Octavio?" I asked myself out loud. "How did you go from the man in this picture to the senile hobo I knew?" My head hurt just thinking about it. He was a doctor, like my parents. Even in his current state he was trying to help people who were down on their luck in his own eccentric way.

Footsteps creaked along the floorboards downstairs, putting a stop to my investigation. Someone was still here.

Chapter Three

I floated down the stairs to avoid alerting anyone of my presence. Whoever was still here could be a survivor — or a potential threat. I told myself I shouldn't be concerned. Noah had prepared me for situations like this. I just had to stay focused and keep a clear mind.

The footsteps were slow and heavy; someone was carrying out their own recon. Sneaking around buildings like this was an unwanted habit, but one I was getting good at. Most of the apartment doors had been taken off their hinges, making it easier to scope out the basic floor plan with a quick peek. I followed the graffiti-laden hallway to the last place I'd heard the footsteps and landed with my back against the wall to listen. There was definitely still someone inside the next apartment. Again I wondered whether this was the person responsible for what had happened. Was the amount of noise they were making sloppiness? Or were they just so strong they didn't need to bother with stealth?

I never would have been able to guess the sight that greeted me around the corner of the doorframe. A hooded man was kneeling in the ashes of some poor Outsider and praying to the rosary in his hand. The act alone was curious enough, considering that the undead consider themselves cursed by God, but the man's clothes were what really puzzled me. Maybe "clothes" wasn't the right word to describe what I saw.

A flashlight's blinding glare pierced the room. I'd been spotted already. How annoying. "Oh, you're not one of *them*." He spoke flatly and turned off the flashlight, putting it back in his pocket. "What are you doing here?"

The man before me was no more than a few years my senior at most — and completely human. He was thin and relatively nondescript except for a pair of blue eyes and auburn hair that stood out against his pale skin. Maybe he smoked, or just hadn't slept in days, because his face was unusually drawn for someone so young. But it was the costume he was wearing that I couldn't figure out. Dressed in a combination of brown leather and chainmail garb, he looked as though he was headed to a renaissance faire. The heavy footsteps earlier were from a pair of medieval-esque boots. A sheathed sword and dagger etched with inscriptions were strapped to his side. If not for the weapons' immaculate craftsmanship, I would have laughed him off as some roleplaying weirdo come to see the "haunted house" at a really inconvenient time. Of course, if he had been supernatural, I have viewed him as a threat considering the age he would have to be for those clothes to be authentic.

"I was told it was safe to crash here. I'm homeless." One thing the Archios taught me by example: lie and deny *everything*. While it wasn't technically a lie, I doubted he had any involvement with what was going on in here and I wanted to keep it that way.

"This place is far from safe. Who told you that?" Unfortunately, I'm a horrible liar.

"Um, other homeless people?" Why couldn't he be an eight-foot tall abomination so we could fight and get it over with? Somehow this was so much worse. "Why are you dressed like King Arthur?"

He wasn't as amused by that as I was and pushed past me into the hall. "Would you call yourself a man of faith?"

"Sure, yeah." I *had* defeated two demons, after all. That should count for something. I never put much thought into God's existence when I was growing up. My parents were very scientific and I was never left looking for answers to life. When the Strigoi explained that the undead had come about through God's curse on the first demon-tempered mortals, I accepted it as fact. All of these other supernatural beings were real; why not God? "Why?"

"This place is evil."

I had to hold back a laugh. "You mean like drugs? Prostitution?"

"The Devil." He was so serious it made me question how far he was prepared to take this whole act. What could this guy possibly know about evil demons? "This place is a nest for the damned."

"I don't see anyone." I looked around skeptically.

"Because it looks like the place has been cleansed. Someone was here ahead of me. All the hellspawn are gone."

"Oh? Who would that be? A friend of yours?" I hoped he didn't have friends with him. All I needed was some guy dressed in a wizard outfit joining in.

"No. I don't know who it was, but you should thank God for watching over you. Whoever sent you here was leading you into a trap. What did they look like?"

"I don't remember, but they seemed nice." I forced myself not to cringe as he walked over the ashes of a poor Outsider.

"That's how they lure you in. They play to your sympathies and tempt your desires." He wasn't wrong. The problem was that not *all* of them were like that.

"Look, I don't know about all this demon stuff. I'm new to the area and was just here for a place to sleep."

"Take my advice and go back to where you came from. This city is a land of sin." He took something out of his pocket and shoved it into my hand on his way out. "There is a church close to here if you need somewhere to go. I'll pray for you."

"Thanks." He'd given me some bills and a few coins. Eight dollars in Euros. What was I supposed to do with Euros in Manhattan? Still, it was a nice gesture of charity. I pitied the poor guy, hoping he never ran into any of the "damned" he was looking for. I doubt he'd have even been a match for Octavio.

There was a loud crash over by the entrance. I headed over to see what the man was up to now and found him pushing broken furniture away from the door.

"By the way." He addressed me without turning around. "How did you get in here? I barricaded this when I came in and the windows are too high to climb to."

"Yeah, I thought the door was locked so I used the fire escape." I hurried outside to end the conversation as quickly as possible. All this lying was making me feel guilty. But how would he react if he found out what I really was? Or was his distain reserved for the undead alone?

Daylight was almost finished encroaching on the horizon. My body decided that had I put off sleep long enough. I waited alongside the apartment building to be sure I hadn't been followed. The streets up in this part of the city were coming to life again. No one stopped or was even aware of the murders taking place right in front of them. The supernaturals' own veil of anonymity was causing them to suffer and fall in silence. My hands were also tied by that charade, making it impossible to find the same help afforded to the masses we interacted with every day. They controlled our fate, while most of them were none the wiser as to who we really were on the inside. The hatred of the few had poisoned the minds of the many into apathetic quiescence over the years.

I sat against a dumpster and stared vacantly at the ground, too tired to get up and find a safer place to rest. I had been looking at the same manhole cover for ten minutes when I was reminded of the Archios by Times Square. What if some of the Outsiders had managed to escape? I had to take the chance and go down there.

The cover flipped into the air and I was gone before it landed back in place. I hit my head in the first tunnel and lost Noah's sunglasses in the sewage. The ceilings were too low to levitate in some areas, forcing me to wade through muck up to my ankles. It wouldn't have been an adventure without me smelling like something nasty; the stink indicated that coming down here was the right decision. I wished I didn't have to search for survivors alone, but waiting for Noah would waste precious time.

Maintenance lights scattered along the winding paths provided a momentary respite from the darkness. I had no idea what direction the Outsiders would take or if they had an emergency hideout. I'd probably have tried to leave the city altogether, but I doubted they were organized enough to have any formal escape plan.

Venturing into the subterranean labyrinth of New York City was as fruitless as it was foul. I couldn't find anything besides rats the size of a small dog. There was no way for me to tell how long

I had been in the sewer tunnels, but the further I traveled the more hopeless finding anyone seemed. What would that Archios from before even do down here? They weren't the most robust and would probably have a meltdown if they got dirty, even if their life depended on it.

I was definitely going about this wrong. I should have found other Archios to question when it was still nighttime. With all their connections they must have an idea of who was after them and how to stop it. The only other covens were the Strigoi and the Carpathians, but the Carpathians had to still be licking their wounds from their defeat three years ago ... right?

I crawled out from the sewers and into the raw morning air to find I had only traveled about thirty blocks north. I was hoping to have covered more ground. Doubts plagued my mind. Should I have kept searching underground? I needed some rest and a change of clothes before I could gain an audience with the Archios. I hated stealing, but I'd have to do it again to get by as I had in the past. The opportunity presented itself a block away with a clothing donation box. I supposed that was better than taking from someone trying to make a living.

After donning a white hoodie, a pair of unintentionally ripped jeans, and beaten-up sneakers, I was set to find somewhere to sleep — preferably someplace warm. I was right outside Highbridge Park, but it would be too cold to stay there for any length of time dressed like I was and I didn't want to take warmer clothes away from anyone who needed them more. Except for the noise, the subway tunnels were a great place to take refuge.

I wasn't too familiar with this part of the city, but it didn't take long to find a subway stop nearby on 168th street. I settled in on a bench and had barely closed my eyes for more than a few minutes when I felt a tap on my shoulder.

"You can't sleep here," a man in dark blue pants with a handgun and handcuffs at his waist announced. "We'll talk more when I'm home. Go back to the apartment for now. I need to train this newbie."

"Wh—what did you just say?" By the time I looked up and my eyes adjusted to the light, the man was walking away.

"Lyle?" I shouted at the back of his blond head as he left through a turnstile. He didn't stop, but I knew it was him. Those were the last words he said to me. The turnstile stuck when I tried to follow him. People were standing around, but I didn't care. I forced open the gate with my powers and ran until I caught up with him. He turned. Before I could see his face, the flashlight in his hand blinded me.

I woke up back on the bench, disoriented and drenched in sweat, as a train roared by. It had been a while since I'd had a panic attack in my sleep and I didn't miss them. I told myself that it was only a dream, but it still left me rattled. Even after all my recent training I was losing people and had no control over it.

The clock above me read 4:34 PM. I had slept through a good part of the day. The sun would be going down soon, and that meant the Archios would be awake and I could finally get some answers. I hopped on the next train going downtown to avoid being seen. The dream still had my mind scrambled and I was distracted by guilt. When staying with Lyle after the war I had made the same immature mistake that cost my parents their life by bringing trouble to their doorstep.

I got to Times Square by sundown, but out of the millions of people not one Archios was to be found. Circling the area brought me to Fifth Avenue. There *had* to be Archios here. Fifth Avenue was the epicenter of luxury and extravagance; they ate this stuff up. An uneventful couple of hours staked out along the strip paid off in spades. A black Lexus pulled up in front of a Tiffany's jewelry store across the street right as the lights turned off inside. Like clockwork three impeccably dressed people emerged from the store and marched to the car. A petite blonde woman in a business suit and glasses locked up behind her while she talked on her cellphone, a tall African-American man carrying a briefcase and wearing an earpiece opened the back door of the car, and between them a rather fit and well-manicured gentleman in his early forties locked eyes with me for a moment before entering the car.

Jackpot.

I shot up to the rooftops in private to tail them more easily. Now my only hope was that they wouldn't take me out of state. It looked like tonight was my night, though; after only three blocks the black Lexus pulled into the parking garage of a very fancy high-rise. I shouldn't have been surprised, but this guy really needed an entourage to go three blocks? From what I could tell they were all human except for him, which meant the escort was more for show than security. There wasn't a doubt in my mind that the penthouse was his so I went up ahead to the balcony.

I perched on the head of a stone gargoyle, from which I could see perfectly into the penthouse. The apartment door opened after a few minutes and in walked my Archios. His eyes went to me immediately and before his assistant could walk in behind him, he ushered her back out and closed the door.

"Not very subtle," he mocked and went to his bar to pour a drink as I let myself in through an open balcony door.

"I wasn't trying to be. I'm here for information that could help us both."

"I would ask you to sit, but the help just finished cleaning the upholstery this morning and we're fresh out of plastic covers." His attitude was getting on my nerves, especially because of how undeserved it was. I shattered the glass in his hand to show him I meant business and his reaction was worth every overpriced cent that glass must have cost. "I see a bit of civility is out of the question. I don't suppose the Strigoi could have programmed you with some manners in their laboratory."

I raised an eyebrow and shattered the wine bottle he was pouring from, letting wine splash all over his suit.

"Do you have any inkling of how much this suit cost?!" he bellowed. "What am I saying? Of course you don't."

"You know who I am?" I asked.

"Not by choice. I was one of those in charge of cleaning up the aftermath from your brawl with the Carpathians that almost ruined the city. Did you think that sort of evidence would just erase itself? Humans are everywhere and they get into everything you don't want them to. Social media has only made it harder on us. Mortals may have short, fragile lives, but the Internet never forgets."

"Fragile? You're not supposed to kill them, you're only supposed to erase their memories."

"Yes, yes, absolutely. Time is money, though and when you are in the diamond industry like myself money is everything. The needs of the many outweigh those of the few. Unfortunately for them, I have just too many in need of my time."

"I was worried about *saving* the city, and all you were interested in was hiding behind a computer. It's easy to pass judgment when you're at a keyboard and not out there facing the world."

"My apologies. How ever can I help you then, great hero? Maybe you would like to break a mirror or two?" There was an undertone of necessary caution in his sarcasm. I wanted to deck him.

"Just tell me what you know about the killings that started last night. I'm sure *you* must be in the know about everything happening around here."

"There isn't a bounty out yet, but I admire your ambition. I should think you'd know more about that matter than me, anyway."

"What are you talking about?"

"Rumor has it the one hunting us is one of us, a particularly swift and stealthy hunter with an eastern flair. That should sound familiar to you, no?"

"Your sources are wrong. I've heard better rumors in a high-school cafeteria. He's been with me the whole time," I lied to see what else I could get out of him. "What reason would he have to start randomly killing his own kind?"

"Orders are orders, I suppose. I try not to question things over my head; it's bad for business." Orders? Noah wouldn't take orders from anyone except Aurelia, and that hadn't wound up going her way in the end. Did this guy not know that Aurelia had finally been destroyed? I thought news spread fast, but I supposed it was possible people thought she had just hidden away after her mansion was demolished by her sister. "Now, if you'd be so kind as to uninvite yourself, I have dinner guests on the way."

I left the balcony without a word and headed back to Fifth Avenue. Could Noah really be doing this? Was that why he had wanted to come back so suddenly, and why everything had started as soon as we returned? I had seen his sword kill the Archios in Times Square with my own eyes, but since then I'd been trying to deny it. I didn't want to believe he could be responsible for something like that of his own volition.

Finding more Archios wouldn't be worth it if they didn't know anything, and I couldn't deal with another attitude like the last one in the same night. I could trail the jeweler instead and wait for him to be attacked. But sitting around like one of his bodyguards felt demeaning even if it was for a good cause.

"Urgh!" I couldn't withhold my disgust as something soggy whacked me across the face and then plopped into my lap. "What the hell?"

"Nice catch." Noah was crouched on a parapet above, looking quite amused with himself as always. "If that had been an enemy you'd be dead right now, or at least temporarily in a few pieces."

Whatever was in the wet paper bag smelled good. Inside was a mess of melted cheese and tomato sauce. "Is this ... pizza?"

"Yeah, I didn't want to hear you whining about being hungry all night like on the flight here."

"I said it *once*. That's hardly whining. But thanks." I was starving. Even if I didn't have to eat to stay alive, I still got hungry, and right about then I would have eaten out of the garbage if I had to. "I'm just going to ask straight out: have you been killing people?"

"I'm always killing people. It's what I do. How do you think I got that pizza?"

"I'm being serious. Someone has been killing both the Outsiders and the Archios in the city and they seem to think it's you. I saw someone with a sword like yours killing Archios in Times Square."

"Did you get it for me?"

"Get what for you?"

"The sword."

"No. They disappeared before I could even see who it was, which made me think it might have really been you."

"I get you pizza and that's how you repay me? You know I like sharp objects. Where are my sunglasses, by the way?"

"In a sewer uptown." I lowered my eyes guiltily as I picked at the pizza.

"I'm going to strap you to a boulder and throw you into the ocean. But first we have a flight to catch."

"We can't leave yet. Someone might be impersonating you and killing a lot of innocent people."

"So what?"

"You seem like someone whose reputation would matter to him. Unless it really is you."

"It's *not* me. When have I ever misled you?"

"Okay, fine. You have to help me solve this, though. Lyle is missing and may be in trouble too."

"I don't have to do anything." He jumped down and loomed over me with his arms crossed, trying to intimidate me. "I don't answer to anybody, especially you. And who gives a fuck about that cop or this city? Let them handle their own problems."

"I care." I stared back at him defiantly.

"Then I guess this is where we part ways. Probably for the best. It's grossing me out watching you eat that slop."

Appealing to his sense of humanity was the wrong approach. I should have known that from the start. "What's the point of training me if we just run away at the first sign of a challenge? Why are you so anxious to leave? Are you scared whoever is impersonating you might actually be better?"

Noah turned back toward me and glared. "Seriously? *You* are trying to manipulate *me*?" I hadn't been scared of Noah for some time, but the way he was looking at me made me slide back as he advanced.

"Did it work?" I asked, hoping some humor would interrupt his pending rage.

"Was it a nice sword?"

"Um, I don't know ... maybe?"

"Useless. I guess I'll have to see for myself. I wouldn't expect you to know quality if it stabbed you in the forehead anyway."

"Thanks," I said, unsure whether it was greed or sympathy that had changed his mind.

"I meant what I said about the cop. Forget him."

"He's the only other friend I have besides you."

"We're not friends." I expected him to say something like that. I wasn't sure if he even meant it or if he was just taking another dig at me to cover up the fact that he was doing something nice. "People you like tend to end up dead or missing, so for my own sake let's keep this strictly business. The cop either moved on with his life, or he's dead. Either way, you can't change that. If you go after him when he doesn't want to be found you'll just be causing him trouble. I say good for him if he managed to escape this life."

"What if he was kidnapped to get to me?" I asked.

"Don't you think if someone went through the trouble to set a trap like that they'd know where you were already? If he's still alive he's probably got a new life and forgotten who you even are. Don't be so self-centered. Not everything is about you. It's about me." He smirked. "Now show me where you last saw my new sword."

"Follow me," I told him. I didn't realize it sounded like an order until it slipped out. He didn't react and we made it to the street without an issue. "He was right there. At least I think it was a he." I pointed and retraced my steps into Times Square where I had last seen the person on the billboard.

"Then what?" Noah asked at the end of my tour.

"Then I went back to the Outsiders who asked me for help."

"And they were all dead?"

"Yeah."

"Wow. You're either a cold-blooded sociopath or an idiot, and the fact that you have me out here trying to save some nobodies has me think it's the latter. You keep making the exact same mistake. How many people have to die before you learn not to bring trouble back with you?"

"I was trying to protect them! They were already dead when I got there." I knew Noah was right. It was time to let Lyle and the Outsiders go, if any of them were still alive.

"Because whoever did this was faster than you. You knew that already when you thought it was me. And there was nothing left at their place? No footprint in the ashes or anything?"

"Not that I could tell. There was this weird human dressed like King Arthur sniffing around, but he didn't know anything."

Noah squinted at me questioningly without a word.

"He was going on about God and demons and then gave me money because I said I was homeless." I pulled out the eight Euros to show him. "I think he was just some weirdo who likes to dress up and go to haunted houses. He probably saw a lot of strange things going on in that building."

Noah snatched the money out of my hand. "This'll go to the new pair of sunglasses you owe me. So, did you kill this guy?"

"No, why would I? He was harmless."

"I don't know, why not?"

"Because you taught me not to kill without purpose and there's no honor in killing the weak," I said, and shoved more pizza crust in my mouth.

"Oh, you actually bought that?"

"Of course I did!" Hearing him say that made my heart sink. It was those teachings that had given some much-needed serenity in this bloodthirsty world.

"I'm kidding. Calm down. I'm surprised you paid attention. It isn't easy to tell with you." Noah laughed from the shadows. "I already have a plan for luring out this wannabe. All we need is bait."

"Ooh, I have the *perfect* person."

Chapter Four

"This was your big plan?"

"Eh." Noah shrugged. "I felt like keeping it simple."

He dropped the body of the jeweler I had had the pleasure of dealing with earlier to the floor and removed the *wakizashi* embedded in the man's heart.

"You can't do this! Do you know who I am?" The Archios sputtered and looked around in disgust at his surroundings.

"I hate it when people ask that. Obviously I know who you are: you're bait." Noah cleaned his sword and sheathed it at his hip. "Now, either you stay here or I cut something off for every attempt you make to escape."

"What is this place? Why bring me here? You're an Archios too, you lunatic!" The man continued to complain.

"It's the Outsiders' old hideout, from before they were all killed. Which is what we're trying to keep from happening to the Archios," I explained. "The imposter is more likely to come back to a place he already knows."

"I can't be the bait if the killer is impersonating me, dumbass," Noah added. "They're not going to want to blow their cover by letting us be seen together."

"I thought you were the killer! And why are *you* helping him? Weren't you here to save us?" The jeweler turned to me from where he cowered in the debris. His arrogance had melted away to expose the sniveling coward he was, and it was so satisfying.

"The needs of the many outweigh those of the few, right? Think of it this way; your sacrifice will serve a greater cause." I smiled down at him and walked out with Noah, who slammed the door, locking the man inside.

"We're not really going to let him die though, right?" I had to ask to be sure.

"I don't know, whatever." Noah dismissed my concern flippantly. "I'm gonna take off. You got this. Don't forget to get me that sword."

"Where are you going? You were supposed to be hiding out with me to ambush the imposter!" I panicked at being sent back to square one again. "I can't do this alone."

"About that, I'm not really in a patient mood. Just get a vantage point and wait to disarm him like we practiced in Japan."

"Don't you think if I could do that I would have in the first place?" I shouted at nothing. Noah was already gone. He wanted me to do what I knew I had to from the start. No excuses.

I sat around for hours watching from the rooftop next door as the jeweler nervously paced the rooms of the apartment building, occasionally checking to see if I was still on duty. And then it happened, right as night turned to day. The jeweler strayed further from the windows to avoid the first beams of sunlight and find a spot to sleep. I saw a tiny glint of light in one of the windows. It was reflecting off the sword I was looking for.

I flew down in a hurry and crashed through the window with my focus on the sword. Wielded by a shadowy figure, the blade pierced the jeweler's chest. I tackled the shadow and grabbed the hilt of the sword to pull it from the jeweler, but it was too late. The man's wide-eyed expression of pain and fear as he was reduced to ash would be burned into my memory. It was one evil taking out another, but I felt the weight of guilt in my heart. I had failed and doomed this man through cruelty, not justice.

It didn't make sense. The undead could take far more punishment than that and walk away from it. Why had a single stab wound finished him off?

Up close, I could see the blade wasn't exactly like Noah's. It was a full-length *katana* that seemed to pulse with energy although there were no visual effects to confirm this. The shadow dispersed into nothingness and I had been holding the *katana* for only a few seconds when Noah appeared. He stayed just out of reach of the sunlight coming in from the window behind me.

"Good job. I'll be back tonight," was all he said before disappearing again and taking the *katana* with him. "Good job" was not something I was used to hearing from him and it was even more rare when it wasn't laced with sarcasm. Normally, his praise would have excited me — a mark of progress or skill. However, all I could see was the man's face as he died.

I left the apartment building, now in broad daylight, and took refuge beside the dumpster in the adjacent alley. I was tired again, more mentally than physically this time. I curled up on the cold concrete, hugging myself as my stomach growled. I listened to pedestrians' conversations to take my mind off everything.

"Call me tomorrow?" a woman's voice asked from the sidewalk. "It would be nice if you'd call me for a change."

She was probably on a cell phone since I couldn't hear a response. Footsteps came down the alley in my direction. I was in a huge city and yet someone had to invade my miniscule piece of it when I was trying to sleep.

"Oh." She was standing over me and I could hear her much more clearly. "Your father and I have a surprise for you when you come back for the Fourth of July."

I knew that voice and yet I didn't want to look up. It was my mother's voice, repeating the last conversation I'd ever had with her. I squeezed my eyes shut until they hurt, but I felt someone nearby put something on me. There was a nudge. The intruder shook me until I opened my eyes. When I did, I saw a familiar pair of leather boots in my face and a blanket wrapped around me.

"Oh no," I moaned, instantly recognizing who they belonged to.

"I think you were having a nightmare."

"I'm fine," I muttered and pulled my hood over my face as far as I could.

"I saw what you did."

Crap. Like the jeweler said, humans were everywhere and saw everything. But why did it have to be this human again?

"What are you talking about?" I asked, hoping he meant he'd seen me take from the clothes donation box.

"You killed that creature."

I closed my eyes again to see if I'd get lucky. Maybe this was another dream. How much had he seen? I was worried.

"Don't worry. I'm not going to tell anyone."

"There's nothing to tell," I said and looked up at him. Except for the boots, he wasn't wearing his medieval getup — just blue jeans, a white button-down, and a parka. I would never have picked him out of a crowd as the type to dress up and pretend to be a fantasy hero.

"I know your secret. You don't have to hide it from me."

"What secret is that?" I was starting to get a little nervous.

"You're the one who cleansed this building the other night. I knew it when I saw you hadn't moved the barricade. You were in there the whole time, before me."

"I told you I don't know anything about that." If only I could tell this guy the truth. It would blow his mind. He was persistent, but I'd be out of the city by tonight, and with no way to erase his memories all I could do was deny it.

"I know you're troubled because you've seen things that others wouldn't believe, but I do. You're doing the Lord's work and I'm here to help you."

My conscience was making me feel bad for pretending this guy was crazy, but I couldn't confirm anything that would motivate him to get involved. "What exactly did you see?"

"I wasn't far when I heard glass shatter. When I got there you were holding your sword in the creature as it died, then another came and stole the sword." I didn't know if it was because he seemed to be in awe of finding someone he thought was like him, or if it was just that he wasn't in his costume, but he came off meeker than he had before — like he didn't have much of a presence to him. "It's no coincidence that we met. I prayed for a way to fight these demons and the Lord answered with an ally."

"I wasn't there to kill anybody or fight any demons. I was trying to score drugs, okay?"

"Then where are they?"

"I ate them. I don't know! Just leave me alone."

"Then it's a miracle you're still alive," he half-joked. "You can lie to me, but you can't lie to God. You don't have to fight alone. We're brothers, after all."

"Brothers ... ?" I didn't know why, but that word struck something in me.

"We're all God's children. Those chosen to enact his will, like us, are closest of all."

I remained silent. This guy wasn't going to give up and I'd never be able to change his mind. He was going to get himself killed, but I didn't want it to be my fault. It was amazing he wasn't dead already. Part of me wanted to tell him the truth so at least he'd have a fighting chance.

"What's your name?" he asked. I still didn't answer, so he held out his hand in greeting and introduced himself. "William."

"Thanks for the blanket," I mumbled, and curled tighter into a ball under it to avoid shaking hands.

"You're welcome. If you won't tell me your name, at least let me take you somewhere to get a hot meal and a shower."

"No. I'm fine." My stomach growled and completely blew my cover. "Do you do this with every homeless person you see?"

"Whenever I can. I didn't think you were really homeless at first until I saw you sleeping here."

All this talking, especially about food, was making me feel weak with hunger. My eyelids felt heavier by the second and the cold wasn't helping. I wanted to fall asleep, but William wasn't letting me.

"Are you okay?" I heard him ask, followed by something else I didn't catch. Everything went dark for a brief moment. William was still there when I opened my eyes, only now he was holding a paper bag.

"Since you won't come with me so I can help you, this will have to do." He held out the bag, which contained something that smelled delicious. I hesitated taking it from him, but it smelled too good to resist and he probably wouldn't give up anyway.

"Why are you so insistent on helping me?" My eyes lit up when I saw the cheeseburger, fries, and bottled water inside the bag. Best of all, he didn't throw it at my face.

"I know what I saw and I know what's out there."

"I didn't kill anyone," I repeated.

"Okay, I believe you."

"You do?" I asked between bites.

"That *thing* wasn't technically alive, so you couldn't have killed it. But you did save plenty of lives by banishing it from this world. You're going to be in danger now that the one who took your sword saw you kill one of its brethren. That must be their leader. It was a good thing the sun came up when it did. Assuming it is the master of that nest, you won't be able to fight it by yourself should it come back for you. Together we can banish the creature back to Hell."

It was a good thing Noah didn't believe in killing the weak or this guy would be screwed. "I'm not going to be here much longer. I'm just passing through."

"So am I. I need to get back to my brothers soon. It might be best to have them help us. There are more of the damned in this city than I thought."

"You travel with your family to go looking for monsters?"

"They aren't my birth family. We're hunters that operate as a brotherhood."

"What does your real family think about you doing this?" Every shred of common sense was telling me not to get involved any more than I already was. But if this guy wasn't just some crazy roleplaying geek that meant that there were humans out there surviving in the supernatural and mortal worlds simultaneously. How long could they really last before ending up on the backs of milk cartons or in a grave marked "John" or "Jane Doe?" I remembered being told about how hunters helped with the anarchy left by the Carpathians during the Black Plague. Had a new generation of hunters taken up the mantle of their ancestors in the wake of the Carpathians' most recent plot?

"They don't," he answered abruptly with a hint of spite in his voice, but he immediately returned to his amiable demeanor. "If I get you a place to stay for a few days, will you wait for me to return with my brothers?"

This was the nicest anyone had been to me in a while, and yet I knew the kindest thing I could do in return was keep my distance. What if he and his "brothers" truly did know how to take care of themselves? They could be allies, friends ... family. But what about Noah? How open would they be to the idea that not all of the undead were bad — just most of them? And what would they think of me and my powers?

"I can't promise that," I said after some consideration. "Let's just say these monsters you're talking about are real. How do you fight them if they have magical powers? Do you have your own?"

"No, not exactly. We use our God-given ingenuity. Sorcery defies the Lord's will. If He wanted us to have it, we all would. It is a temptation of the Devil to take the easy path through our trials on Earth. Those who turn to magic corrupt their mortal souls and may never reach the gates of Heaven because we did not live as God intended us to."

This was going to be a problem. Maybe he just hadn't met anyone supernatural who wasn't evil yet and would change his mind if he found out.

"Where are these brothers of yours?"

"England." He seemed to perk up at my interest.

"That sort of explains the Euros."

"Sorry," he apologized. "I didn't realize when I handed them over. I've only been here a few days and that's all the cash I had left on me from my other travels. Were you able to use them anywhere?"

"No. Someone took them."

"Oh," he said dejectedly. "Then let me get you that room to make it up to you."

I was cold, dirty, and exhausted, and I knew what was coming once Noah returned. He'd throw me in the ice-cold river to clean me off so he wouldn't have to smell me on our flight.

"One night." I agreed to compromise.

"At least two," he bargained.

We walked to a motel near Highbridge Park where I had been earlier. "How come you don't have an accent if you're from England?" I asked on our way there.

"I'm from Canada originally."

"Don't you have a job? How can you take time off to go fight the forces of Hell?"

"You have a lot of questions for someone who won't tell me his name."

He had a point. "I'm Dorian." Immediately I realized I should have used a fake name, but it felt like lying to a priest. It was bad enough I was deceiving him about what I really was, but the truth would come out when I was ready.

"I'm a photographer, so I can set my own schedule. Money isn't really a problem. We all help each other out and there's enough of it to go around."

"That must be nice. Do you ever take pictures of supernatural stuff? You could make a lot of money, I bet." I was hoping he would be smart enough not to paint an even bigger target on his back.

"No. No one credible would believe it. Photography is my escape so I like to keep it separate. Nature is my favorite subject matter. I love the beauty in all of God's creations and always find something new to capture."

I expected us to stop at the motel's front desk to check in, but William already had a room. I was under the impression that someone who was so free with his money would spend more lavishly on himself. The room was small, with only a single bed and fading décor that probably hadn't been thoroughly dusted or updated since the motel opened for business thirty or so years ago. That was also about how old the matching TV and VCR set was. Everything about the room was sad. Even the moth-eaten pastel curtains made the windows look like they were crying. If I thought the stale, recirculated air in the room was hard to breathe, the bathroom was worse. Running water was all I really cared about, though, and the thought of a hot shower was as exciting as Christmas morning for a kid.

William's costume was laid out on the dresser next to the TV. He probably didn't have to worry about room service coming through and asking questions here.

"Does dressing like King Arthur really help you fight crime or is it just to look cool?" I motioned to the outfit.

"It's blessed." He smiled admiringly at the clothes. I still wasn't convinced how serious he was. "I'm serious. The armor has magical properties that protect whoever wears it from evil."

"I thought you said magic was a no-no."

"I'm not the one using magic. The divine enchantment was a gift from God."

"Who made the armor in the first place to be enchanted then?" I wasn't sure I bought all this, but after seeing what the Strigoi could do, anything was possible.

"It's been handed down for generations in the Brotherhood. I assume one of the founders crafted it centuries ago."

"And the weapons?"

"I made those." He said it in such a matter-of-fact way, but I would never have guessed this skinny photographer from Canada was involved in all this. "I ... have a lot of free time."

"I wouldn't think you had any after fighting the forces of evil and keeping a job. How many have you actually killed?"

"Seventeen this week. In total, I don't know, but it isn't enough. I'm going to run some errands before I have to leave for England, so you can have the room. It's paid for until Tuesday." His shift in conversation was a bit awkward and I had a feeling I might have hit a nerve, as I had when I'd mentioned his family. I had to stay optimistic that I could change his mind about the undead being evil.

"I have no idea what day it even is." I had only been immortal for a few years and already time had no meaning anymore.

"It's Saturday," he answered and headed out the door.

"You're leaving me here with your holy relics?" A bit surprising, but I couldn't exactly see myself trying to pawn them on the street.

"I trust you."

Chapter Five

Shedding the remains of the past few days' adventure felt as refreshing emotionally as it was physically. The hot shower couldn't have come at a more welcome time. Looking back, I didn't know if I had accomplished anything at all aside from adding another layer of dirt to my body. I had disarmed the stalking shadow that wielded that odd sword, but wouldn't he find another weapon with which to continue his extermination? One more Archios had died, even if his death was warranted for killing human witnesses. I myself only had played witness to it despite William's perspective.

And then there was William himself. A potential ally, but I had done nothing to merit his trust except being in the wrong place at the right time. He didn't even know what I really was but he had already made up his mind. I felt like I was misleading him. None of this was going to sit well with Noah. There needed to be some compromise. I thought if anyone were going to budge it would be William. All I really had to show for myself from the past few days was washing down the drain.

I had just finished my shower when I heard a commotion from the hall, followed by the sound of a fire alarm. So much for getting any sleep. I threw my clothes back on and left the room. People were evacuating, but one woman was left standing in front of her room looking in and crying at the billowing smoke. I ran over to see what was wrong, but the smoke quickly turned thick and black, making it hard to breathe.

"It's my friend Michelle," she sobbed. I checked the room as flames spread to the bed from a static-displaying TV. There was a lump under the covers. I ran in and pulled off the sheets to find my parents' bodies, contorted by rigor mortis, staring back up at me. Not again, not here too ... This had never happened when I was still in Japan. Why was I seeing all of these things now?

I turned to leave the room. The sobbing woman was replaced by Minerva, who scowled at me. She was my worst nightmare on two feet. The same Strigoi turned demoness who orchestrated my creation and then abduction was staring me in the face.

"You can *never* stop it!" she hissed. The door slammed, trapping me in the fire. I could feel the pain of my skin burning as I went down with the room. It was so real, yet I had to keep telling myself it wasn't until I blacked out.

I awoke back in the shower. The water was scalding and the steam choking. Without my regeneration I would have been in the hospital burn unit for sure. Semi-conscious, I dried off and dragged myself to bed. I wasn't even sure if sleep was what I wanted. Regardless, I succumbed to temptation and drifted off.

It was dark out when I woke up again. I paced the brown carpet of the small room trying to decide what to do. William would probably be back any minute. Did I really want to enable the insanity of a mortal hunting evil by joining him?

I left the motel and rushed down the street to the park so I wouldn't run into William. "I'm ready to get out of here." The voice came from above me the second I passed the park gates. Noah was kicked back in a tree with his arms behind his head, the new *katana* on his lap.

"What about the killings?"

"Who cares?" Noah jumped down to face me. "A swordsman without a sword is merely a man."

"That doesn't make sense. He can get another weapon."

"I'll still have his pride. If he wants it back he'll have to come get it. Any swordsman worth his weight will follow his blade to the ends of the Earth."

Smart. Noah and I would be drawing the killer out and away from any more potential victims in the city.

"Remember that guy I met who was dressed like King Arthur? I kind of made friends with him."

"And now we have to put him down?"

"No! He's a … hunter, and I think —"

"You *think*?" Noah interrupted. "You never think. You get all needy for a friend like a puppy and then when it goes wrong you can't understand why. Now it's not even a normal human, but a hunter. Real smart. Does he have any idea what the hell you are?"

"No … I mean not yet."

"You're a moron. First you're whining about wanting to save every piece of shit this city has to offer, then you buddy up to someone who kills our kind. Pick a side. You either trust me or you don't."

"Why do you have to berate me any time I'm friendly with someone? You keep telling me to trust you, but you never reciprocate that trust. There doesn't have to be two sides. We can work together. He's already aware of the supernatural world and how to survive in it. It isn't like I'm pulling him into something unknown that will get him killed."

The more Noah insulted me, the more I was motivated to rebel. He was jaded and refused to see there was still good in the world. It didn't all have to be loneliness and solitude.

"You're pissing me off." He poked me with his *katana* in an attempt to be playful. "When are you going to —"

A blinding flash pierced the dark shroud of night around us in the empty park. Noah grunted in pain. His exposed skin had been charred down to the bone with third- and fourth-degree burns. I had seen that same intense light before. When I looked behind me I saw William in his armor holding out some sort of amulet in Noah's direction. I put my hands up to stop him, but Noah beat me to it. He dashed into William and punched him clear across the park. William's body smashed through the door of a car parked on the other end.

"No!" I shouted. There was no way William could have survived. If his neck hadn't snapped, the broken ribs puncturing his internal organs would do him in within seconds.

"It was a mistake ever trying to help you," Noah snarled. His body looked like a statue made of charcoal. "When your new pets find out what you really are and turn on you, don't come looking for me. I want you to remember that you did this to yourself."

Noah was gone, along with our friendship. I saw the pain in his eyes mixed with anger before he left. I wanted to apologize. He was the last person I had ever thought I would put in danger, and now somehow I had screwed that up, too.

I ran over to check on William's body. Nobody even came over to see what happened. The world was cruel and unforgiving. How was anyone supposed to know the right decision before it was made? At every turn something out there was trying to twist the good will of others.

I kneeled down beside William's slumped body. He was still breathing. How was that even possible? I knew I shouldn't move him in case anything was broken, which it surely was. I yelled for help as I checked his pockets for a cell phone.

"Stop," he protested weakly. "I'm all right."

"How are you alive? How are you *conscious?*"

"The armor. I told you. It's blessed." He sat up easily for someone who had just been thrown a hundred feet and crumpled like a rag doll. He wasn't making it up. He was the real deal. "Do you see now why I want you to come with me?"

What other option did I have? Stay in the city chasing my tail?

"I didn't think we'd be taking a private plane *and* a limo," I said as we pulled away from Bristol Airport. I was trying to seem captivated by the novelty, but the flight would have been a lot more enjoyable if William hadn't read passages from the Bible the whole way. I admired his dedication to his faith, though. Anything that gave someone a sense of direction and inner peace had my respect.

"It makes travels a lot more simple. Otherwise, I'm not a big fan of luxury in excess." William still had his nose buried in the Good Book. I, on the other hand, was in complete awe of the scenery Bath offered as we drove through. *I could have finished my degree in architecture by now*, I thought. Bath was famous for its Roman architecture, which was always my favorite. This trip was turning out to be such a tease. But who was to say I couldn't return to school when all of this was over? The Archios mingled in human society. William maintained a normal life along with his supernatural one. Noah was angry at the world and dealt with it by hiding, but I didn't have to. As long as I kept to myself, like I used to, others wouldn't be in danger. Life wasn't easy for anyone, but trying to sequester myself wasn't a solution. The world was meant to be explored, no matter how much I had let myself be convinced otherwise.

"You said you'd tell me about that amulet." William had promised to tell me everything once we got to the Brotherhood, but the anticipation was maddening. I was anxious to know what could have done that much damage to Noah and how it had gotten into human hands. Most of all, I wanted to know the details of what I was getting myself into.

He fished the mysterious trinket from his backpack and held it out for me to see. "I call it the Archangel Amulet."

Appropriately named, the amulet comprised angelic feathered wings made of silver that folded over to hold a milky-white teardrop gemstone. Even at rest the gemstone had a soothing ethereal glow and appeared to be moving as if it were made of liquid.

"Where did you get it?" I asked.

"It was entrusted to me by the Holy Spirit in a dream one night shortly after I joined the Brotherhood. It's how I knew my purpose was with them and I was destined to help purge the evil from this world."

"No wonder you're so confident."

"It's my faith that gives the amulet its light, not the other way around. Beings of pure evil don't stand a chance against Heaven's wrath."

Did that mean Noah was evil? He was a lot of things, but once I'd gotten to know him, it had never occurred to me to think of him as evil. What would this amulet do to someone like Emilia or Octavio? I was sure they weren't evil.

"When did you join the Brotherhood?"

"I was sixteen." His answers about his personal life were always so abrupt for someone so friendly.

"That's pretty young to be out there hunting, isn't it? What about school? Your parents were okay with that?"

"I went to school." Again, another short answer.

"Are the others like you?" I wasn't sure quite what I was getting at, but I figured if I left it vague he might be more apt to open up.

"My age? Some of them. There are only a few of us where we're going. Chapters in other English counties have more members I've heard, but I've never visited them personally. You'll fit in fine, don't worry. Best of all, you'll never be cold or hungry again."

We continued our drive through Bath in silence until we reached the countryside.

"Here we are," William announced more cheerfully as we rolled up to the gatehouse. The road branched off to a collection of moderately sized mansions scattered about the grounds. I was *not* dressed for this — not that I ever was, but I had been under the impression we'd be going to some monastery or a church.

"To your place, sir?" the driver asked William.

"No, we're stopping by Carter's first."

The limo dropped us off at the second house from the left. Compared to Aurelia's enormous chateau, these mansions resembled quaint dollhouses that could fit in her ballroom. Still, the stone façade, mahogany doors, and bay windows of the immaculately restored nineteenth-century country villa were magnificent in their own right. Inside was similarly breathtaking. I spent more time eyeing the wood paneling and detailed molding than noticing the rather dapper-looking gentleman in a smoking jacket who had come to greet us.

"William, my boy! Good to have you back. How was your trip?" He was in his mid-to-late fifties with slicked-back salt-and-pepper hair.

"Not too good, Carter. New York —"

"Splendid! And this must be young Daniel," Carter interrupted, offering me his hand.

"Dorian." I corrected and shook his hand. He promptly cleaned it on his velvet jacket. It was almost like he knew I had been swimming in sewage prior to coming here. I didn't think I had ever seen someone wear a smoking jacket in person.

"Right then. Well, I won't keep you boys from … whatever it was you came here for. Just remember the rules, William." Carter strolled from the foyer. I wanted to find something nice to say about Carter, but it wasn't in his ability to leave a good first impression.

"What rules?" I asked William after I was sure Carter was gone.

"Nothing. House rules. Standard stuff." That wasn't convincing. What did Carter think William was going to do, play baseball indoors?

The earthy smell of scotch wafted in from a room to our right preceding the entrance of a woman William greeted as Amy.

"Darling! Welcome home!" Amy trotted over sloppily in heels and a sleek cocktail dress. She was at least fifty and desperately clinging to her long-expired image of youth, or plastic, judging by her lack of facial expressions. "Boys! William is back!" she shouted to the rest of the house.

"Only Micah is home next door," Carter shouted back from the room to which he had retreated. He didn't seem thrilled with her presence either. Maybe I shouldn't have taken our warm reception from him too personally.

"You are simply precious!" She smiled at me. "How cute! William, you didn't tell us he would be this cute."

"Thank you." I smiled back, a bit scared.

"About New York —" William began, but was again interrupted — this time by something truly terrifying.

The front doors flew open and in walked the very specter of death, dripping with blood from head to toe. The ghastly reaper wore black body armor made of leather that fitted tightly over his muscular frame. The armor, a hybrid of assassin and executioner, concealed everything but his fingertips and a pair of sharp hazel eyes. It wasn't until he threw off the hood and face mask that I saw his real appearance was far from horrifying. He was handsome, blond, and clean-shaven, and I knew exactly who he was.

"Back so soon, Owen? How was the hunt?" Amy asked. He was twenty-eight. I knew his exact age because I had been a fan of his for years. Owen Blackbourne was a boxing prodigy turned professional mixed martial arts champion by the age of twenty. My friends and I had been obsessed with MMA in high school, and Owen was my favorite fighter. My junior year, I had even convinced my dad to take me out late on a school night to see one of his matches because it was the first time he had come to the States. He was billed as "England's Greatest Export." I saved the ticket stub for years. As a boxer he'd been nicknamed "Pretty Boy" because he looked more like a model than a fighter. I had been called the same thing as a slur because of my youthful appearance and my inability to grow facial hair. Owen beat down every last competitor, and some part of me lived vicariously through his wins. Later when he crossed over to MMA he earned the nickname "Platinum Kid" and "Diamond Fist." He had had the most consecutive wins at the time and was the youngest pro fighter in the sport. His specialty was striking moves from his boxing career. People said he "punched like his fists were made of diamonds."

"I need a bloody smoke." Owen stormed past us, throwing his blood-soaked gloves to the floor. "I know you have one in here," he said as he rummaged around in the drawer of a desk in the hall.

"Clean this up, you little wanker! I'm not your mum!" Amy barked and left the three of us. Owen ignored her outburst, victoriously lighting a cigarette he had found and continuing to peel himself out of his upper-body armor. He wasn't quite as chiseled as Noah — I didn't think that was physically possible — but Owen was still impressive.

"This the fresh meat?" he asked, checking a minor scrape on his cheek in the mirror. I was hoping to keep our interaction at a minimum so I wouldn't make a fool of myself. I had never been the type to be starstruck by celebrities, but Owen had been my teenage ideal of coolness. Suddenly I felt validated in my decision to go with William.

"This is Dorian, yes." William spoke up.

"Hey." Owen nodded to me through the reflection. "Hope you're more fun around here than Willy."

"I hope so too," I said, not even noticing the jab at William.

"I like this one already," Owen chuckled. "If you want a word of advice, mate, just do whatever Willy here says not to and you'll get along famously with the rest of us."

"We should talk about going to New York. I think there's something there you'll like." William tried moving the conversation back to business.

"Oh yeah? What would you know about things I like, Willy? Did they add fanny pictures to the Bible yet like I requested?" Owen asked, still checking himself out in the mirror for damage. By now there was a significant pool of blood at his feet that evidently wasn't his. "I'm joking around, Willy. We can talk after the party tonight."

Owen scooped up his discarded clothing from the floor and made his way up the cantilevered stone staircase. "Good to meet you, mate. Hope to see you tonight," he called back to me.

"You too," I replied, trying to sound casual.

"I guess you've heard of him before." William glanced over at me.

"Hasn't everybody?"

William and I left the mansion and walked back across the grounds to his place. "He's a good person. He walks a dark path, but there is light inside him. Fame and fortune led him astray, but I know I can help him as long as he keeps doing God's work."

"None of this was what I expected. I was picturing clergymen and crosses everywhere."

"I admit things have become less pure. Some of us are going through a crisis of faith. But it's what's on the inside that matters most. They'll repent by continuing to take action against the world's greater evils, and God will forgive them. I don't suggest you go to the party tonight. I never attend. You'll see things that will tempt you from your path."

"I'm not much of a party person anyway."

"I figured." Coming from William, that sounded more like praise. I had already done battle with the forces of Hell, so I wasn't worried about something like alcohol at the party being a negative influence. I guess William was just being overly cautious.

"I've got to be honest with you. I'm not a devout Catholic like you are." It meant so much to him and I felt his perception of me had been skewed since I'd told him I had faith back in the Outsiders' apartment building. I also wanted to see how this would affect our friendship and if he'd be able to handle the rest of the truth. "I respect it. I think it's great. It's just not who I am."

"I see." William's return to abruptness didn't give me the reassurance I was hoping for. "There were probably not many opportunities to practice on the streets. It's the core values you live by that are important."

William's residence strongly reflected his tastes. The wood paneling was darker, and there were swords, shields, crosses, and religious statuettes everywhere. This villa definitely had a more gothic medieval feel.

"So what was Owen hunting?" I asked. "I didn't notice any weapons on him."

"Wolves most likely. They're common around here. He only fights them barehanded."

"Wolves?"

"Lycanthropes. Werewolves."

"He fights *werewolves* with his fists?" I remembered Noah's startling description of them;

they were at least seven feet tall and hit like a speeding train. He was so proud when he killed a pack of them on his own that he had a claw mark tattooed across his side.

"Yup. He's good at it, too. He uses a serum made from hormones in their blood. It's like a super steroid that increases strength and reflexes without any major side effects. There's a pharmaceutical company that makes it for him. He and another brother, Micah, are pretty big investors."

"I thought the Brotherhood only fights evil. I didn't think werewolves were evil."

"They are abominations of nature. Man is meant to lay with woman, not a beast."

"Is that really how they're made? That doesn't sound right."

"It's how they began. God cursed the first man to lay with a beast, and from their offspring lycanthropy spread."

"How do you know it's a curse? Maybe it's a blessing."

"God created man in his image. Those fiends are nothing like us. They feed on men and are cannibals at best. If that isn't evil, what is?"

"I didn't know they ate people, or at least, no more than a bear or a lion would if you stumbled into its home. But if lycanthropes are born that way, does it make them evil if they are just trying to survive the only way they know how? Couldn't some of them be good?"

"You have a lot to learn." William opened a closet in one of his bedrooms. "I don't mean that as an insult. You'll learn everything you need to know here and you'll always have the Brotherhood watching your back."

There seemed to be a disconnect in what he believed the Brotherhood was and what their actions showed. It was like he *wanted* them to be this pious sect of hunters, but they didn't take him seriously. He had very specific views on the undead, some of which I knew from my experiences to be wrong. I had my doubts about his knowledge of the werewolves' origin, too. His fervent hatred for anything supernatural, not just the undead, was making me nervous again.

"Carter and Amy don't seem too interested in me," I said.

"They have a lot on their mind with the upkeep around here lately. Up until a couple of years ago Carter was the sole person responsible for the finances of our chapter, kind of like the patriarch of the family. He had a failed run for political office and took it hard. Micah has stepped in now that he's finished his schooling at the university. He takes care of all the banking and investments that keep the estate where it is. I think Carter feels he is being pushed out by the younger members and resents it. I pray every night that he will find the strength to conquer those inner demons."

"What about Amy? She seems pretty ... lively." I stumbled trying to find a polite word to describe her. "When you said Brotherhood I wasn't expecting there to be women. Does she hunt?"

"Women weren't allowed membership in the Brotherhood until the turn of the twentieth century. She used to hunt, but now just spends her time ... indulging. Many of the senior members took their seat at God's side recently and Amy doesn't feel like fighting to keep up with the younger crowd. Instead she cemented her place as this chapter's matriarch and handles business between the other houses in England. She also takes care of internal affairs and human resources, like hiring and managing the help." William pulled a few shirts out of the closet he was staring into and tossed them on the bed. "This is all stuff she bought for me with the Brotherhood's money that I never wear. She likes to shop. Don't be surprised if you hear a lot of arguing between her and Micah when you meet him. I try to donate as much of it as I can but the closet just keeps getting refilled. Help yourself to whatever you want."

"These are all different sizes." I picked through the pile of designer clothes. They still had their tags. One of these shirts could have paid a month's rent in Manhattan.

"She never remembers my size. I think she just gets a rush from buying things. Anyway, I've got some stuff I need to do, so why don't you make yourself at home. You can take this room, but feel free to have a look around. This is your home now."

"Thanks, Willy."

"Don't ... don't call me that," he sighed on his way out.

Part of me wanted to run around like a little kid and explore. The other part of me was hesitant, as though I shouldn't have been there. I wondered if I should be stockpiling food and bottled water from the kitchen. It was going to take a while for me to get used to living comfortably again. I took a quick peek into the other rooms adjacent to mine. They were all unoccupied and decorated in more or less the same way. I would have been lonely living in such a big house by myself.

Almost every wall had a framed photograph of a local landscape, presumably taken by William. They were all remarkable. He had some serious talent. You could tell what he'd been feeling at the time he took each picture just through his use of lighting and angles. Perspective was a powerful thing.

As fascinated as I was with my new home, I was most interested in my king-sized bed. Maybe I'd finally be able to sleep more than a couple of hours at a time.

Chapter Six

The antique grandfather clock outside my room chimed twelve times. Had I really slept for seven hours without any hallucinations or night terrors? I rolled around the bed with a huge smile on my face. I hadn't felt this alive since Japan. The bed was so large it was like I was on an island in the middle of the room.

William was nowhere to be found. He'd said not to, but I was curious to go check out Owen's party. I didn't want to be rude and I couldn't turn down an invite from Owen Blackbourne. My second shower in two days was a luxury that I still couldn't stop smiling through. There was even deodorant and a toothbrush!

I picked out the most expensive-looking matching warm clothes, and ended up with a gray cashmere V-neck cardigan, a white oxford, designer jeans, and black Italian loafers. William hadn't been kidding — there was quite possibly every size available. The waste of money was depressing, but it was to my advantage so I couldn't complain. For once I would be dressed appropriately and not get gawked at.

I realized I had no idea where the party was until I stepped outside to see one of the houses all lit up and a fleet of limousines parked in front. I could see my breath as I hiked across the lawn and was glad I'd be spending the night somewhere warm.

"Your name please, sir?" An elderly man in a tuxedo greeted me at the door.

"Um … Dorian?" I wasn't used to a guest list at a house party — not that I had been to very many.

"Are you not sure, sir? Because that name is not on the list, I'm afraid."

"Because he is family, Richard." A platinum-blond man about my age in a well-tailored suit stepped forward. "It's all right, let him through."

"Micah." The blond man introduced himself and extended his hand. We exchanged pleasantries and walked in together.

My smile faded slightly after I looked around at all the guests dressed in swanky formalwear.

"I didn't know this was a black tie affair," I said dejectedly.

"Nothing to worry about, the tie is the first thing to come off anyway. You clean up quite nicely, very smart. I heard from William the state he found you in. Pity. The young and beautiful should never have to go through that."

What a strange compliment. I didn't think anyone should be homeless, regardless of how old or attractive they were, but I thanked him.

The mansion was laid out in an open floor plan and had been turned into the Blackbourne's own casino, complete with blackjack, poker, and craps, two full bars, cocktail waitresses, and live music.

"Wow," I whispered to myself, trying to take it all in.

"Like it?" Micah asked, amused by my reaction.

"Yeah, it's really impressive!" I paused when I noticed some of the girls in the crowd of socialites walking around in matching lace lingerie and heels. "What is that about?"

"The birds?" Micah signaled one of the waitresses to get him a drink. "A bit of entertainment for the party. 'Companionship,' you know? That is, if you can get one Owen hasn't claimed."

"Is any of this legal?" I was a bit bewildered by the whole scene. When William had told me not to go, I figured he was being overly cautious with the homeless guy because there would be some drinks. When I'd realized at the door it was a formal gathering, I wondered if William had thought I would feel out of my class level and be drawn in by the glitz and glamor. But what I saw in the first five minutes of the party blew all of that away. To my right, an older man with a cigar dangling from his mouth who'd been stuffed into his suit had a hand firmly attached to a lingerie-clad girl's backside. His fat, sausage-shaped finger was trying to wedge itself between her cheeks while he carried on a conversation with some other guests. To my left, two younger men sat at a booth with their ties loosened and shirts unbuttoned. The scantily clad girl sandwiched between them looked to have had so many drinks she couldn't even feel their hands groping every inch of her bare skin.

"Does it need to be? When you're one of us you live by your own rules. It doesn't hurt that most of Parliament has been through here at some point."

I spotted Owen at a blackjack table with Carter, but Owen was too busy with the girls in lingerie on his lap and at his side to do much gambling. He dipped his finger into his drink and traced one girl's lips with the liquid, letting her suck it off. No one at the table seemed to mind that they were in the middle of a game when he found better entertainment by making the girl on his lap giggle and squirm by burying his face in her neck. Nor did anyone bat an eye when his hand traveled so far up her inner thigh it treaded salaciously close to crossing the lace border of her undergarment. Nobody cared when he exchanged the girl for the brunette beside him and sat her on the table. There wasn't a word of protest as his eager mouth found its way to her breasts — one patron courteously slid over and gave them some room.

The dealer's stoic expression indicated that this was not a rare occurrence. He maintained his professional demeanor as he collected the cards strewn about by Owen's rising passion. What the hell had I walked into?

"What can I get you, mate?" Micah offered and waved over another waitress. "Pick your poison, we have it all."

"No, it's okay, I'm good," I declined, sounding more nervous than I wanted to. I wasn't much of a drinker to start with and this was the last place I felt comfortable letting my guard down.

"You'll have a much better time if you relax a little," Micah insisted. "You're in good company here, but we can't get to know you if you're all wound up. Wine at least?"

"I guess," I accepted with some apprehension.

"The claret," he ordered the waitress. "You know, you look familiar. Did you used to model?"

"No."

"Hm. Well, you should. You're a pretty lad. It got me through university and you'll have to pull your weight around here." Another shot at modeling was the last opportunity I'd expected to have here. Maybe it would be a return to normalcy amidst this group of debauched hunters. I hadn't originally wanted to be a model, but now modeling seemed more enticing as a regular lifestyle than living on the streets or in the wilderness. It would have made my mom proud. "I'll make some calls this week and see what I can set up for you."

"Your drink, sir." The waitress returned with a smile. Suddenly I felt like a million bucks. Micah led us to a table to continue our chat. Owen glanced up from his guest's chest to acknowledge me with a friendly nod as we passed, but Carter made sure not to look our way.

"Do you want in on this, Dorian?" Owen yelled to me over the din. I couldn't believe he actually remembered my name. Hearing him say it in his English accent gave me chills. It took me a few seconds to realize what he was asking as he stood up to leave with his shirt untucked and his arms around the girls.

"No, no ... no. I'll, uh, pass. They already look pretty warmed up to you."

"Suit yourself, mate. More for me."

"Smart choice," Micah said as we sat down. "Tag teaming with Owen can be tiring if you're trying to keep up. He's broken a few hips and even more headboards."

I kept my head down and stared wide-eyed into my glass of wine. "This is a lot different than the impression William gave me."

"I imagine so," Micah rolled his eyes. "Don't tell me you're a good ol' altar boy. I don't take you as the type. You have too much style. William can't even match a tracksuit."

"I'm not. I don't see how he — what's the word — fits in here. This is more of a high-society frat house than a holy Brotherhood."

"Jesus died for our sins and all that. We're just making sure his sacrifice doesn't go in vain.

You're not wrong though. Willy's on his own quest." Micah rolled his eyes again.

"You're all out to fight evil, though."

Another waitress stopped by to replace Micah's drink. I had barely taken more than a few sips of mine.

"Evil?" Micah smirked. "Sure, why not? We give it a go once in a while."

"What about the blessed armor? That amulet of his that hurts evil beings? What do you hunt?"

"Whatever's fun. It's all about the thrill, the rush you get when it's your life or theirs. The bigger the game, the greater the rush. Did Willy happen to leave out how our little family got its start?"

I shook my head. I wasn't sure if this was good or not. On one hand I was relieved that the whole Brotherhood wasn't fixated on destroying anything different than them on the grounds that different meant evil. On the other hand, killing innocent people for sport was just as bad. Thinking about it made my stomach hurt.

"The founders were highborn men from across England who vacationed in Bath for the summer. There wasn't much fun to be had back in the early 1400s I suppose, so the men would gather in hunting parties. Their presence disturbed the sanctity of the woods and they were chased out by packs of wolves that attacked their summer homes each night. The men thought to put the wolves down while they slept during the day and ventured into the woods to find their den. But what they found were no ordinary wolves. Most of the men were torn apart by the enraged werewolves they blundered into, but four of the men made it out alive and with the body of a lycanthrope to prove it.

"They didn't know that after a lycanthrope dies, it reverts to its human form. Their 'proof' turned out to be evidence they were murderers and the fact that most of their hunting party was dead didn't look good either. Being rich and powerful has its perks; they covered up the deaths and rallied a new party to go back in again and again for revenge until every last one of the beasts was slain. Most of the men died, but the handful that survived had become addicted to bloodlust and secrecy. This house was built on the site of the first hunting lodge created by our founders."

"So the werewolves *aren't* evil?"

"No more than any other animal," Micah shrugged "They're quite a bit more entertaining to hunt, though."

"But if they have a human side to them and they aren't evil, you *are* murderers."

"If you find one that wants to join us for tea sometime to talk about it instead of tearing off your bloody face, I should be glad to invite it over."

Micah and I looked over at a man causing a ruckus at the poker table.

"Tch, the Prime Minister is always sore when he loses. Amy threw a drink in his face once for accusing her of cheating."

"Was she?" I watched as security tried defusing the situation — the "situation" being the Prime Minister trying to flip over the poker table.

"Of course she was. She was only offended because he called her an amateur."

"What about the undead that William is so obsessed with?" I asked once the scene was over.

"What's there to say? They aren't much fun, if you ask me, with their mind games and such. There isn't much of a hunt to it either if you know how to get in close enough to stake one. When Amy hunted, the undead were her fancy. Didn't require much sport.

"Some of the other chapters in England that don't have wolves near will use undead to fluff their points."

"Points?"

"We keep score. Just like any other sport. Brother against brother, chapter against chapter. It's all in fun," Micah explained. It was all fun for them, not the poor victims. This whole operation was so much bigger than me, but if I could change the mind of even one of them it would be a success. If I could get them to focus on only fighting evil ... "Damn Willy would put us back on top if he'd stop chasing the goose to help his wife and go after bigger marks with us again."

"Wait, what? Willy, er, William is married?"

Micah stopped talking as though he shouldn't have let that slip. Why was being married such a big secret for a good Catholic boy?

"Ah, bad metaphor. They get a bit sloppy this late. He's married to his crusade, I mean."

"You're lying." I called Micah out. He took out a pack of cigarettes and offered me one.

"Tell me. When I ask him about it and he wants to know who told me it's going to come back to you anyway."

"Blackmail on your first night? Cheeky little bastard," Micah snickered, but I could tell he was uncomfortable. "All right, then. Willy joined us when he was sixteen. He was thrown out when he shagged his girlfriend, at Bible camp no less, and got her pregnant. She was from England and convinced him to stay with her. She was cast away too. They don't believe in abortion and all that nonsense."

"William?! I can't picture him defying his religion like that. How did he end up here? Where's his wife?"

"Emily got him to marry her so their baby wouldn't be a bastard. The marriage didn't last long. They were living on the streets, Willy doing whatever it took to get by and provide for his happy family. He came back to whatever shitter they were staying in one night to find her on the ground and a man at her neck. When he ran in to save her the neckbiter disappeared. She was dead, along with their unborn child."

"That's horrible. No wonder he's so adamant they're evil."

"Carter found him and took him in, even officially adopted him on the down low. Kiddies are a great tax write-off. Willy was worth his weight in gold for years, killing everything in his path. Best hunter this house had seen in years, Carter said. But now it's just preaching 'monster this' and 'evil that.' He's got no off switch and is driving himself bonkers."

"How is that helping his wife if she's dead? You said he's chasing the goose to help her."

"I don't know, mate. Avenging the fallen soul of a loved one? The boy's missing a few upstairs if you ask me."

"You're lying to me again. I think you know."

"You like to play it rough, don't you?" Micah took a long drag off his cigarette and looked at me slyly through the corner of his eye. "That's all I've got for now. You'll know the rest tomorrow; you have my word. Just keep this to yourself until then. Willy gets a bit sensitive."

"Another drink, sir?" The waitress stopped by our table. I didn't realize her question was directed at me until I noticed my glass was empty.

"No, thanks." I excused myself so I could go to the bathroom and decompress. Micah grabbed one of the lingerie girls passing by and sat her on his lap for company after I got up.

The bathroom door was half open and the lights were on, but there was so much noise from the party I couldn't hear whether anyone was inside. I walked in to see Amy and a few guests having their own private party. Each of them was taking turns cleaning white powder off the counter with their nose.

"Sorry," I said and backed out just in time for Amy to push the door closed in my face. There had to be another bathroom in a house this size. I went through a back hallway, around the perimeter of the first floor, and past several sitting rooms filled with people who wanted to chat away from the congestion in the casino area.

In the last room I walked by, Owen had found a more comfortable place than the blackjack table to continue entertaining his two lady friends for the evening. Eyes closed, head back, pants down, Owen was in heaven on the couch. One girl knelt over him; the other straddled him. He had pretty much all the bases covered and, like any gracious host, was making sure no one was left out by keeping a good rotation going. I couldn't imagine what he would want a partner for. He didn't look like he needed any help or encouragement. It was time to return to the other house.

I had to climb over several alcohol-saturated socialites to reach the front door. To my surprise, William was standing by the entrance dressed in his hunting armor.

"Are you okay?" I asked. Up close I could see he looked exhausted. There were dark circles under his eyes and his face was even more drawn than usual. He looked me over, but didn't show how he felt either way. I expected him to preach against luxury and falling to temptation.

"I just came to see if you were here," he said, dodging my question as usual. He was so uneasy here I could see it written across his face.

"I was on my way out. I came to say hi and meet Micah so they wouldn't think I was being rude."

William nodded and left. For some reason I felt guilty for being at the party, even though I had no reason to. I followed William out and walked with him back to his house, but there wasn't much conversation.

"The twins must like you," were the first words out of his mouth after five minutes of silence.

"Twins?"

"Micah and Owen. We all take the same surname upon joining the Brotherhood. I call them the twins. They look and act the same, and they're inseparable. Micah is even Owen's manager as of last year. The two of them brought in more money for this chapter than it's seen in decades."

"How can you tell they liked me?" I asked. "Owen was a little preoccupied. Did you speak to Micah?"

"No, but if they didn't, you wouldn't be here right now. It takes a majority of the house to officially vouch for new membership. Carter and Amy won't vouch for anyone younger than they are."

"What would have happened if none of them liked me?"

"You'd be bound, gagged, and drugged, then left in the middle of the woods for the wolves."

I wasn't shocked by how close I had come to dying; the joke was on them. But how could William be okay with it?

"That doesn't sound very pious," I pointed out.

"It's a tradition I don't participate in." William brushed me off. "It was started generations ago so that new recruits wouldn't speak of what they saw in their time with us if they weren't accepted."

"I didn't know I had to be officially accepted. I guess I'm glad that's over."

"It's not," William stated as he flipped through a photo album on his dresser. "Not until you clear a hunt with us tomorrow night."

"Great. I can't wait." That meant I had less than twenty-four hours to 'fess up about what I really was ... or run.

Chapter Seven

It was late afternoon when Owen finally dragged himself in his underwear to our meeting to discuss the night's hunt. I had spent a good part of the day with William; we'd chatted about everything except what I really wanted to know. I noticed that he wasn't wearing a wedding ring. There was no way I could ask him about his wife.

"Good morning, princess," Micah jabbed at Owen, even though he had only joined us an hour earlier.

"Sod off." Owen collapsed on the bed and covered his face with a pillow.

"You're getting old. You don't bounce back as quick after getting pissed anymore. You'll be in bed by eight and trading those boxers for a nappy in no time." Owen received Micah's continued digs by throwing the TV remote at his head.

"I'm going to knock your bloody teeth out as soon as the room stops spinning," Owen groaned from under the pillow.

"New York is in bad shape." William tried yet again to pitch his plan. "There are dozens of the undead crawling the streets and their leader has taken notice of Dorian."

"How'd you manage that?" Micah asked, twirling a dagger between his fingers.

"Wrong place at the wrong time," was the best I could come up with.

"He killed at least one of them in a building where the homeless take shelter," William interjected. It was pointless to keep trying to deny what he thought he'd seen. I'd be better off taking credit for it and trying to get them to see that not all supernaturals were evil or simple beasts to be hunted.

"I was defending myself," I added.

"No one's judging you, mate. You lived, it died, that's what counts," Micah told me.

"How many of those things have you ashed, Dorian?" Owen asked from under his pillow.

"One," I answered.

"Brilliant! He should take point tonight. Don't you think, Willy?" Owen's comment seemed to get under William's skin based on the twisted expression he got in response.

"You're not the first Willy has brought on a hunt without much experience," Micah whispered to me while the other two bickered. "They're buried a few miles from here now. Real nice funeral. Willy gives a good service, very respectful."

That was not reassuring.

"Are you dim? If you would just shut up," Owen yelled at William. "Micah, tell this arse what we found so he'll stop his yapping."

If there was this much dissent in the Brotherhood already I was scared to see how they'd fare on the battlefield together. They must be amazing to have stayed alive this long.

"*I* found the lord's manor," Micah explained. "It's been right under our noses this whole time."

William's eyes lit up. "Where? How?"

"Let's not get on about the details. What you need to know is the neckbiter is here in Somerset. We haven't seen anything during day recons because the manor only appears in moonlight."

"Of course! It figures the monster would use wicked magic to hide in plain sight," William exclaimed enthusiastically.

"Right. Whatever." Micah rolled his eyes. "The manor is between Wells and here. I'll mark the location on GPS."

"So close to the cathedral. The ungodly arrogance of these creatures is disgusting," William declared angrily. "Is there nothing they won't try to spread their corruption to?"

"I need a drink." Owen sat up and looked around William's room. "Never mind, I forgot where I was."

"I'll drive," Micah announced. "We'll take the Lamb."

"The hell you will," Owen protested. "You're not laying a hand on her. I just need a few drinks in me and I'll be good to go. I drive better drunk."

How were any of them still alive? There must be a God.

"What if he's not evil?" I asked. "What if he's just hiding because he wants to be left alone and isn't hurting anyone?"

The three of them stopped what they were doing and stared at me, then each other. "They're *all* evil," William answered. "Hiding or not, they are cursed by God. They feed on the blood of regular men like you and me for sustenance. What part of that could be considered good?"

"Have you ever asked any of them or gotten to know one? Maybe some of them are just regular people that fell victim to someone passing on the curse."

"Don't go soft on them or they'll have your throat. Your heart has to be as cold as their bodies if you want to keep the blood in your veins," Owen cautioned me.

"You can't talk to them without their mind games playing with your head," Micah added. "If we kill the lord in this area, then the curse on all of his offspring will be lifted."

William was getting frustrated with my stalling. That wasn't how it worked though, I was sure of it. Noah hadn't changed after Aurelia was killed, and neither had Vance after Minerva died and was sent to Hell.

"How can you be sure?" I debated. "Maybe the lord is innocent and that's why he's hiding. If he's good and can help us find the bad ones we'd be doing something better than just killing indiscriminately."

"You're taking all the fun out of it. That sounds like so much more work," Micah objected. "You know this is a hunters' group, right? We *hunt* things. It's what we do."

"Can't we just hunt the bad ones? I'm sure there are enough of them. At least you can talk to them more easily than you could a werewolf."

"He has a point there," Owen agreed. William stared at him.

"What would happen if one of you got turned?" I asked. "Would you kill each other?" Micah and Owen exchanged a sideways glance.

"We don't have many rules, but we don't hunt our own," Micah explained.

"I would put Micah in the ground for a gin and tonic about now." Owen grabbed Micah and put him in a headlock.

"Get off me, you drunkard!" Micah shouted and punched him in the stomach to break free.

"So we agree then? No killing unless evil?" This was probably too easy, but there was hope.

"Whatever, let's just get on with it," Micah shrugged. "We'll let you do the talking, so when he's ripping your throat out we'll know it's okay to attack."

"We should have a safe word," Owen commented. "Micah, what's one of yours?"

"I don't know what you're talking about," he grinned.

"I wonder what it would be like to bang one of them." Owen always seemed to have his mind in one of two places: sex or alcohol.

"It's quite cold, but the lads have the birds beat if you like them feisty," Micah divulged on our way out.

"And how would you know that?" Owen asked.

"Interrogation is my specialty. I had to get the info about the manor out of them somehow. I thought I was being rather creative," Micah boasted. My eyes nearly popped out of my head at Micah's sudden candidness about his fluid sexuality. William could be heard whispering prayers to God as he pulled away from the group to go on ahead.

"Did you save one for me?" Owen asked Micah, amused by William's discomfort with the topic. "Female, of course."

"No, didn't you see the ashes in Willy's bed? I couldn't let them give us away after I finished, could I?"

William spun around, giving Micah the most menacing glare possible for a human. "I'm just having a bit of fun, Willy." Micah put his hands up innocently. "You know I take them to Amy's room if it's going to be dirty. It's not like she would notice."

"Micah and I have to get suited up," Owen said. "Wait for us by the gate."

"What about me? I don't have any way to defend myself." If I had no weapon it would look awfully suspicious if I escaped any violence unharmed. The undead could still sense me differently so I had to hope it wouldn't come up. I wasn't ready to say anything yet.

"I thought you were going to hug them all to death with the power of love?" Micah teased. "Here." He tossed his dagger to me a little faster than necessary, but I caught it in one hand with ease.

"Did they teach you that on the street?" Micah asked. He and Owen looked impressed.

"I'm, uh, used to having things thrown at me." *By Noah*, I thought.

"Good thing too. The pointy end's a bitch if you miss." Owen laughed and flashed me a thumbs-up over his shoulder. "I knew I liked this one."

"How much for the night, pretty?" Micah came screeching around the corner in the latest silver Lamborghini with Owen in the passenger seat. The both of them were dressed in matching black leather armor. No wonder William called them the twins. Except for Owen's slightly larger build, the two were indistinguishable with their hoods and masks up.

"I don't come cheap," I laughed and got into the backseat with William.

"Doubt that, but it was Willy I was talking to." Micah puckered up in the rearview mirror, much to William's chagrin, and toyed with the GPS. "Hm, must have already put the address in."

"When were you in my little Lamb?" Owen asked defensively.

"She's cheating on you, mate. She loves how I make her purr." Micah leaned into the steering wheel and revved the engine. "I must have been pissed the other night and put it in ahead of time."

"Are you guys normally this carefree before going to face certain doom?" I asked as we flew down the driveway and swerved onto the road.

"What's to be all serious about? After we stop at the market we'll have enough garlic to take care of a full house of neckbiters and make my famous sauce for dinner." If Owen wasn't joking, we were screwed.

"Don't take this the wrong way, but I can't picture you cooking."

"I love it. It soothes the beast within," Owen answered dramatically. "You shouldn't judge like that. Only God can judge me. Isn't that right, Willy?"

"I wish you *would* take this more seriously when my wife is at stake," William snapped. "Wife?" I asked. Finally, time for some answers.

"Life. I said *life*," William whispered. It was a poor cover-up. The twins remained quiet, so I'd have to try a different approach.

"So, how did you guys become hunters?" I asked. Micah gave me a subtle smile in the mirror.

"Carter took me in when I was sixteen." Owen spoke up. "I had just emancipated myself from my parents. Boxing was my life growing up, but none of the universities they wanted me to apply to offered boxing scholarships."

"You left your family for boxing?" I asked after his silence.

"His dad was an angry lush." Micah picked up for Owen. "Their money came from an inheritance when his mum's parents died. He pissed away Owen's tuition money and expected Owen to make it back by winning prize fights against people twice his age when he couldn't get a scholarship."

"I took up boxing when the beatings started," Owen added. "I was eight. It made me feel strong, but then it just gave the old man an excuse when he left marks. Carter reached out to me when I earned a full scholarship for rugby and made the newspaper. I was making decent money from legitimate fights when he approached and asked if I wanted a match that would leave me set for life.

"He took me to a cage they had set up for matches underground. The other guy didn't look like much, but halfway through our fight he changed into a bloody werewolf. Carter throws a silver knife into the ring and says 'Slit the beast's throat. Let out your anger so you can become a new man'."

"Do you ever see your mom?" I asked.

"Lost her four years ago to lung cancer. She was a big smoker. It was the only way she could deal with that lush."

"What happened to him?"

"He met a truly unfortunate end in a private cage match. Let's just say no one threw him a knife."

The Brotherhood was as full of surprises as the supernatural world. I'd thought my high-school image of Owen was ruined after I saw the delinquent he was in person. But he had fought for his place in the world since he was a child. His self-destructive habits weren't an indulgence, but a coping mechanism.

"What about you? Don't you have family, Dorian?" Micah asked. The speed at which we were tearing down the open road made me nervous. Even I wouldn't be able to walk away if we crashed.

"No ..." Guilt was weighing heavily on my mind. Everything I wanted was before me and yet I couldn't manage to tell them what I really was. The Blackbournes were my age, living in and understanding the supernatural world. They had taken me in and opened up to me, but I couldn't return the same courtesy. I felt the hairs on the back of my neck stand on end and my skin bristle with anxiety whenever I got close to opening up. "My parents passed away a few years ago."

"Sorry, mate," Micah apologized. "Mine threw me out. I fell into the Brotherhood the year after Owen."

"And you cried every bloody night for a week. I had to sleep in the room next to this crybaby." Micah punched Owen in the arm to shut him up.

"I had just survived an attack in the woods while on a camping trip with my junior hunting club."

"He ran like a big girl's blouse at the first sight of a werewolf," Owen laughed. "I was trapped in a cage with one and fought it to the death."

"Sod off!" Micah yelled at him. "My bloke Nicholas had just been torn to shreds in front of my eyes. We weren't supposed to go out as far as we did, but we wanted some alone time. Nobody believed me when I told them what I saw. They said it was just a wolf. My family was the stuffy 'old money' type. It wasn't 'proper' when I was in the papers talking about monsters in the woods. They thought I was making a mockery of our good name.

"Nicholas' family was threatening to sue. They thought I had coerced him and was responsible for his death. It broke my heart. When I told my parents why I had snuck out into the woods with Nicholas they wanted me sent away. It was like I had some disease that they hoped I would recover from if they kept me away long enough."

"If you pray to God for the strength to resist those urges you can stop them from happening again. I wish you would see that by now," William cut in.

"What about you, Willy?" Micah asked. "Tell Dorian how you came to us."

"We're almost here," Owen said, citing the GPS in an attempt to diffuse the situation.

"That's okay, I can pull over," Micah said with malice in his voice. He glared at William in the mirror. "I want to hear the story again, it's been a while."

"Here we go." Owen sighed and lit a cigarette.

"I repented for my sins," William answered and left it at that.

"What sins?" I asked quietly.

"They are between me and God. He has forgiven me." William evaded the question again.

"Really, Willy?" Micah's voice was full of venom. "Is that why your fiancée is chained up so you can 'bleed out the evil' by cutting her? Didn't God forgive her for getting knocked up at sixteen at Bible camp?"

"WHAT?" I couldn't hold in my disbelief and disgust.

"Micah, stop," Owen murmured.

"Why? We're all sharing right?" Micah continued to press the issue. "Why don't you tell Dorian about Emily, William? Why don't you tell him why we're going all the way out here for a bloody neckbiter? How she's one of them now, how you think that you can change her back by doing God's work? I've got news for you, Willy: *He* isn't listening!"

"I feel sorry for you," William whispered. "I'll still pray for you."

"Save your breath." Micah started to calm down. "Prayers and threats of divine wrath won't change who I am and who I'm perfectly happy being."

"We're here," Owen announced, sounding relieved to put that conversation to rest. Outside my window a three-story Elizabethan mansion stood solitary against the night sky. Lights were on in nearly every window, casting a glow onto the clearing surrounding the house. Owen and William leapt from the car before it made a full stop.

"Are we going to walk right up?" I asked Micah as we got out.

"No point in trying to be sneaky about it. They can sense us approaching either way. Probably already have the welcoming party prepared. As soon as we're at their door, they'll be at our throats, so stay alert."

"So is William married or engaged? You called her his fiancée back there," I asked Micah when the other two were far ahead.

"Engaged. He refers to her as his wife, but no Catholic church would marry a pregnant teenage runaway. It gets to him when he's reminded about that." Though I could only see his eyes, I could sense his remorse. "He's not a bad guy, just very … narrow."

"He doesn't think you're bad either. He told me so. It sounds like he wants the best for everybody, even if he's not sure what that is."

"I should apologize for putting you in the middle of that. Bloody hypocrite gets under my skin, you know? I don't care if you're a sinner or a saint, but don't look down on me when you're sitting there too."

The four of us stood on the stone steps of the palatial residence. We paused uneasily for a moment, waiting for an ambush or a full frontal assault to pour from the entrance. People moved about inside the towering windowed walls. The building was certainly occupied.

William reached for the handle of the walnut doors. "Wait." I stopped him. "I'll take point."

"I was kidding," Owen whispered. "You have no armor. Just stay alive and keep your neck covered."

"I'm not scared," I reasserted. "Besides, I'm the least threatening and we agreed to leave if they weren't evil." I also wouldn't die if we walked into a trap.

Chapter Eight

A woman's scream greeted us as soon as we stepped inside, followed by two more. Three women dressed in nineteenth-century housemaid's clothes dropped the piles of fresh linens they were carrying and ran at the sight of us.

"What the bloody hell is this?" Owen walked in next to me. William entered next. He grabbed a startled butler, who had come over to see what the disruption was, and took out his amulet.

"William, don't!" I shouted. A bright light shone from the milky-white gem but had no effect on the butler. The man tried to pull away, but William overpowered him and took off his own glove.

"He's human," William announced after checking the butler's pulse and letting him go.

"No kidding, Willy," Micah groaned as William flashed his amulet at fleeing servants to no avail. "You know the biters keep pets."

"We're here to save you," William told the panicked residents. "You're free now."

"Save us?" a woman asked, nervously creeping closer to pick up the laundry the others had left. William took her by the arm, trying to pull her away. "Let go of me! Someone get Master Belanger!"

"I am already here, my dear. There is no need to worry." Across the marble floor and up a grand staircase stood what could be none other than the lord of the manor, dressed in his Victorian finest. He was tall, maybe six feet, and stood with remarkable posture and authority. "Our guests mean us no harm."

"Please." He looked at William's hand where it rested on his servant. William released her. She scurried away. William stared at Master Belanger with daggers in his eyes.

"The door please. We don't want to get a chill, now do we?" The lord's gaze was on me now. I felt compelled to grant his request. The honey color of his eyes was anything but sweet. They pierced me like a frigid wind, far worse than any chill from outside.

"Be judged, *monster!*" William ran up the stairs holding out the amulet.

"William! No!" I tried to stop him, but was too late. The blinding flash burst forth.

"Well, that was quite rude." The lord straightened his tailcoat and cravat. He was completely unhurt. He had the sharpened incisors and accentuated pallor that marked him as undeniably one of the undead. But the amulet had no effect on him.

"Impossible! It must be some sort of dark magic interfering with the amulet. It's never failed me before." William tried again.

"I would ask you not do that. It is rather annoying." The lord took the amulet from William's hand and placed it back in his pocket for him. "There we are. Now what is all this about evil and monsters and dark magic?"

"We are so sorry, Master Belanger." I apologized and pulled William away. "He thought you might be evil and um ... holding these people against their will."

"Please, call me Castile, and it is quite all right. I have grown used to these accusations by now. After three thousand years you would think the mortals would learn, but still they surprise even me." Three thousand years? He was almost as old as Aurelia, which meant he was an Ancient too. An ancient that wasn't evil. "Supper will be ready soon."

"We aren't here to be your meal, monster." William drew his sword. "We are here to cleanse this place."

"I have maids for that, thank you. I was offering an invitation to be on the guest list, not the menu, but if you are to be rude about it then I will be forced to recant. A pity; the roast pheasant is outstanding."

"We're leaving," Owen said. "Come on, Willy. No evil here, you saw for yourself."

"I'm not going anywhere." William stood determined on the stairs as Castile walked past him.

"May I ask the nature of this intrusion?" Castile never took his eyes off of us. There was something unsettling about the way he stared. His gentle mannerisms and soft voice had me on edge. I was waiting for the other shoe to drop — for us to be thrust into battle. *Am I just letting William and my past experiences jade me?* I wondered. *Maybe I'm looking for the monster in people when there is none.*

"Willy here thinks if he kills the neckbiter who turned his lady into one of you she'll be cured," Micah explained.

"Ah." Castile sat staring into our souls for a moment before he said anything else. "I can assure you it wasn't me. I haven't brought a child into this world since I was turned myself. I wouldn't wish this upon even the worst of you. Whoever told you there was a cure to our condition is playing you for a fool."

A maid came in holding a serving tray with a teapot and small porcelain teacups. "Would you care for some tea?" Castile offered as the maid served him.

"How is that possible?" I asked as I watched him drink. It was very clearly hot tea and not blood. I'd witnessed some of the Archios in the past coyly sip from wine goblets and bottles – but they were drinking blood, not alcohol. "How are you drinking that?"

"With my mouth," Castile answered in a matter-of-fact tone.

"Do you have anything harder?" Owen asked. "I could go for a gin and tonic."

"I'm afraid not," Castile apologized flatly.

"Damn. I was starting to like him," Owen said, taking off his mask and hood. "Do you mind if I smoke? I hate hunting the neckbiters. It's always all talk. I need action. I get anxious when I'm not pissed or punching things."

"Outside," Castile answered.

"Can we go now, Willy? Are you satisfied yet? I think we've bothered this bloke long enough." Micah tried pulling him away from the stairs.

"He's still an abomination that doesn't belong in this world. Not killing him would be an insult to God." William refused to budge.

"Ah, I see now. You seek redemption for your sins." Castile spoke between sips of his tea. "Will your resolution to unwavering acts of carnage buy back His love? Paying for your sins with spilled blood. What an interesting notion. Sadly, not an original one."

"You don't know anything about redemption, devil!" William spat.

"We're leaving," Owen announced and walked to the door with Micah. "Come on, Dorian. Willy, if you don't want to walk back home you'd better move."

"I have no need for your particular brand of redemption," Castile answered. "I have never conceived a child out of wedlock against God's wishes. Do come back to tell me how your solution plays out for you."

As soon as I heard Castile say that, I knew the results would not be good. William lost his last shred of self-control and charged at Castile, who didn't move from his chair. I grabbed William by the arm as he ran by but was knocked down by his blind fury. Micah and Owen bolted from the doorway to stop him, but it was too late. William swung his sword wildly, striking the maid who had just returned to collect the serving tray. She fell to the ground in a pool of her own blood. William had struck a lethal blow to her neck.

"What did you do?!" I shouted at William.

"Mama!" a tiny voice cried from the top of the stairs. A boy of about six sobbed as he looked down at the body. The butler and other servants came in to try and help the poor maid, but it was too late.

"Will your penchant for murder ever allow you to atone for your sins?" Castile asked. He spoke calmly, but I could hear a growing agitation in his voice. "You slay the good, the innocent, the mortal and immortal alike, and yet I am the monster?"

"That was *your* fault." William tried placing the blame on Castile. "These people shouldn't be here serving a creature like you."

Two of the housemaids covered the body over with a sheet while choking back tears. The butler went upstairs to pull the boy away from the sight.

"Shut up!" William screamed at them. "You aren't supposed to be here! You should be free! How can you raise a child in the presence of the Devil?!"

"Right now the only monster here is you." I glared at William as Micah and Owen dragged him away.

"Perspective and reality are a funny thing," Castile said, remaining stoic. "Which truly influences the other? Does the world we look upon merely reflect what we believe it to be because we are told it is so? Mortals can only see through their own eyes. How can they tell their senses aren't deceiving them? Is it trust in teachings? Faith?"

"I have seen through the eyes of many and even something as simple as the color of the sky can be refuted endlessly. How can any one man's perspective be superior to the next when none are ever the same? Reality is malleable and tempered by our perspective. From where you stand I am the monster. Even your comrades entertained the thought because you poisoned their minds to think so. But now your actions have changed that perspective. Does that no longer make me the monster? Or are we both? Which is the reality? Or are there many realities combining into one?"

"Is murder for a cause as noble as love any more justified than indiscriminate slaughter? Is it the victims who temper that reality by passing judgments of innocence or guilt? Does their verdict change the universe or do they simply assuage their own need for resolution and accept it as their new reality?"

"How many of the damned can you slay before you risk becoming worse than they? What do you call yourself now, man or monster?"

"I am a man of God!" William shouted. "Your riddles mean nothing to me. Your mind games will never break who I am! I will beg for His forgiveness and He will understand because I am His loyal child!"

"I wonder ... what path will you choose this time?" Castile asked as the servants carried the body away. "Will you spare your beloved further indignity and release her from this immortal coil? Will you wield that periapt as an instrument of mercy or hatred? Will you set free the rage boiling over in your soul and take revenge upon a world that tempted you beyond the limits of your faith?"

Castile's eyes gave off a faint glow, turning their honeyed color to gold. "Leave us now and retire for the evening. When you awaken, our encounter will be gone from your memory. Until next time."

The Blackbournes turned and left without a word or further resistance from William. "Stay," Castile said as I went to follow them. "There is much we need to discuss."

"They're kind of my ride," I said as I watched them walk away. The clocks in each room struck one at the same time, almost making me jump out of my skin. I hadn't realized how long we'd been at Castile's mansion. "And it is getting kind of late." I inched toward the door.

"They are under my control at the moment and no good to you. We've played out this very charade many times before. This is the first time they have brought me someone like you, however." Castile stood and placed a hand on my back, leading me to a sitting room. He hadn't torn William's head off; that fact put me somewhat at ease that he wouldn't lash out at me either.

"What do you mean you've met them before?" I asked.

"For ten years these three have been at my door with the same purpose. Each time I send them away with no memory of our meeting."

The GPS. That was why this place was already in the GPS when Micah checked. He erased their memories, but without the memory they wouldn't know to look it up until they came back here.

"Why?"

"Their visits help pass the time. It is a game I have played with their Brotherhood for generations. I enjoy the insight they offer into the mortal realm."

"They aren't exactly the best representatives for humanity." My eyes strayed nervously around the room to avoid his penetrating gaze. I was afraid to ask what he wanted with me. An oil painting above the fireplace mantle caught my eye. It was a portrait of a beautiful woman with the same chestnut-colored hair as Castile, but her brooch was what struck me. It was the Archangel Amulet.

"An angel in every facet, isn't she?" he asked.

"Yes, but that amulet ... it's the same as William's." William said he awoke from a dream where the Holy Spirit gave him the amulet. Was his dream related to this woman and the commands Castile had given him to return home to sleep in the past?

"It is the very same one. It was I who gave him the amulet, as I have given it to many before him. He came to me a frightened child searching for answers at the end of a blade. Now look at him. A fearsome warrior who wields his faith as a weapon, striking down all those who cross his path. Power is a terrible thing.

"How many souls has he reaped to feed his thirst for death? Do answers even hold importance to him anymore? He, like those before him, claimed to seek a power to appease their God, yet it was their own selfish lust they sought to fulfill once they had that power. Does God look down upon him now and smile? 'Bleed dry the corpses of my creations, go forth and soak my grounds with their blood.' Is that His message to the devout? A most interesting God indeed."

"Why give him that power?"

"Because I too knew love once. The woman in that painting was my bride. She warmed the cold heart in this body after centuries of loneliness. I granted dear William use of the periapt during his first visit to see what choice he would make; accept his bride for what she had become and know true love, or turn it on her and spare her from the cruel injustices of a world that scorns the unfamiliar."

"I don't think he made a very good choice," I said, thinking of what Micah had told me in the car on the way.

"That is your perspective. His faith is stronger than ever and he is filled with purpose. Maybe saving his beloved was never what he wanted in the first place. Perhaps he wanted someone upon whom to project his guilt."

"Why did you want me to stay?" I finally worked up the courage to ask. Knowing my reputation with Ancients so far, the answer was likely because he wanted to use me for my power.

"There is a great darkness coming straight from the bowels of Hell," he said. Those words alone made me shiver. It was something Aurelia's sister, Rozalin, had said when we defeated her. She was another lunatic obsessed with power. Rozalin even went as far as to destroy her own physical body so she could become an incorporeal phantom to better seek revenge on her sister over a sibling rivalry. "It surrounds you and I both, all creatures living and not. Those more in tune with the universe, such as myself, can sense it looming closer. I can see past, present, and future. This darkness has risen before and soon it will rise again."

He sounded more concerned. When it had come from Rozalin, amidst her deranged fits of laughter, the statement had seemed threatening.

"What do I have to do with this? Don't tell me I'm fated to stop it or anything like that. I'm getting real tired of hearing what my powers can do when I can't even live a halfway normal life for a day."

"No. Your existence is inconsequential to the cycle. You are powerless to stop it and will most likely perish a hundred deaths to make it through to the other side."

That was a bummer. I was expecting a rousing speech telling me how one person could change the world. Even if I didn't believe I was that person, it would have been nice to hear. He sounded like Minerva, when she'd told us we were powerless before the great cycle we could never stop. All the Ancients seemed to speak in the same voice, as if they shared some universal consciousness. Maybe they just lived long enough to see history repeating itself.

The clocks struck two and I had to hold on not to be jolted out of my seat. There was a joke to be made about waking the dead somewhere in there.

"That was a quick hour," I said, checking the clock.

"Was it? I find it fascinating that something so ephemeral as time can dominate so many. What is it about the unseen that enthralls us to the point that we base our lives around it? To me, it was an hour as any other. To you it was faster, and to the clock it is all the same. Our perspective guides our concept of time, like everything else. Reality is what we make it."

"Why did you want to talk to me about this coming darkness?" I asked to get back on track and away from the philosophical mindfuck. "The other Ancients I've met have brought it up too. Some of them seem excited that Hell is going to spill onto the

Earth and others are talking about how we're all going to be destroyed or enslaved."

"Apocatastasis. A belief the world will be reset to its original state. Tabula rasa, another clean slate. A cosmic cleanse that knows no end. But when it is through what will it mend?" Castile rhymed without the usual tone of frivolity you'd expect from a poem, although the subject matter didn't necessarily call for lightheartedness. He had stayed civil so far, but I wasn't about to drop my guard. Aurelia had been every bit as hospitable and then some when we first met.

"I assure you I am nothing like the wicked princess."

"What princess?" I asked, a bit confused.

"I dare not honor her with a greater title. The wretched matron of the Archios." He sounded disgusted, but remained polite.

"I never said anything about her."

"Your unspoken words are just as loud."

"You're saying you can read my mind?" No one had been able to get inside my head since the ritual that had bonded me with the parasite. "The others, they can't ... I don't understand."

"I am not like the others." Castile glanced around the room, preoccupied. "Our powers are akin to one another. I control the mind without limits, and you control matter. You are someone with the ability to bend reality to your will. Why put your life at the mercy of others? Why the charade with the Brotherhood?"

"They took me in. I was feeling them out to see if they were dangerous or if we could be friends."

"Ah, a friendship based on deception. Truly poetic. You will make a marvelous Ancient in time. Aurelia will be so proud."

"Why would I care about making *her* proud? She's dead and I couldn't be happier about it."

Castile snapped his attention back to me. "Dead? I think not. She is no more dead than I. Our mutual enemy is quite well. Isn't that right?" Castile directed his question to an empty wall.

"Who are you talking to?" I asked.

"Come now, don't be rude," Castile continued talking to the wall. "Skulking about in the shadows is no way to be a houseguest, uninvited or not."

Dispersing his veil of invisibility, Noah stepped out from where Castile was gazing. "Noah?! What are you doing here?" His wounds from William's amulet had healed and his tattoos had been redone. I was happy to see him. Even after everything he'd put me through I did sort of miss him when he was gone.

"Has your fair lady finally entrusted you with the task of assassinating me? Or is it to reclaim your investment?" Castile was visibly amused for the first time that night.

"What investment? Is that true? Is she still 'alive'?" I asked.

"He's lying." Noah's teeth were clenched tight and his eyes were fixed on Castile.

"Go on, tell him," Castile coaxed. "It is an easy thing to prove. The boy can simply travel there himself. Surely she is still prone to making herself a spectacle."

"No!" Noah demanded with his brow furrowed, still glaring at Castile as he spoke to me. "You were told what you needed to know."

"Tell the boy how you never would have earned his trust without the guise of her death. How could he trust the puppet while the puppet master still pulled his strings?"

"What is going on?" I yelled. "What happened to all that talk about trusting each other?" Noah didn't answer. He wouldn't even look at me. My anger was quickly coming to a head.

"Because you were to be his replacement," Castile answered. "A trade." Noah's muscles tensed and his hand hovered over the hilt of his *katana*. "The boy deserves to know, does he not? The companion he once stood beside and looked up to was only teaching him to be an obedient slave."

"You need to leave. Now," Noah ordered, and vanished. I knew what was coming. He would strike out with lethal speed to behead Castile. First would come a horizontal slash across the midsection to cleave him in two, followed by a spinning slash to the neck from behind.

"Kneel," Castile commanded. Noah's attack was halted. He reappeared on one bended knee, growling and struggling against Castile's mental dominance. "Turn the boy into a mindless killing machine and barter him for your freedom. Isn't that right? Why else would dear sweet Aurelia allow you to stray so far for so long with someone she once wanted dead? Someone she once viewed as a threat to her immortality and wanted under her heel?

"Best of all, it was his own idea from the start." Castile gripped the back of Noah's neck as if he was holding a dog by the collar. His eyes glowed eerily as he continued to probe Noah's mind. "She thought the Strigoi creation an untamable beast to be put down, but he convinced her to let him try in return for his own freedom. How cruel to doom another to the same fate he laments each night."

So he was evil. That was why the Archangel Amulet had burned him. Anger turned to rage inside me, but it would not take over. I wouldn't allow it. *I am not a mindless killing machine. I am not a monster*, I thought.

"I knew you were an asshole on the surface, but I didn't think you were anything like this." I said as I stood in front of Noah, who remained stiff. His nostrils flared as he stared at the floor, still fighting Castile's hold on him. "I thought there was a good person buried deep under those rotten layers."

"How I detest the Archios and their crass schemes. Aurelia and her subjects are amateurs at best, yet still they persist. Petty children playing a man's game." The doors to the mansion flew open as Castile cursed the Archios. A figure shrouded in crackling shadows dashed for us. It was the same person that I had taken the *katana* from in Manhattan. The enigmatic figure had replaced its lost sword with an ornate Asian-styled polearm.

"More uninvited guests." Castile maintained his composure as he grabbed a walking stick from beside where we were sitting and used it to parry the shadow's weapon. The two exchanged a barrage of blows. Castile didn't move a foot out of place until finally his walking stick was snapped. Castile reached behind him and retrieved a sword from a suit of armor against the wall I would have sworn hadn't been there a moment ago.

"We're leaving." Noah grabbed me by the back of shirt. He'd been freed from Castile's hold without my noticing.

"Get off of me." I pushed him away. "I'm not going anywhere with you."

I went to Castile's aid, using my telekinetic grip on the shadow's polearm. The figure swung over it in an acrobatic leap to dodge Castile. The polearm released a stream of electricity that coursed through my body. Castile's sword was knocked from his hand, leaving him defenseless. His eyes turned bright red as he stood his ground. The servants came into the room, clamoring as they got closer. Their eyes glowed red to match.

"Bear witness to the true horrors of the mind." Castile stretched out his arms and the servants began to transform into hideous floating monstrosities with empty eye sockets, contorted faces and deformed appendages. Their skins dripped off like liquid and snaked across the floor. They converged on the shadowy figure as Castile took a step back and melted into the wall to become one with the mansion. All the lights in the house were extinguished, leaving us in total blackness for a moment. I could hear the distorted shrieks and screams of the servants as the figure swung at them in the dark.

"I can see your fears." Castile's voice echoed from the walls. The room lit up red as innumerable eyes of various sizes opened from the walls and focused on the figure. The shadows concealing it were banished by whatever terrifying power Castile used. The figure was revealed as an Asian man with very long hair dressed like an ancient warrior.

"Remain in obscurity, fallen prince." Castile spoke again, his voice sounding much more demonic. The marble floor swirled beneath the man like quicksand and pulled him down. I was floating far enough away to avoid being sucked in too. I noticed none of the furniture or anything else was affected.

Only the man's head remained above ground as the building began to quake. A bolt of lightning crashed through the ceiling and exploded upon making contact with the warrior. The monstrosities and ocular manifestations were purged by the blast and the building began to crumble. The once-beautiful house was no more than an illusion that dispersed to show the truth that lay underneath. A dilapidated ruin caked with dust and left for centuries in disrepair was all that remained. The paintings and furniture had been transformed by the illusion; now it was obvious that they were neglected and forgotten. Castile had been living in his own reality. His will was so strong that the world itself bent to his will to create his ideal home.

Castile fell from the wall, his body disintegrating to ash before it reached the ground. The one peaceful Ancient had been destroyed by the same killer I'd failed to stop in Manhattan. If this person was strong enough to destroy an Ancient, I did not have an easy fight ahead of me.

The Asian warrior leapt at me, but was taken down in mid-air by Noah, who had reappeared on the scene. The longer they fought, the faster Noah struck to try and get a hit in, but the warrior parried his every attempt. I couldn't see Noah's movements anymore. I could only hear the clink of metal after each attack landed. At the speed he was going his strikes sounded like a machine gun. I had no idea how the Asian warrior was keeping up. He didn't move anywhere near as fast as Noah, who was completely invisible because of his incredible speed, but somehow he preempted every strike.

I'd had the chance to get rid of Noah once when fighting the Carpathians and I chose to save him instead. That had been a mistake. But now I had the chance again. If I killed Noah I would be done with his deceitful games, and the other warrior would be worn down from the two battles he'd already fought.

The rhythm of Noah's strikes varied on purpose to try and throw off his opponent, but it also made it hard for me to predict where he'd be. Then again, what reason did I have to be accurate? I got a vague glimpse of Noah in the blur around the other man and unleashed a telekinetic blast. The polearm-wielding warrior was thrown through the wall and tumbled helplessly down the clearing, smashing most of his armor along the way. I flew through the unearthed dust to follow after him, hoping I'd hit Noah too. Strangely, none of the debris landed outside the mansion. It all just seemed to disappear past the outer wall.

"Nice hit." Noah emerged from the dust cloud unscathed.

"I was aiming for you," I retorted.

"I know! Just like old times." It was just like him not to take any of this seriously. He vanished again as a whistling sound approached. I looked to where the other man had been thrown just as his polearm streaked across the grass and went right through me, pinning me to a wall back in the mansion.

"You should dodge that." Noah appeared over me. I pulled the polearm from my body as a lightning bolt crashed through the ceiling and struck me. I was so infuriated I didn't even feel the pain. Plus, the last change of clothes I'd probably have for days had just been ruined. The Asian man seemed surprised I was still alive when he came to reclaim his weapon. Noah took the opportunity to stab him in the back while he was unarmed and I used my chance to smash them both between two bookcases. I sent them back outside, but the bookcases disappeared past the walls of the mansion just as the debris had. How much of this place wasn't real?

"You think that *guandao* would look good above my bed?" Noah shouted from a balcony above. I pulled the crumbling balcony out from under him, expecting him to reappear behind me. He did just what I'd planned, but as I struck he turned back into mist. My blast traveled through him and hit the other man, who was charging for us.

I was letting myself get too caught up in the fight, something I'd been taught not to do. I had to be smarter about this. I flew up above the field and out of reach to force the other two to go back to fighting each other. The polearm was again thrown toward me. I had the advantage of height and it missed me by several feet. The Asian warrior must be tiring out, or so I thought. The polearm continued to soar until it pierced the clouds. There was a loud crack of thunder as the clouds swirled around the sky where the polearm had vanished. This was going to hurt.

The sky lit up and lightning razed the ground, hitting me several times as I spiraled downward out of control and hit the ground.

"Remember when I taught you to fly and I said the high ground has the advantage?" I heard Noah's voice and felt a nudge to my side before I got my vision back. "I didn't mean against someone who can call lightning."

I couldn't hold in my anger any longer. "Don't worry about me, I'm just getting warmed up," I coughed.

"Really? I'd say you're more well done." Noah laughed at his own bad joke and disappeared again. He made it easy to want to hurt him. I no longer wondered whether I'd feel bad or not after I got rid of him for good.

He and the other warrior went back to their stalemate as I sat on the grass and watched. "Are you going to help?" Noah asked between slashes. "I feel like you're mad at me."

"Are you serious? You betrayed me. You're selling my soul to the Devil incarnate for your own gain."

"Oh come on. Don't be so sensitive. You just have to trust me."

"Trust you?" I yelled. "I want to *kill* you!" I took the dagger Micah had given me from my back pocket and threw it at his heart at the first opening. It passed right through him again as he turned to mist and stabbed the other man in the forehead, giving Noah the opportunity to finish the job with a slice across the throat. The warrior collapsed in a ball of azure light and faded away, along with his polearm. That was something I had never seen before. If he wasn't undead, what was he?

"Thanks. I was getting bored of that." Noah stretched and sheathed his *katana*. "Let's go."

"I'm not going anywhere with you," I snapped. "Everything you told me was a lie. What makes you think I'd ever trust you again, let alone be in your company?"

"I told you, you just have to trust me."

"That's not good enough for me, sorry." I got up and went back into the mansion to look around. "You aren't even denying that what Castile said is true."

"Because it is, sort of. It's not what you think. Perspective, remember? Isn't that what this prick said? You're not in any danger, not any more than you were wandering into the home of some Ancient or trying to pretend you're human to a group of hunters. Now stop being a whiny brat and let's go."

"Get lost," I told him as I walked up to Castile's ashes. *I wonder if that man we just killed had anything to do with the coming darkness the Ancients were all talking about,* I thought. Noah didn't seem that surprised by his strange death, but I wasn't about to ask him. I scooped up a handful of Castile's ashes in my hand and walked back outside.

"You're starting to piss me off, kid," Noah complained. "I'm fine with doing this the hard way and you know it."

I opened my hand when I reached the grass. The ashes were gone. Not even a speck. Noah picked me up under his arm. Before I could fight back, the world became a blur as he tore across the land at light speed. This wasn't over, but there was no running from Noah. Maybe for now it was better to play along.

Chapter Nine

"You're unusually quiet." Noah sat across from me, kicked back like everything was great in life. "I like it."

"Where are you taking me?" Those were the first words I had spoken to him since Castile's estate. My head was still spinning from traveling at breakneck speed. He had dragged me all the way to the airport and snuck us into the cargo hold of a plane.

"Japan. You like it there."

"I liked it there before I knew what you were planning. What makes you think I want anything to do with you aside from killing you?"

"If you could kill me, you won't have anything to worry about from Aurelia. It's not like you have anything better to do than practice."

"I have *friends* now. I can think of plenty of other things I'd rather be doing."

"Those aren't friends, those are pets. Pets that are going to get themselves killed any day now."

"Nothing lasts forever, but that doesn't mean I can't enjoy it while it does."

"That's deep. I guess it's an improvement from your usual whining." He got up as the plane started to take off. "Well, good night!"

"Where are you going?" I asked. If I could have staked him in his sleep and thrown him out of the plane I'd have been only too happy to do it.

"Nice try, but I'll be somewhere you can't get me unless you want to crash a plane full of innocent people. And you might want to go through all this luggage and look for something else to wear. You look ridiculous and smell like a forest fire. You know I have a very sensitive nose." With those kind parting words he disappeared in a cloud of mist. I needed to get back to the Blackbournes, but I had no way to contact them. With William's amulet I could beat Noah, or at least give him a very bad day and get him to leave me alone for awhile.

Once, when we were in Japan, I thanked Noah for everything he'd taught me. He told me not to thank him. The best thanks a student can give a teacher, he said, is using the teacher's lessons to surpass him. Was he trying to tell me something when he said if I could kill him I wouldn't have to worry about Aurelia? Or was this another lie to keep me complacent a while longer?

"Why are we getting off here?" It was hard to tell sitting in a pile of luggage, but we had only been flying a few hours at most when the plane landed and Noah brought us to the entrance of the airport. There was no reason for us to have left the boarding gates if we were changing flights on our way to Japan.

Noah took a map out of a passing tourist's hands to look it over. Judging by all the signs in the airport it appeared we had taken a pit stop in Germany.

"Everyone's looking at us," I whispered to him. The tourists and travelers gawked at Noah in awe as he nonchalantly inspected the map in the middle of the crowded waiting area. It probably wasn't often that a six-foot-three, two-hundred-and-thirty-pound man who could be the fitness champion of the world stood shirtless in an airport. It was probably even less often that that man radiated a supernatural magnetism that would cause even the chastest individual to drop to their knees in worship.

"They're looking at *me*," Noah smirked. "Nobody wants to see your nasty charbroiled carcass."

I hadn't put on new clothes on purpose just to bother him. Even if I did, they wouldn't last more than a few hours anyway. He turned to the befuddled woman whose map he'd pillaged and spoke to her in German with a wolfish grin.

"I didn't know you spoke German," I said to him after he handed back the map.

"There's a lot you don't know about me. Just the way I like it." He grabbed me and prepared to take off running at Mach speed again.

"I thought we were going to Japan." I yanked my arm back.

"Yeah, I lied."

"What?! What's in Germany?" It took me a moment and then I remembered: the Strigoi.

Why would he bring me to them? All they ever want to do is experiment on me or use me. Wouldn't that be counterproductive to his plan?

"Don't worry about it, trust me."

"Vance!" Noah pounded on the door to a run-down gothic chapel. "Open up, I'm here with your science project!"

I scowled at him. "Science project" was the most derogatory term he could call me after learning about my past. Leave it to Noah to come up with it.

"See if you can get inside." Noah hit me on the shoulder. "They have some magic crap that won't let me in."

"Gee, I wonder why. Maybe I should get that too."

"You'd need a house. You don't even own a cardboard box." A harsh reality. I wished I was back with the Blackbournes.

My hand was magically repelled from the door handle, preventing me from opening it. Telekinesis worked just fine, but I couldn't walk through the doorway without being bounced back. A somber-looking man around Noah's age, dressed in ceremonial robes, stepped into the candlelit hall before us.

"Why are you here?" he asked.

"Is that any way to treat an old friend, Vance?" Noah grinned and picked me up by the back of my shirt. "I want to turn this in for a newer model. This one keeps talking back, I think he's broken."

"Free will is not a defect ... just an oversight," Vance said, and set down the stack of old books he was carrying.

"Vance, let us in or he'll never go away." I tugged free until Noah set me down.

"The sun has to rise eventually." Vance started to close the door. Noah picked up a rock and threw it through a stained-glass window in protest. "Must you always be so juvenile? I haven't forgotten your explicit orders to destroy me after my involuntary aid at your chateau. Why should I open my doors to danger?"

"Don't worry about that. I took care of her."

"Really?" I squinted at Noah through the corner of my eye.

"I can tell you're lying." Vance wasn't entertained by Noah's ploy. "Why does your sword have an aura?"

An aura? Only things with souls had an aura. Auras were the invisible light that radiated from the souls of both living and undead, and some supernaturals were able to see them.

"It's a long story. Let me in and I'll tell you," Noah bargained.

"Come in." Vance's insatiable curiosity was too great to resist such an offer, even if it could cost him his head. At his command, the repelling barrier dispersed long enough for us to enter. The dimly lit chapel was small, but the high arching ceilings made it seem so much grander. Though the building had been a place of religious worship, there were no statues or ornamentations depicting such. Musty scrolls and stacks of tomes were scattered on every surface.

"Vance, I think you have a hoarding problem." My joke fell on deaf ears.

"What have you been up to? Mixing up anything good in your creature cauldron lately?" Noah swept a bunch of books onto the floor and took a seat on an old wooden chair that didn't look like it would support someone his size.

"This is a peaceful arcanum. We don't conduct experiments here, only research."

"That's boring." Noah flipped through a tome, then threw it over his shoulder. It seemed like he wanted to say something, but was holding back.

"Show me the sword." Vance collected the displaced literature and tried reorganizing it amongst the clutter. "We've been working on recreating the tethering of a soul to an inanimate object as we did when we defeated Aurelia's sister. With the *Grand Grimoire* lost to us it has been difficult to achieve."

"I thought you said you don't conduct experiments here," I reminded him.

"Theoretical research for now," he mumbled. "You appear to have become stronger since we last met. Your aura has grown and shines brighter."

"He's been training with me." Noah sounded like he was boasting, but was it about his teaching skills or my results? "If you find any of the others like him I can use my Midas touch on them too."

"Show me the sword." Vance ignored the comment and repeated himself. Noah shot up and grabbed him by the throat, slamming him down on the rickety table.

"I wasn't saying that to hear my own voice." Noah bared his fangs. "Where are the others?"

I wasn't a fan of Vance, but I liked Noah even less lately. This sudden outcry of aggression wasn't completely out of character for him, but it was uncalled for.

"I don't know," Vance choked.

"Bullshit. You saw what this kid could do. You said yourself he was a success. I'm not gonna believe that you didn't go looking for the others and I'm not leaving until you tell me where they are," Noah threatened.

"Why do you want them?" I asked.

"He wants his own army, or Aurelia does," Vance choked out again.

"Don't you wanna know where they are?" Noah looked over his shoulder at me.

"No," I answered. "If they're not already part of this world I don't want to be the one to get them involved."

"Oh." Noah released his hold on Vance and helped him up in a questionable display of a truce. "Never mind then."

Vance and I exchanged equally uncertain glances. I was perplexed. Noah had dragged me here to see if Vance had found the others like me the Strigoi had made? If he didn't want to hand them over to Aurelia, why would he care?

Noah placed his new *katana* on the table. "You can look, but don't touch," he warned.

"Where did you get it?" Vance cautiously inspected the sword. "It's fascinating. I sense a very dark energy from it."

"Some guy on the street." Noah summarized quite a bit. "So you stole it."

"No, technically the kid stole it."

"The guy who had it was killing people for no apparent reason," I explained. "Innocent people."

"Totally unrelated, but you wouldn't happen to have a way to banish spirits, would you?" Noah asked coyly. "Really angry guardian spirits. Besides that tethering thing. I mean banished for good. Far away somewhere. Like Japan."

Vance froze and turned to Noah. "This sword wouldn't happen to belong to such a spirit, would it?"

Noah shrugged. "I don't know, maybe?"

"What did you do?" Vance cried out. I should have known Noah was so interested in this *katana* for a reason.

"Yeah, I screwed the pooch on this one. I admit it. I might have unleashed an ancient curse on the world when we were back in Japan."

"That's what the guy with the polearm was? A spirit? No wonder the killings started the same night we arrived back in New York. It followed us back there. You're the one responsible for all those deaths!" I shouted.

"What did you want me to do?" Noah yelled back. "I got bored watching you roll around in the mud all day. I had to find some way to entertain myself! I was poking around this Buddhist temple when I found the *katana* lying there."

"Lying there?" I doubted that.

"Okay, maybe a few hundred feet underground in a sealed vault. What's it matter? I'm trying to fix it now. I already killed that guy."

"*We* killed him," I corrected. "And if he's dead, why are you worried? Why did we come here?"

"There may be more. Probably one or two ... or four." Noah smiled slyly. "I'm a bit rusty at reading ancient Japanese inscriptions."

"If it is a spirit like you say then it won't stop until the curse is broken. You have to give the sword back," Vance said.

"Uh, no? It's mine now. They'll just have to get over it. And that's why I need you. In case they can't." Noah pointed at Vance. "I'd get to work if I were you, because they're usually right behind me."

"I cannot believe this," Vance fumed.

"I know. It's getting pretty annoying." Noah took a seat again and kicked up his feet.

"I mean I cannot believe I've allowed you to suck me into your lunacy once again."

"Hey, the heart wants what the heart wants. If it makes you feel any better, you were the first person I thought to come to."

"Why didn't you just go back to Aurelia?" I asked. Noah stopped flipping through another dusty book.

"That's the smartest thing you've ever said, brat." He sat up in his chair. I couldn't tell if he was being sarcastic or not.

"What's that sound?" I asked. Something outside sounded like a speeding train going in circles around the chapel.

"Your time's probably up," Noah said to Vance.

"Archmage!" A very youthful-looking Strigoi girl came running in. "Oh, I didn't know we had visitors. You should know there is a ... a tornado surrounding our arcanum!"

"Yes, I can see that Heather," Vance said as all of us except Noah peered out the broken window to see the winds whipping around the building. Out of the vortex stepped another obscured figure, but this one willingly dropped his disguise to show himself to us. It was another Asian man. This time he was dressed in only the lightweight pants of a martial artist's *gi* with one black and one white leg and spikey black-and-white hair to match. He cracked his knuckles and smirked at us from the windstorm. His cocky expression was very similar to Noah's and he had a body that almost matched Noah's as well. The man stood there for a time, then crouched and touched the beads around his neck as if in prayer.

"I'm giving him the sword," I said and went to grab it. Noah snatched it away and put it beside his seat.

"Don't be such a coward. You wanted to kill the guy back in Manhattan because he was hurting Outsiders."

"That was before I knew it was all your fault!" I shouted.

"Minor detail. It shouldn't matter what the reason is for a fight. Just suck it up and go out there."

"You're the one who always told me there's no honor in a fight without purpose." I nailed him with his own philosophy.

"Goddamnit, why do you always have to pay attention when I think you aren't? Then sit here and wait until the bookworms figure something out. No one can get in here anyway with that magic bullshit blocking them."

"It doesn't stop the wind," Vance said as a gust tore through the windows, sending books and papers everywhere. The winds picked up and ripped bookshelves and tapestries down from the walls.

"This is *your* fight, Noah. What are *you* so scared of?" Noah didn't seem the least bit concerned, but I'd take any jab at him I could get. Maybe if we all got lucky we could get Noah out of our lives for good. " 'A sword is useless in the hands of a coward.' It's tattooed on your body."

" 'Know thy enemy,' " Noah quoted and reclined again. "Remember that? I'm not wasting my time until I know what I'm dealing with. *That's* why we're here."

" 'Those who cling to life die, and those who defy death live,' " I quoted back one more of his tattoos before we were interrupted.

Three more Strigoi women and a bald man, all wearing ceremonial hooded robes, joined us in a panic. "The walls are collapsing!" one of them screamed. "The arcanum will surely be blown from its foundation at any moment!" another cried. "Our years of research will be for naught!" a third shrieked.

"I'll go secure the specimens in the laboratory, Archmage," Heather offered and ran off.

"Specimens?" I glared at Vance. "What happened to a peaceful arcanum with no experiments?"

He pretended not to hear me and went back to Noah. "There's no way to do our research if the arcanum is destroyed."

"Fine. The kid and I will keep him busy."

"No, I won't. I don't want any part of this. *We* are not friends, remember? You kidnapped me. I'm flying out of here and going back to my friends."

"Good luck with that, because if I die, guess who they're coming after next?" He poked me in the chest. "And if they're coming after you, you can bet your 'friends' won't last more than a second. That is, if they even let you leave here."

"If you die, which would be great, they'll have their sword back," I snapped.

"The curse doesn't end until everyone who's tainted the *katana* dies. Anyone who's touched it will be on the list." Noah suddenly knew more about the situation than he had pretended to earlier.

"That's why you had me steal it for you, isn't it? I never should have trusted you."

"I warned you," Vance chimed in. The rest of the windows shattered, throwing shards of glass at us like knives. The wind itself became painful against my skin. It was hard to breathe.

"Let's get this over with." I headed for the door, knocking Noah's feet off the table on the way out.

Chapter Ten

"What's he saying?" This new spirit was a lot more fun than the last one. I couldn't understand a word he said, but as soon as Noah and I walked out he started flexing and kissing his biceps, then snickering and pointing at Noah to mock him.

"Something about you smelling bad." Noah had his hands on his hips, trying to play it cool, but I knew him and could tell he was seething on the inside. The man came closer, pointing to his incisors like he was trying to show us they were normal. Then he pointed to Noah's fangs and indicated with his fists that he was going to knock them out.

"I don't speak Japanese, but if you can understand me, I'm all for that!" I shouted over the gale-force winds.

"He's speaking Korean, dipshit." Noah crossed his arms. *He still had a couple inches and a few pounds on this other guy, but I'd love to see Noah taken down a peg,* I thought. *Out of my life for good would work, too.* The man clapped his hands in laughter and crossed his arms, mimicking Noah. Up close, I could see his eyes were almost pure white, like an albino's ivory orbs. They were striking against his very tan skin. He had a tattoo of a tiger sweeping across most of his body from front to back. He compared it to Noah's tattoos with animated gestures of mockery.

"Isn't Muy Thai from Thailand, not Korea?" I asked, after taking note of the rope hand wraps that ran the length of the spirit's forearms and another set around his upper arms that were common to that style of combat.

"Who cares?" Noah said something in what I assumed was Korean. It must have been rather rude, judging by the man's change in expression. Noah smiled and held out the prized *katana* to gloat over it. He flipped it around to hold it by the blade and offered the hilt to the spirit. Maybe he had finally come to his senses. All this trouble over a stupid sword wasn't worth it.

My faith in him was misplaced as usual. In a flash, Noah was behind the man, driving the sword through his back. The spirit didn't bleed, but he winced in incredible pain. He transformed into a gust of wind, throwing Noah and I into the air, before Noah could chop off his head.

Taking flight wasn't an option in the storm. It was arduous enough trying to get back to the ground without being thrown off course. The chapel was ripped from its foundation and smashed to pieces, adding large amounts of dangerous debris to the vortex. There was no sign of the Strigoi, who must have taken refuge underground.

Noah had been thrust out of his mist form as he tried to stop spinning helplessly. He was left at the mercy of the spirit, who showed he was able to move deftly through the storm. The man struck Noah with his fists repeatedly, sending him careening around the speeding winds. Noah struggled to get his bearings, but adapted well to being off the ground for someone who couldn't fly. He managed to keep the *katana* in his grasp and counter the spirit's oncoming fists with tempered steel.

Noah grappled with the man as both of them tumbled through the air. The spirit had Noah by the arm as it tried to wrench the sword away, while Noah used his free arm to try and snap the spirit's neck. The two fought until finally the sword fell at my feet. I thought the spirit would dive for it, but he continued to trade blows with Noah, turning their battle into a disorienting mid-air brawl. I was getting dizzy keeping track of their movement around and around until the wind came to an abrupt stop. Noah landed on his feet a second before the spirit's body crashed to the ground.

"Amateur." Noah spat blood at his fallen opponent. His cuts and bruises healed away as he sauntered over to claim his prize again. A bolt of lightning struck between us, blocking Noah from the sword.

"Not again," I moaned as the shadowed figure appeared with his polearm and showed his true self. Behind Noah the wind spirit got to his feet and cracked his neck back in place. "Oh, come on! You can have the sword. Do what you want with Noah. I'm not part of this."

I threw up my hands and went to walk away, but a gust carried the wind spirit to block my path. I tried motioning with my hands up that I wasn't involved as I sidestepped around him. My attempt at peace was met with a bone-breaking punch to my ribs that sent me sailing past Noah, who just waved to me. I had to lie there for an agonizing moment to let myself regenerate. I watched through tears as both spirits converged on Noah.

The added challenge of fighting two-on-one invigorated Noah. I didn't want to admit it, but seeing him take on both spirits at once was amazing. He wasn't just holding his own, but punishing them with devastating blows from his blades and fists at every opportunity. Most of the time the man with the polearm was able to parry, but the raw strength behind Noah's attacks caused the spirit to recoil and left him vulnerable.

It didn't last long, sadly, as Noah made a grave mistake by turning to mist to dodge a strike from the polearm. The wind spirit turned into a small-scale twister that caught and trapped Noah. The other man stabbed the ground in the eye of the storm with his polearm and electrified it, sending Noah's sizzling body tumbling.

Noah couldn't recover fast enough from the paralyzing bolt. The wind spirit leapt from the twister and grabbed Noah by the arm as he fell. The spirit pinned Noah's face in the dirt with one foot on the back of his head and violently twisted Noah's arm in an attempt to dislodge the *katana*. Noah couldn't break free without using his mist form, which he knew would only land him back in the same unfortunate position. The struggle ended with an excruciating crunch as Noah's shoulder, elbow, and wrist snapped.

He reeled in pain, letting the wind spirit take possession of the *katana*. The wind spirit plunged it through Noah's heart. The man sat on Noah's chest laughing and slapping him in the face as Noah lay there lifelessly impaled to the ground. Droplets of blood left Noah's body through the wound and traveled up the blade, turning it red. I had never seen a sword do that before. *That must be why it's special enough to be cursed*, I thought. Noah's golden tan turned gray as the blood was slowly drained from his inanimate body.

I wanted him out of my life. He was dangerous and untrustworthy, but my conscience felt differently. I tried to tell myself that I was only helping Noah in order to help myself as I watched the man with the polearm kick him. The anguish on Noah's face was evident as he lay there helplessly. I wouldn't be able to take on both of the spirits myself. I needed Noah, for now. That's all this was. *I won't let myself trust him again. If I help him here I can use that to bargain a truce later.* Not that that had ever worked in the past.

I tried to call the *katana* from Noah's body and immediately the wind spirit stopped punching Noah in the face to hold it down. The lightning spirit threw his polearm at me, but I was ready this time. I caught it with my powers and snapped it in two. With one forceful telekinetic blast I launched the warriors away, counting on them to take the sword with them. They didn't fall for my ruse and left the *katana* in Noah. When I went to pull it out, the wind spirit grabbed me from behind in a crushing bear hug, then transformed into a small cyclone. I knew what he was trying to do. I summoned pieces of the collapsed chapel walls to buffer the winds and shelter me from the lightning.

From underneath my makeshift hiding spot I had a line of sight on Noah. Both spirits were too distracted breaking down my walls to notice me pull the *katana* from his heart. Noah vanished the second he was unstaked. I threw off the rubble around me to cause a distraction. I knew Noah would go for the wind spirit first to settle their rivalry, so I took the lightning one. I also knew they were deadlier together since their powers were complementary.

As soon as Noah engaged the wind spirit with a sword to the back of the skull I began putting all my focus into crushing the lightning spirit. I envisioned a bubble around him collapsing from all sides. It felt like he was made of metal, but I gradually made progress, dooming the man to a slow, torturous demise. He let loose bolts of lightning in retaliation. I blocked them with floating rubble. I couldn't concentrate on everything and had to let him go.

Noah was in the distance. The *katana* exchanged hands between him and the wind spirit a dozen times. He still had both his *wakizashi* at his hips. That gave me an idea.

I summoned both *wakizashi* to me and spun them together like propeller blades. The lightning spirit had no weapon to parry with, but he dodged the blades with ease as I got him used to a simple pattern ... and then separated the blades. The lightning warrior dodged away from one blade and right into the other. All it took was one full turn to sever his head from his shoulders. He exploded in a wave of azure light. I shot the *wakizashi* outward, missing Noah by a hair, and plunged them into the wind spirit's eyes.

"Give me this." I flew over and grabbed the *katana* from Noah's hand. I beheaded the spirit, letting him explode into a white light.

"Um ..." Noah stared at me, befuddled.

"If you ever interfere in my life again you better be damn sure you know how to kill me first." I shoved the *katana* back in his hands and stormed off to pull Vance from his rabbit hole.

"The sword is called *Juuchi Yosamu*, Ten Thousand Cold Nights, although some refer to it as Muramasa, the name of the sword master who forged it." Noah sat on a crate in the Strigoi's underground bunker, disclosing all he knew about the *katana*. He was pretty beaten up and I knew he needed blood, but it wasn't coming from me. It surprised me that he hadn't demanded it already. "I found it in a hidden shrine under the Kiyomizu Temple in Kyoto. There are several legends about where it originated from and how it got its power. All I know is that it drinks blood and cuts sharper than any blade I've ever handled."

"Why would you need a sword that drinks blood when you already do that yourself?" I knew I shouldn't bother asking just to get some half-assed answer.

"I can think of a few applications," Vance said. "It wouldn't be used to harvest food, but to wear down those more impervious, blood-reliant opponents when a quick death isn't an option. Say, a particularly troublesome undead?"

"How do we stop the curse?" Noah asked, wiping the blood from his nose. "And don't say give it back. This is all I have." There was something melancholy in the way he said it.

"Spirits aren't necessarily tethered to objects in order to exist on this plane like ghosts are, but they can be summoned," Vance explained. "It isn't as simple as breaking a tether and banishing them back to their dimension. You would need magic more powerful than the kind protecting it in order to cast a counter-spell. I would have to know more about the sword, the curse, and its origin. Go back to where you found the sword and find the truth so I know what we are dealing with."

"You're coming with me. I'm not really the research type," Noah said to Vance.

"I'm not really the field type, and I will be warding this place against the elements in case we get another visit while you are gone."

"What's wrong, Noah? Scared you've lost your edge?" I had to get one more jab in.

"I don't get scared." Noah's eyes cut like daggers. "And you're coming with me, kid."

"Like hell I am," I laughed. "Let them come after me. I think I proved I can handle myself. As far as I'm concerned you owe me, *again*, so you and I are done." I waited for a snappy comeback, a threat — anything.

"I need blood."

"Good luck with that," I refused, throwing his own catchphrase back at him.

"Our synthetic reserves are low," Vance said. "I'm afraid you'll have to go elsewhere."

"Happy hunting," I smirked. Noah left without another word. "A swordsman without a sword is just a man, but a man with his pride is nothing," I recited his line from the other day back to him.

"You handled yourself admirably tonight," Vance commented. The other Strigoi passed by the small concrete room carrying books and various research supplies and trying to salvage what they could from the wreckage above. "This is more like the power you were created to have."

"Yeah, thanks." Without even wanting to, I had fulfilled the purpose I was designed for: protecting my creators. "Nice place you have here. Sorry about your house."

"It was only a dupe to mask the laboratory. Nothing important was lost. If you wish to repay me, however, you could donate a sample of blood or tissue, or an organ or two." The harsh fluorescent lighting made Vance's undead flesh appear even more sickly and conspicuous.

"Fine, but first I want to know more about this looming darkness Rozalin talked about. I met another Ancient that mentioned it too."

"Another Ancient?" Vance looked concerned.

"His name was Castile Belanger. Do you know him?"

"Ah, the ex-Archios. There aren't many Ancients in the first place, but his name is fairly well-known because of his very public falling-out with Aurelia. They were uneasy allies for a time until she usurped his rule in England."

"He mentioned the darkness coming and resetting the world, like when you mentioned the battle between Heaven and Hell spilling out on to the Earth."

"I suppose it would be a dark time for us all, yes. Whether literal or metaphorical, I can't say. I am no theologian, but many human religions believe similarly in an end and rebirth to the world. It would be impossible to efficiently prepare for such an event."

"Minerva didn't think so and I can't believe you would just accept the end like that. What exactly are you working on down here?" I asked as a bald Strigoi man passed us for the fifth time carrying equipment. He was wearing strange goggles that looked like an exaggerated version of a watchmaker's glasses. This time, his clothes were spattered with blood.

"Oh, some things. Uh, nothing too interesting. Certainly nothing to worry yourself over. A lot of reading, really. Minerva was convinced that the denizens of Hell would reward her for her loyalty, but they will tempt you with whatever you desire most to add you to their ranks." Vance dodged the question with the finesse of a four-year-old. "Now about that sample?"

"Yeah, sorry," I said as I made my way up the ladder to leave. "I lied."

Chapter Eleven

Six days later I dragged myself onto the Blackbourne's property. I was cold, hungry, and most of all, exhausted. I hadn't eaten or slept for a week as I backpacked across Europe, sans backpack. Without Noah to sneak us onto planes, I could only fly short distances at night. By the fourth day I became paranoid, waiting for an ambush that never came. Maybe Noah had broken the curse, or the spirits were too busy chasing him. Either way it meant peace and quiet for me. Lonely peace and quiet. I was looking forward to being back with the Blackbournes, even if they were a bunch of deviants.

"Dorian!" William ran up to me after I was let in through the gate. His face was wearier than ever. His quest against the undead must have been taking its toll on his body, and undoubtedly on his mind. "Thank the Lord. We were starting to think we'd never find you."

"I'm sorry, it's a long story." I was so out of breath it was hard to express my joy. In spite of having sufficient time, I wasn't able to come up with a good excuse for my disappearance. It was time to come clean with the truth. "Why's your pocket glowing?"

William looked puzzled and retrieved the amulet from his pants pocket. A shining light overpowered the morning sun and immediately ignited my skin with searing flames. I tried to shield my eyes, but all I could see was William's silhouette in the glare before everything went black.

The single overhead light wasn't enough to reach the perimeter of the dark room where I woke up. I tried to move, but my arms and legs were restrained with iron shackles fixed in the stone wall. I tried to make sense of what had happened as I came to. Why had the amulet burned me?

Something was moving in the shadows next to me.

"Hello?" I groaned. "Who's there?" There was no answer except the sound of rattling chains. Using my powers, I felt out the shape of a body in the direction the sound was coming from.

"Emily?" I asked again, but there was still no response. I swung the hanging light to catch a glimpse of who it was and gasped in fright. The body of a girl hung shackled to the wall. Her dark brown hair was stringy and matted. Clumps were missing from her scalp. She was motionless except for a sporadic twitch that made her body spasm and shake the chains. Her dead unblinking eyes stared straight down and her skin even more gray than the Strigoi at their worst. There were numerous cuts all over her body, but worst of all was the wooden stake that penetrated her heart. I removed it from her with my telekinesis and called out her name again.

"Who are you?" she cried in fear. "Where's William?"

"I'm Dorian. Emily, did William do this to you?" I already knew the answer, but I didn't want it to be true.

"You are the first visitor I've had. Other than William, of course."

"Visitor? Emily, I'm chained to a wall. We're prisoners."

"No, that isn't true! He loves me. He's keeping me here to contain the evil I hold inside until he finds a way to cure me. If you are here too that means you must be a friend in need."

Love is blind, but she's delusional. She must have been here for almost a decade in this condition. How could she be so complacent about being imprisoned? I wondered.

"Just because you're different doesn't mean you're evil, Emily. What he's doing to you isn't love, it's torture."

"You don't understand. William would never hurt a fly. You have to have faith in him. I know he can save us."

"He's been hurting you. So do you consider yourself less than a fly?"

"He just needed to remove as much of the bad blood as he could. I deserved it, for I have sinned." She didn't even hesitate with her answers. It was like she was reciting a script.

"The way I heard it you both sinned, so he's equally responsible. Yet you're here and he's free."

"Because ... it is my fault I lost our child. I am marked by the Devil. I don't belong out there. William repented and God forgave him. He is doing the Lord's work now. If I have faith in him he will save me too. It won't be long now."

"That isn't love, Emily. You aren't evil because of what you are. You didn't ask to be this way. Only your actions can make you evil and you didn't do anything wrong. Nothing you did merits being treated like this. You have every right to be treated with kindness if you are a good person." What did my actions say about me? What had I done for the amulet to burn me? Was I destined to become the evil instrument of destruction my creators had intended me to be? "He should love you for who you are. I don't think there is a cure, but if there is you should be finding it together."

Was this punishment because I left Noah to fend for himself when I knew he needed me? I had even taken pleasure in seeing him humbled because I wanted revenge so badly for his betrayal. It didn't make a difference who he was. My own actions that must have changed the amulet's judgment of me.

"What are you doing?" A door flew open and William rushed in wearing his armor. "Stop talking to her, monster!" He picked up the stake and replaced it in her chest.

"I'm not a monster, William. How can you do that to someone you say you love?" I looked at Emily's limp body dangling from the chains.

"I knew there was something different about you the first time we met. You weren't the hero doing God's work back in New York. You were the monster killing your own kind so you'd be the only one."

"What is it with you and hating anything that's different? I never did anything wrong to you and now you're treating me like this. Who are you to judge me?"

"You've been lying to me and my brothers this whole time, pretending to be some innocent homeless boy. I don't know what you are, but your trick to hide yourself from the amulet has failed. I know you're no undead or the amulet would have killed you instantly. That can only mean you are a demon."

"I'm not a demon. I don't know what I am, but I'm not evil and neither are all the undead. Neither is your girlfriend here. Have you ever tried the amulet on her?"

"Don't pretend you know anything about her!"

"But you can pretend to know me? And all the innocent undead you've killed just because they aren't like you? Give me a break. You have no idea what real evil is." Unfortunately, I was still shackled.

"Is that a threat?" He drew his sword. "You would be dead right now if I didn't have questions. Who else are you working with? I know you must have left to inform others about the Brotherhood so you could take us out."

"No. I'm saying there's real evil out there you could be banishing if you opened your eyes a little. Can you let me down now? I'm not going to hurt you."

"You aren't leaving this place. I should have known I wouldn't get a straight answer from a demon."

"This is hopeless. There's no getting through to you." I broke free from the shackles with ease.

"Stay back!" William yelled and held out the amulet. My skin caught fire and I had flashbacks of being burned alive. I knocked the amulet from his hand, but in my frenzy I smashed him into the wall and shattered it.

"I'm sorry! I didn't mean to." This wasn't helping my case. He swung his sword at me to no avail as I plucked it gently from his hands. He looked terrified as I kept trying to calm him, but words weren't helping. I ran after him as he fled the room. It wasn't worth it. He might never change his mind and I didn't want to fight him.

I went back to Emily and removed the chains and stake. "You're free now."

"Where is William? What did you do to him?" Emily cowered against the wall. What was wrong with this girl? This wasn't love or faith. This was brainwashing.

"I didn't do anything to him. He ran off on his own. Emily, there are others out there like us. They're good people that won't judge you and don't want to hurt anyone. It's a dark world out there, but maybe your faith can bring them a little light without your being chained up and tortured. Don't you think you've suffered enough?"

"But what about William?"

"If he truly loves you then he'll stop this obsession. He isn't as pure as you think. He kills with hate and prejudice. He has to find his way and you have to find yours. Isn't that why God put us all on this Earth? How can you repent your own sins by hiding away?"

"Where — where do I go?" she asked as she crawled out from the shadows.

"You can try New York. There is a group there called the Outsiders. They are like you. They're good people." With Noah out of the city the threat against them should be gone too. Hopefully some of them had been spared. "If you find someone by the name of Octavio tell him I sent you. He, uh, also goes by 'Grampy.' Don't ask."

"New York is so far. How will I get there?"

"Come with me." The door led to a narrow staircase, which climbed to a small wine cellar. A giant cask hid another staircase to William's room. I went first in case William was waiting to jump out, but he was nowhere in sight. Luck was on our side; night had fallen. I grabbed money from his dresser and clothes from his extensive wardrobe and gave them to her.

"I can't take this. It's stealing," she refused.

"Consider it a charitable donation. Besides, weren't you two a couple?" She took the clothes and money and looked around the room in awe. "Yeah, he enjoyed all this while you were down there just because you were 'evil.' Fair, huh?"

She didn't come back with a reason for why he deserved the luxury, so maybe we were making progress.

"You're going to need blood. You won't get far looking like that." I offered her my wrist. "Just do it. Time is of the essence." She bit down nervously. I realized I didn't know what coven she was. Noah bit me once years ago, and the Carpathians had bitten me in battle. They were both very different sensations.

The bite hurt, but not more than that amulet. I turned away so she couldn't see me grimace. Afterward, I lied and told her it hadn't felt bad. The last thing this girl needed was an eating disorder. Looking at her made me even sadder once she had taken on a more human appearance. She looked like a totally average doe-eyed teenage girl, aside from the fangs and pale skin. She should have been in high school, not chained up in a basement. I wished I could have done more to help her, but she had to learn to be strong and independent, not to follow me around. My tendency to attract danger would only make things harder on us both.

I brought her outside after she had changed and washed up a bit while I guarded the door. "Jump the guard wall and follow the road east. You'll reach Bath before morning if you run. You have enough money there to buy a small house. Get a room at a hotel to sleep through the day and then take a taxi to the airport near Bristol. Make sure to get a flight that won't arrive during the day. You can get a map of New York City when you land at the airport. Also try to remember to exchange currency there. This money isn't going to get you far in New York." I thought of writing this all down for her as she stared back at me with her eyes glazed over. "Got it?"

"Yes! Do you think I'll have enough money here after all that for an umbrella in case I get caught in the sun?" Coming from anyone else I would have taken that as sarcasm.

"No, don't go in the sun. *Ever.* Nothing is going to help you with that." I sent her on her way and wished her luck.

"Thanks, I'll add you to my prayers at night!" she said cheerfully. I watched as she attempted to jump the eight-foot wall. Next, she tried to climb it. She looked back at me, unsure of what to do. I flew her over to speed things along.

"Thanks! Which way is east?" she shouted, probably alerting everyone on the property.

"Your left," I whispered back loudly.

"Okay, thanks!" she whispered. I waited until I heard the sound of her footsteps fade into the distance across the dry leaves.

"Look who it is!" A voice startled me. I whirled around to see Micah and Owen in their full hunter gear.

"Is Willy dead?" Owen pulled off his mask.

"No?" That was a strange first question. "Why would he be?"

"Oh." Owen lit a cigarette. "He told us you were some sort of thing now and he had you locked in his basement. I figured if you got out you must've gone through him."

"I'm not here to hurt anybody. I scared him off and he ran."

"Good enough for me." Micah shrugged and bummed a cigarette off Owen.

"You guys don't care that I'm ... not human?" I was a bit confused. I waited for them to turn aggressive.

"I knew the whole bloody time," Micah confessed. "And so did Owen."

"What? How? I never used my powers around you."

"Well first, you drank enough elephant tranquilizer at the party to kill a herd. We wanted to have a bit of fun and drive out to werewolf country with you to see if you could make your way back."

"And second, your neckbiter friends aren't as good at covering their tracks as they think they are. After Willy called us to say he was bringing you over from New York he sent a picture from his phone. He was always suspicious of you. It was kind of strange for you to be hanging around that biter-infested building and kill one yourself."

"You're more twisted than I thought. And to set the record straight, I didn't kill him."

"Whatever helps you sleep at night, mate. Because it sure isn't tranqs," Micah laughed and took a drag from his cigarette before he continued explaining. "I remember seeing that pretty face of yours fighting some nasty winged buggers on a street camera a couple years back. We heard about the headache over there, but by the time we checked it out it was over."

Noah's lost love Vivian had been in charge of covering up the events in Manhattan. When she had fallen the task passed to the other Archios, like the jeweler, who had obviously done a piss-poor job. Outsourcing at its finest. How many more people had seen that footage?

"You're not going to hunt me?"

"No fun in hunting something that doesn't want to fight back," Owen shrugged. "And we don't hunt our own."

"What about William?" I asked. "You didn't seem too concerned that I might have killed him."

"He broke the rules. He already admitted he attacked you. It's on bloody camera, for Christ's sake." Micah motioned to the perimeter wall by the gatehouse. "I have a feeling we're not going to be seeing much of him around here from now on. This isn't the first time we've had non-human brothers. They don't typically stick around long. I suspect that's Willy's doing."

"You're still gonna have to pull your weight around here. Don't think you're special now," Owen chimed in. "Do you grant wishes?"

"I'm not a genie."

"How about presents for good boys and girls?"

"That's Santa Claus, and no. I don't think either of you would make the cut."

"You're damn right about that," Owen laughed. "Let's go in so we can make a toast."

"A toast to what?" I asked.

"I don't know? Thursday? I just need to get out of these clothes and into some liquor. Don't worry about Willy. We'll serve him the eviction papers personally if he can't handle the rules. I never cared much for the wanker anyway."

"I appreciate it, but you don't need to do that. I won't be staying long either. Bad things always happen to people around me," I said, feeling a bit of remorse for having come back at all.

At least I had helped Emily.

"Stay the night, then. You look like you could use it," Micah offered. I accepted and went with them to Micah's house on the estate.

"You knew about Emily, right? How come you never did anything?" I asked them. "Wasn't she one of you?"

"She wasn't. Willy would have had our heads if we interfered," Owen answered. "It's not like we didn't say anything to him, but that was his headache. None of us agree too often about anything. It was just another log on the fire."

"She was an innocent girl."

"A lot of girls and boys come here innocent and leave anything but," Micah said. Was he talking about himself and Owen? "It's over now. I'm sure she'll be fine out there, mate."

"You know?" I thought no one had seen Emily's escape. Micah took out his phone and showed me how it allowed him to watch the cameras around the property. I felt pretty stupid. Someone was always watching.

Next, Micah played an audio recording for me. It was of our trip to Castile's. "You remember that?" I asked.

"No, that's why I recorded it. Owen and I thought something was a bit odd before we left. I wanted proof. One of the bloodsuckers I interrogated seemed to think I had been there before. Then the GPS was already programmed with the location. It wasn't just in the Lamb, either. I know I drive pissed all the time, but not enough to forget going there in five different cars. Good thing the old chap doesn't keep up with technology or he might have known he was being recorded."

There was a constant high-pitched interference throughout the recording, and Castile's voice sounded strange and demonic, as though multiple voices were speaking at once. You could barely make out what he was saying. The longer the recording went on, the more it creeped me out. I was reminded of Castile's battle with the longhaired spirit, during which he'd turned his mansion into a house of horrors.

"I told you I hate going after the neckbiters." Micah turned off the recording. "They're always playing games."

Chapter Twelve

I said my goodbyes to the Blackbournes the next day as their housekeepers were setting up a gigantic Christmas tree, and left for Bath clean and clothed. I promised I'd visit, but I knew the best thing for all of us was to stay away. They may have accepted me for what I was, but I still felt I didn't fit in. I couldn't change how they lived their lives and it wasn't my place to try, but maybe with William shamed and at least temporarily out of the picture they wouldn't be so prejudiced toward the supernatural community.

The trip to Bath was another sobering experience. During any time I had to myself, my mind ran wild. I wished I could turn off my thoughts. Where was I going to go now? What was I going to do? Was this what the rest of my immortality would be like? Wandering from place to place, always saying goodbye, fighting to be left alone and then starting it all over again? I had asked myself these questions a million times before and still I had no answer. Sometimes I just wanted to lie down and let the world go on without me. These were my darkest, immutable thoughts. I could escape spirits, the undead, and demons, but not what was in my own head. I hated being alone and I hated saying goodbye even more.

I made it to the city by the afternoon. I had wanted to explore when I first passed through Bath on the way to the Blackbournes' estate. It was a grand city with an Old World feel that you wouldn't find back home in Boston or New York, but most interesting to me were the famous Roman baths. In my travels I had been to France, Germany, and Japan, but I was never able to enjoy any of the cultural beauty those places had to offer.

My first stop was in the heart of the city to visit the baths before something catastrophic happened. They might have been around for two thousand years, but with my luck that day would be the day they got wiped off the face of the planet. The bubbly museum staff greeted me as soon as I set foot inside. My heart broke a little when they asked if I was a student. There was nothing I wouldn't give to have my biggest problems be midterms, research papers, filling my portfolio, and pulling all-nighters at the library.

I strolled through the interactive museum, wading through the horde of exuberant children running amok. Each consecutive exhibit added to my itch to start sketching. In my human days I never would have called architecture a serious interest of mine. I liked it and had always found it interesting that a pile of ordinary wood and stones could make something both functional and artistic, but it never lit a fire in me. Nothing did back then. My choices were based on how I could hide and go through life unnoticed. If I had enjoyed math I would have picked accounting. Architecture was more of something I'd chosen on a whim for a college major — my discomfort around blood had ensured I wouldn't be following my parents' footsteps into medicine. *It's almost ironic how every step I take seems to be soaked in sanguinary humors*, I thought. If I could go back in time I would tell myself not to regret a single mundane second studying or drawing.

"Beautiful, no?" A man's heavy Italian accent stood out amongst the crowd of jabbering children and curious visitors. I loved other languages and dialects. Maybe it was the mystique they generated thanks to my own woefully inept attempts at learning a foreign language in the past. Maybe it was just that the exotic was always sexy to me, whether it was British, French, or Italian.

I inspected a miniature replica of the Roman Forum that showed what it must have looked like in its prime until I heard the Italian accent again.

"You have been here before? To Roma?" A hand pointed to the replica. It wasn't until I looked up that I realized the man was speaking to me. There was something about the way he looked at me, but I couldn't quite place what it was.

"N-no," I stammered in awkward response. "Not yet, at least."

It was more than my severe lack of social skills that caused me to be caught off guard. The man himself was disarmingly gorgeous. He was slightly taller than Noah, with jet-black hair and stubble, olive skin, and jade-green eyes. His masculine beauty wasn't supplemented by any hypnotic aura, or an entrancing gaze that caused a feeling of blissful intoxication. Thankfully, there was also a complete lack of fangs in his brilliant white smile. His eyes, while the same color as Noah's, lacked Noah's steel-sharp soul-penetrating gaze. Instead, they were friendly, and best of all they were *human*.

"You will love it if you go." His smile was so welcoming, not at all like the cocky grin of Noah's I always wanted to wipe off his face. It was unusual for a stranger to strike up conversation in public in New York, but I noticed a lot of the patrons here would exchange comments or even just a smile as they walked from one exhibit to the next.

The room was so packed there wasn't more than an inch between the two of us. I had to strain my neck to meet his eyes. He was dressed remarkably stylish for a trip to the museum, in black slacks and vest and a pinstripe button-down shirt. The top three buttons were undone, exposing faint traces of chest hair across his pecs. The somber outfit didn't detract from his warm appearance.

"Is that where you come from?" I scrambled to find some way to continue the conversation, hoping I hadn't just offended him.

"Why do you ask this? I am not from here?" he asked seriously. My face must have shown how mortified I was by my own stupidity. He laughed and patted me on the shoulder. "I am teasing you. Yes, it is my home."

"I've always wanted to go there to see the Colosseum." I hurried to recover from my *faux pas*. "The architecture there is my favorite. I made a diorama of it in school once."

Why did I say that?

"Ah, you are a, hm, what is the word? A scholar?" It wasn't just his attractiveness making me nervous. It sounded as if he was using his tongue to make love to every consonant that crossed his lips. There was no rushing to finish a sentence. Every word had its place.

"No, it was in elementary school." I smiled. Maybe my interest in architecture was more deeply rooted than I previously thought. He smiled back. I realized he might not know what a diorama was. "Do they have that word in Italian? Diorama? I don't know what to call it. You make it in a shoebox with papier-mâché."

"Eh, no? Maybe another word?"

"It's like this." I pointed to the replica. "But smaller and not as professional."

"Ah, I see." He was still smiling, but I didn't think I had made it any easier to understand. "How is this? Your favorite." He placed his hand on my back to lead me over to a display of the Colosseum.

"Yup, that's the one." I forced myself to take my eyes off him to look at the exhibit. I wasn't a touchy person and valued my personal space more than most, but when he put his hand on me I tingled. It was a completely natural feeling, without any hypnotic supernatural interference.

"It is my favorite place in all of Roma. Many, many great battles were here. Now, not so much." He stood so close to me as people squeezed by that I could almost feel his body heat, and when he spoke, his deep voice sounded like it was whispering into my ear. I was beginning to wonder whether he worked here because of how talkative he was. He had to be in his mid-to-late twenties, too young to be the owner or curator. Maybe he was a model they hired to walk around and entice people to donate.

"How long have you been in England?" I took a step back to give my neck a rest. He had a slightly leaner build than Noah, but similar broad shoulders and muscular physique — both accentuated by the form-fitting European cut of his clothes. Being short was annoying, even though five foot nine was technically average. Too bad I couldn't fly without causing a riot.

"A very short time. I am on a visit … a tourist. I just learned this word. My English is bad, I know."

"No, no, it's really good," I assured him. "I was just wondering if you worked here."

"You are nice." His smile was so sincere. *Maybe the Blackbournes sent him to keep an eye on me while I'm still in England,* I thought. "I think you work here, no? I see the passion your eyes have when you look at the diorama."

I tried not to laugh at the thought of *me* being passionate about something. Just a few hours ago, I had been fantasizing about lying in a field until the end of the world.

"What?" he asked. "You are teasing me now! You taught me this 'diorama.' Is it not?"

"It is! I wasn't laughing at you. I haven't ever thought of myself as passionate. It's a long story. It's a good thing." He watched my mouth as I spoke. I looked away to stop myself from blushing. The more I avoided his eyes, the more I broke out into nervous laughter, until he joined in.

"Why are you looking at me like that?" I asked. His smile grew bigger and he shook his head.

"Is this bad? I look to your lips to see the English words."

A man and woman in Ancient Roman clothes interrupted us. My initial reaction was that we were either under attack or about to be. I had to do a quick scan to be sure they weren't supernatural before I calmed down. People gathered around as the couple hosted an informative lecture on ancient times in the Roman Empire and the purpose of the Forum. The man I had been speaking with was thoroughly engaged in the assembly, so I took the opportunity to bow out and explore the rest of the museum.

The bath area took up two floors, with a balcony supported by limestone columns overlooking the main pools. It was spectacular. There was nothing there that I didn't love. If I ever had a home I would want at least part of it to resemble the architecture I saw. Gazing down into the tranquil steaming water and immersing myself in the serene ambiance was therapeutic. For a moment the raging storm always swirling in my head was quelled. I heard a group discussing how during the summer months the baths were opened later by torchlight. *That's something I'd like to experience*, I thought.

I carried on toward the sound of music until I found its source in a tea room adjoining the museum. Being around all that water was making me thirsty and I hadn't had anything to eat in days. The Blackbournes had given me money before they left, and I couldn't think of a better way to use it. While they were hospitable hosts, I hadn't gotten the feeling they acted the way they did out of concern. I was more of an investment for the Brotherhood than a friend they cared about. They treated William the same way.

The hostess seated me at a corner booth in the back and presented me with complimentary pastries and a menu. This was almost too classy for someone who would be scavenging for food in the dirt in twenty-four hours, if I even ate at all. I wanted something refreshing after passing through the heated areas, but the waitress stared at me like I had ordered blood when I asked if they had iced tea. The English take the sanctity of their brewed drinks very seriously. I settled for the hot tea suggested by the waitress instead, which was as pleasantly relaxing as the orchestral trio.

"Can I sit?" I hadn't noticed the Italian man walk up to my table and was a bit surprised by his continued interest in me. It was difficult to feel him out and I was sure he felt the same. Could he be like me? Maybe he was just a friendly European.

"Sure." He took a seat on the booth closer to me than most strangers probably would, but maybe I was reading too much into it. "How was the speech?"

"Very nice. But I am sad they do not speak Latin."

"I don't think anyone speaks Latin anymore. It's a dead language."

"Ah, I think maybe the scholars do, no?" He watched my mouth intently again when I spoke, making me feel a bit uneasy.

"Maybe," I answered, and quickly sipped my tea so he would stop looking.

"I have not learned your name. I am Gianluca." He introduced himself with another warm smile.

"Dorian." I wanted to dive into the pastries before my stomach joined the conversation. I felt weird shoving food into my mouth and offered him some.

"Dorian," he repeated and selected a pastry. It sounded so much better coming from him. I felt like I had been saying my own name wrong this whole time. "I see you have passion for Roma and the desserts."

I couldn't hold back a laugh, which was dangerous. My second pastry was half in my mouth and I almost lost it when he joined in. It was judgmental of me, but I had assumed because of his appearance that he wouldn't have a good sense of humor. Insanely attractive people were usually stoic, with an air of indifference — but that could have just been my high-school experience. I hadn't really had the chance to socialize much since then and Noah was not the best counterargument.

"Now we have two things together," he added in between our laughter. We chatted about Rome, both past and present, for what felt like minutes, but when the sun set halfway through our conversation I realized we had been talking for hours. It was the best time I'd had for as long as I could remember and, as Gianluca put it, I felt "passion" in my words. I had asked the waitress for a pen so I could draw on my napkin to show Gianluca what I meant when words failed us. After a while my drawings turned into a bunch of silly hieroglyphics — stick people and animals mixed with architectural sketches. When he took the pen from my hand to draw something I swore his fingers lingered as we touched, but it could have just been my mind getting the better of me again. We paused at the sight of a small face peering over the table at us. A child from the family next to us had wandered over to see what the excitement was about.

"Ciao!" Gianluca greeted the child with a wave and offered him one of the pastries. The child's eyes lit up and his grin matched Gianluca's as he snatched the dessert and toddled back to his parents, holding it up like a trophy. The family thanked Gianluca with smiles and clapping as their little boy enjoyed his prize, keeping his eyes on Gianluca the whole time.

"You made a new friend," I said.

"Two, no?" He placed his hand on my shoulder, still grinning from ear to ear.

"Are you always so happy?" I asked and smiled back at him.

"Is this bad? I am happy to come to this place and to meet someone like you." His hand traveled across the back of my neck until his arm was around my shoulder. "I think you are very, very beautiful." He was looking right into my eyes. My heart raced. A minute ago I had caught myself imagining that this would happen, but now that it had, I panicked and didn't know what to do.

I wanted to enjoy the moment, but for once it wasn't the fear of demons or impending doom that had me anxious. It was the other patrons in the room. I felt like all eyes were on me and it was making my head swirl with self-consciousness. The beaming little boy watched us until his mother took note of Gianluca's arm around me and covered her son's eyes. The family whispered to each other and exchanged glances, gawking at us like we were animals at the zoo.

"Please, stop," I said under my breath as our waitress passed by the table. She did a double take and tried to cover it up by removing an empty plate from our table. I watched as she ignored the kitchen and went to talk to the hostess up front, who turned to look at us. "Everybody is looking at us."

"Because you are the most beautiful here," he insisted and caressed my shoulder. "You are shy. I can tell."

"I don't think that's it." My hand started to shake and I put it under the table to hide it, but that probably only made us look worse.

"I do not understand?" Gianluca asked. He was leaned back in the booth comfortably with his arm still around me, completely oblivious to the judgmental stares. The venom spread throughout the room like a plague. It wasn't long until the rest of the patrons and staff joined in observing the freak show.

"I have to go." I pulled away and jumped from the booth, throwing whatever money I had in my pocket onto the table. I had probably tipped the waitress with enough to buy a small yacht, but I would have done anything to get out of the situation.

"Wait," Gianluca called after me.

"I'm sorry," I apologized, trying not to let my emotions take over. "It was nice meeting you, but it's getting late."

"I will walk you —" Gianluca started, but I was already out the door. I ducked around the back of a parking garage and shot up to the roof. From over the edge I could see Gianluca on the sidewalk, looking to see which way I had gone. I curled up in the darkest corner out of sight and begged myself not to start sobbing. I was stronger than this. I didn't need love or romance to be happy. It was a weakness.

I had thought the night couldn't get any worse, and then rain began to pour from the night sky. The nearby sound of people running to their cars didn't strike me as odd until I realized there were no cars on the roof. After a flash of lightning I looked around and saw three shadowed figures crackling with energy approach. The same two

Asian warriors from before revealed themselves to me, this time accompanied by a geisha carrying a parasol. She was dressed in a dark blue kimono with a minimal floral design, in heavy contrast to her white face paint, which gave her a rather solemn, dignified look. Their skin was exuding a pale iridescent glow that they didn't have during our other encounters. The two men spoke to me as they stepped forward, but I had no way of understanding them until the long-haired one held out the Muramasa. They had finally managed to reclaim it from Noah, which meant he must be dead. My heart sank, although I didn't know if I should be feeling remorse or relief.

"Just leave me alone!" I shouted over a crack of thunder. "You got what you wanted. Now go away!"

I knew it would be no use to try and communicate, and even if I could I doubted they would break the curse at my request. *How long will this go on for if I can't die?*

The wind spirit inhaled dramatically. There wasn't anything up here to take cover behind and a lot of innocent people below could get hurt. I knew I could beat two of them, but had no clue what the woman would add. I flew back to bring the fight to a less populated area. The man exhaled a razor-sharp gale that cut down to the bone. I fell from the sky face-first onto the concrete roof and staggered to my feet in a pool of my blood. The wounds healed, but my clothes were shredded.

The rain picked up into a torrential downpour and winds churned to monsoon levels. Pedestrians screamed as geysers erupted from the sewers. The waterspouts flooded the streets and the parking garage roof, which was enclosed by cement walls on all sides. The water was up to my ankles and I knew what was coming as the long-haired man charged a bolt of lightning into the Muramasa. I had the choice between flying and being cut to ribbons, or staying down and being electrocuted. These spirits always had their bases covered and it only got worse the more of them there were.

Visibility was terrible, but I could just make out the trio's faint illumination as they circled. I lashed out at one of them with a shockwave that sent deep fractures across the structure in all directions, shaking it to its core and setting off car alarms. The barricading walls broke and let the water drain out on to the street. For all the damage it caused, whichever spirit I'd hit was unfazed. The two men charged me head-on, alternating fist and sword, merciless wind and brutal lightning. My body was pummeled and torn apart in seconds, leaving me writhing in anguish.

Adrenaline pumped through my compromised veins and culminated in a detonation of psionic energy. The roof caved in, smashing the cars under it to scrap metal, but the three spirits jumped down after me with hardly a scratch. The geisha erected a prismatic shield, negating any damage to herself, and the man in black and white flickered incorporeally into the wind to dodge. I couldn't find the lightning spirit, which worried me. It wasn't long until he made himself known by stabbing me through the back. My body felt cold, yet images of hellfire and brimstone flashed in my head as the blood was sucked from my heart. The

Muramasa didn't just drink blood. Vance said it had an aura and now it was giving me visions of Hell. The sword itself was alive and it was evil.

Flashbacks of burning took over and another, more powerful telekinetic shockwave was expelled in all directions. The *katana* and the spirit wielding it were flung back, along with a hail of rubble. The cars in the lot were thrown like toys. Still the spirits remained intact. They were so much stronger this time. What was going to happen to me when they couldn't kill me — or would they find a way?

I tried again, this time focusing my fury on the spirit with the sword. He was crushed against the stone wall until it broke. The man was forcefully propelled out the hole as the other two spirits bore down on me. Flashing lights and the sound of sirens and hysteria flooded in from the outside. The lights inside grew dim and I knew this would put me at an even greater disadvantage. I flew out and up to another rooftop, from which I witnessed the chaos erupting in the city.

The light from street lamps and buildings dimmed, but didn't shut off. Even people's car lights and cell phones dimmed, as did the moon peeking through the storm clouds. All sources of light weakened to such a point that their radiance served no purpose. This was not a blackout caused by the storm or rushing waters. I had a horrible feeling of dread. This darkness wasn't natural.

The spirits paused in their pursuit of me to take note of the surreal change in atmosphere. They seemed as perplexed as everyone else. If they weren't causing the darkness, who was? The brief respite from battle ended when the wind spirit leaped through the air at me. A fourth shadowed spirit appeared beside me, this one larger than the other three. I flew to the side to avoid them, hoping it was so dark that no one below would see me — not that that mattered anymore.

The fourth shadow grabbed the wind spirit out of the air by the neck. This new shadow wasn't like the others. It took the form of a terribly imposing black knight clad in heavy metal and chainmail armor. This was no human playing dress-up or a hunter donning the garb of his ancestors, but a being of living shadow. The blackness swirling around it was darker than the moonless sky. I had seen this in the past. Rozalin had commanded a form of sentient darkness in Aurelia's chateau.

The wind spirit struggled in the black knight's grasp as an inky black substance was pulled from every one of his pores and orifices and melded into the black knight's ebony gauntlet. The struggle ended in the wind spirit's demise. This time, he faded from existence instead of exploding in azure light. His allies charged the knight. The woman summoned a torrent of water, and bolt after bolt of lightning struck down from the heavens at the other man's signal.

Neither was successful in breaching the knight's armor. The knight stood stalwart without even having to brace himself against the attack. At the knight's command the shadows under the swordsman sprang to life in the form of thick tentacles that ensnared him in mid-air and pulled his body apart piece by piece. His remains, along with the malevolent *katana*, fell to the shadows below and sunk into a tar-like abyss.

This was the power of the ancient darkness Rozalin had threatened, or some manifestation of it. It was already here.

The knight fabricated a long sword to match his armor and hurled it toward the remaining spirit, shattering her barrier and impaling her. The sword dripped like oil and melted around the geisha, dragging her down into the darkness. Now only I remained and the knight turned his focus on me. I put everything I could muster into pushing him away so I could escape. The building shook from the impact and the windows shattered as it crumbled to the street. The black knight, however, was not deterred. He walked through like nothing had happened. I couldn't even lift him. He was heavier than the building I had just demolished.

I retreated into the sky, but kept low enough over the skyline to stay hidden as I left the mayhem in the supernatural gloom. I thought the great war the Ancients had spoken of wouldn't happen for years or even centuries. It was happening now and it was very real.

I narrowly evaded the knight's grasp as he stepped out from the shadows on a rooftop to intercept me. I had to push myself harder and faster than I ever had. *This is a being of darkness, a demon sent from Hell. They can't exist on Earth for long without a host and even then the more powerful ones are too strong for the human host's body to contain for any length of time. If I can stall him out and get to Vance maybe he'll know more about how we can protect ourselves*, I thought.

I checked behind me to see if I was still being followed, but there was no sign of the knight. The lights in the area were normal, as was the weather. In my haste I made a stupid mistake — I forgot to watch where I was going and crashed into a wall. A wall with arms that wrapped around me.

"Please, stop. You are safe now." It was a wall with arms and a heavy Italian accent. I pushed away from "the wall" to see Gianluca standing before me. The last of the black knight's armor morphed into Gianluca's clothes.

"It was you this whole time?" No wonder he was so interested in me. He was another demon hoping to use me as a host. But did Minerva send him, or was he above even her? After seeing what he did to the spirits and how he took my strongest attack head-on I knew I was outmatched. This could be the master that Minerva and the Blighted One served, the one looking to reset the world to zero. "You're a demon? You're the ancient darkness everyone is talking about?"

"Demon? I do not understand. I come to save you because you are in trouble. Why do you look at me like this?" He reached toward me and I backed up, afraid of what he would do.

"You're evil, that's why. I've heard enough warnings to know without having to see it with my own eyes. I'm not falling for your tricks or pacts or whatever you are going to threaten me with."

"I am not evil. Why do you say this? Is this why you run from me in *Aquae Sulis*?"

I wasn't buying his innocent look or hurt expression. I knew too well what manipulation these things were capable of.

"The whole 'black knight controlling darkness' thing doesn't seem evil to you?"

"Dark is not evil. It is good if the heart of the man is good." He took another step forward, but I backed away again. "In the mother's womb we are loved in darkness. We go to darkness to sleep when tired, to hide when scared, no? We make love in dark. Why is this evil?"

"I was born in a lab in some machine, but I'm sure you already knew that."

"No? What are you saying?" He was either genuinely clueless or a fantastic actor. *Come to think of it, if he were a demon he would have had to return to Hell by now. He's been here for hours. When I fought Minerva and her infernal ally they only lasted minutes. He could be inhabiting this body. Maybe it was altered like mine to not break down from the possession.*

"Forget it. Are we fighting or what? I'm not joining forces to destroy the world, so get it over with."

"I love this world. I do not want to fight. I wake up because I think we are maybe the same? I want to meet you, but then you run from me and I thought you had trouble."

"Wake up? Where were you sleeping? In the museum?" Was this guy for real? He wasn't undead, that was for sure, but maybe he also wasn't the bringer of the apocalypse.

"The dark. Many, many years. I feel something I have not before and when I wake up I look around for it until I see you."

"What are you talking about? Where were you sleeping in the dark for years? Here? Underground?"

"No. Another world like this, but only darkness ... *tenebrae aeternae*. The shadows are my windows and my doors. I can see any place on the Earth there is shadow and I can go there, like the tunnel." He demonstrated by stepping back into the dark and then rising up behind me from my shadow. Spooked, I flew away to the other side of the roof. "Please, I will not hurt you."

"Yeah, well I'm a little nervous. My powers can turn a building inside out, but they don't even make you blink."

"Why do you want to use it? I am same person in the museum. Now you see more of me, but I am not different. It was not a lie."

"I've had bad experiences with that same darkness. There's someone else who controlled it like you, a woman named Rozalin. I fought her three years ago. Maybe that's why you felt my power wake you up if it's all connected. She also talked about some great darkness that's going to destroy the world."

"It was not me. I wake up three years past, but I never see you until now. I can stop who uses the darkness for evil. That is why I wake up other times, but this time I feel your energy in my world. It is strong like the wave in the sea. I feel this so I look and look and that is when I see you."

Could this other world he's talking about be the Rift where the parasites are from? "Are there animals in your world? Parasites or things that look like weird bugs and fish?" I asked.

"No, only darkness."

"Who are these other people you woke up for?"

"The ones who made me. They are very evil men. I hide from them for many years, but I become strong and find them to stop their evil. They are dead now, but when I feel you wake me I thought maybe we are the same too."

"Well, I don't control darkness and I'm not evil. Who made you?" *Maybe he is like me. My power is fueled by another world too.* Was he a previous attempt at making a suitable vessel for the demons? I stopped floating and landed a little closer to him to show some trust, but I was ready to escape the second he tried anything funny.

"I see this and I am very happy. In my time I was ... I do not know the English word ... soldier?" He held out his hand and from his palm the darkness formed a perfect Roman soldier seven inches tall. He motioned for me to take it. I shook my head no, but hesitantly picked it up. It was lightweight and cool to the touch, like metal. The details were eerily accurate. It looked exactly like him. Out of curiosity I tried to levitate it, but there my powers had no effect. It was as though the figurine didn't exist.

"You were human once?" I asked.

"Yes. I am now too, I think, no?"

"Humans don't move through shadows and create objects out of darkness." The little soldier disappeared in a poof of black odorless smoke that made me jump.

"I do not know. I am a man. Why does this matter?" He was right; it didn't really matter. I had been so caught up in labels and judging people I was starting to sound like William. "I was a soldier, but now I have no empire to protect. The world is very different for me, but still beautiful."

"How were you made to control darkness? Who were these evil men?"

"Senatus. They lead Roma many years ago. Some of them come to me at night and all drink my blood. When I wake up I become cold like them. They tell me to do things, hurt people, until I say no more."

"You were undead?"

"If this is the word, yes."

"How did you turn back? You can eat food? Breathe? Walk in sunlight? You don't have fangs either." Castile drank tea, but after witnessing everything else in that mansion I was sure that was an illusion too.

"Yes. After I kill the evil men, I become even more strong. They control the dark too, but I take the power away for myself. Then I sleep in the dark world for many years. When I wake up, I am alive. The darkness is part of me now, in my soul. I can feel it, but it is not bad. I think I am the only one now."

I'm not really sure how sleeping in this dark dimension for centuries cured the undead curse, but if there is one exception then maybe there are others. Then again, if he killed all the people responsible for turning him undead that could have done it, according to William, I thought. Maybe it wasn't crazy.

"Sorry for acting like that before. I should have given you the benefit of the doubt, but I've fought demons, ancient undead, and spirits. All of them were affected at least somewhat by my powers. Between that and all these doomsday prophecies I feel like I'm constantly being challenged to save the world."

"But, you are still a boy! You are so small!" Gianluca laughed with a big smile on his face. "Like the baby chicken."

"Hey! What?!" I was more than a little insulted by that. I couldn't help looking like a fresh-faced teenager for the rest of my life. People only value youth when they don't have to be taken seriously. "I'm a lot stronger than you think. I always manage to pull through sooner or later."

"This is not bad. I like it." Gianluca smiled at my scowl. He had a unique way of making me feel happy even when I didn't want to. Right then, I hated it. "I am the soldier. It is my job to protect" - he paused and tried to fight back a laugh- "the baby chickens."

"That's not funny. And they're called 'chicks'." I fought laughter. It was so hard not to laugh around him.

"Yes, these." He made one in his hand out of the darkness and let it pop around silently on the roof. I was amazed by how lifelike its movements were. Aside from its color, it was indistinguishable from the real thing. "In Roma we call them *pullus*. It is also the nice word for the one we like."

"We're not friends anymore," I teased him back.

"Yes, we just start," he disagreed.

"Nope, you blew it." I didn't want to be too enthusiastic about our potential new friendship, but he wasn't making it easy. I had learned my lesson several times over and was about to learn it once more. Out of nowhere, Noah pounced on Gianluca's back, dragging both *wakizashi* across his throat.

Chapter Thirteen

"Don't do it!" I yelled, but it was too late. Noah's blades snapped like toothpicks against Gianluca's skin. Even without his armor, Gianluca didn't suffer a scratch. Noah was a big guy, yet Gianluca didn't seem encumbered by the additional weight. The shadows underneath them shot up to form a spike that nailed Noah to the floor through his heart.

"Please, don't kill him!" I pleaded with Gianluca. "He doesn't know you aren't bad."

"He is a friend?" Gianluca held back from pulling Noah apart by the arms and legs with tendrils of darkness. Noah was already in rough shape, and I feared the slightest twitch would do him in.

"Sort of. Just don't kill him."

Gianluca released him and went to apologize, but Noah grabbed me and dashed away in a blur until we were miles outside of the city.

"Are you stupid? Do you have any idea how powerful that guy is?" Noah dumped me on the ground and shouted. "You can't be left alone for a minute without walking right into the arms of another Ancient. They don't even need to trap you. You just go willingly, you idiot."

"It wasn't on purpose. He found *me* and I didn't know exactly what he was," I corrected. "I believe in treating people equally and giving everyone a chance. Innocent until proven guilty. What are you doing here, anyway? I thought you were dead."

"Disappointed?"

"I don't know yet. Are you here to sell me into slavery for Aurelia?"

"What are you talking about?"

"Do you not remember admitting to that at Castile's? That you took me to Japan to train then planned to hand me over to Aurelia in exchange for your own freedom? Lying about her being dead?"

"I never lied about it. I said 'don't worry about her,' and I meant it. Worrying is only a distraction. She doesn't give a shit about a brat like you. I took you there to give me something to do when I wasn't looking for that sword. Now stop whining and stop running into Ancients!" He pointed at me accusingly like a parent scolding his child.

"Then why did you admit to it at Castile's? Did he make you say that stuff?"

"I don't know what you're talking about. Nobody made me do anything. You're a weak little shit. Aurelia would never want someone like you to replace me."

Maybe Castile did get into our heads to turn us against each other. He hated the Archios and it was the perfect opportunity to sow dissent. These games made me feel hollow inside. If even Noah could be manipulated so easily, then the glass ceiling was higher up than I thought. Would I ever be able to rise above the Ancients' games? *I hope Gianluca is different,* I thought.

"Stop looking like that." Noah interrupted my thoughts in a softer tone — as soft as Noah's tone could get, anyway. "You're not *that* weak. I mean, you've come pretty far since we met ... I guess."

"Are you trying to apologize?" I was amused that he thought I looked sad because of his comment. Anything he had to say rolled right off my back.

"No ... For what?" Noah fumbled through a poor recovery. "The only thing I'm sorry about is how much time we're wasting. I need to find the Muramasa. Those bastards got it from me when I was fighting them three-on-one and had to retreat. The sun will be up in a few hours. We have to get it back before then so we can head to Japan. I've already been there once and got what Vance needed. He gave me something he thinks will help."

Maybe I shouldn't tell him that Gianluca dropped the sword into the shadow world. Noah's unhealthy obsession with it was putting us all in danger, but Gianluca was the only one who could handle the curse without a problem. The problem was that I wasn't sure how much I could trust either one of them.

"By any chance, does the Muramasa have some connection with Hell or a demon?" I asked.

"I don't know." I could tell he was being cagey. He had known more about this than he let on from the start. It wasn't until things started going downhill that he even admitted knowing the sword's name.

"Yes, you do. I think it's poisoning your mind. You said yourself it's bloodthirsty."

"I said it drinks blood. Nothing is controlling me, so get it out of your stupid head and stop asking so many questions. Just trust me, I know what I'm doing. End of story."

"There you are, my friends." Gianluca stepped out from the shadows of a nearby tree and almost gave me a heart attack. "Here, your swords. I am sorry they broke." He handed Noah the pieces, and the expression on Noah's face was priceless.

"What the hell are you smiling at?" Noah growled at me for taking amusement in his misfortune.

"Maybe he could help us?" I asked, looking to Gianluca. "Those spirits won't stop attacking until we break the curse, and we can't handle them on our own like you can."

"Yes, I'd like this," he smiled back at me. I turned away, trying to be serious so I wouldn't be caught smiling.

"What's wrong with you?" Noah asked me in an accusing tone again. "Of course we don't want his help. I can handle them just fine. If he really wants to help make him find the *katana* they stole from me."

"This?" Gianluca retrieved the Muramasa from the shadow he had emerged from. So much for keeping it away from Noah for his own good.

"Not bad." Noah snatched it from Gianluca's hand before he could change his mind. "While you're still playing the good guy and taking orders why don't you go away, like, forever."

"Noah, why do you have to be such an asshole? You've gotten your ass kicked at least twice so far and you're a mess right now. Are you trying to get yourself killed? We can't do this with just the two of us."

"Whatever. I know what I'm doing this time. I learn from experiences, unlike you," he said with a smug look on his face. "How can you trust this guy?"

"He hasn't given me a reason not to, unlike you."

"I will leave. I do not want to make a problem for you. I am sorry we could not be friends, but I am happy we meet." Gianluca faded away into the shadows faster than I could stop him.

"Huh, didn't think it would be that easy." Noah admired the blade of the Muramasa in the moonlight. "I'm gonna need blood before we go."

"What do you want me to do about it? You're a big boy, go get some."

"What's your problem?"

"You. It's always you. I used to look up to you, but now all you do is cause trouble. After this is over, after we break the curse, I'm done, we go our separate ways."

"You should be thanking me. I just saved your life. The best victory is one where you don't have to draw your sword."

"Stop quoting me bullshit. Do you even believe half the stuff you say? Or does saying it out loud help you justify making me miserable?"

Noah zipped forward and grabbed me by the neck with spite in his eyes. "I risked my life to save you when I thought you were being attacked by another stupid Ancient."

"You don't scare me." I flew back and broke his hold on me.

"You only have the balls to stand up to me because I taught you to be strong. You're only *alive* because of me. You aren't as unkillable as you think."

"That's what I was hoping to hear," A voice rang out from the trees. It was William's. He stood off to the side. Who knew how long he'd been watching. This was the second time he'd snuck up without either of us noticing him.

"Perfect timing." Noah smirked at him. "We were just discussing dinner plans."

"Don't you dare," I stated firmly.

"I'll see you dead before I leave this place, monster!" William came toward us, hunched over. His sword was drawn and he wore his battle armor. He looked dreadful. His eyes were crazed and his skin was so pallid the veins were distinctly visible. He had let himself deteriorate for far too long. Had I been mortal, his image was most likely a reflection of what I would have looked like. "You are an unnatural abomination and an affront to God!"

"I'm not fighting you, William. I'm the same person you knew before. I'm not a monster, or a demon, or whatever. I'm Dorian."

"You *are* the creation of undead mad scientists, a parasite from another dimension, and forbidden demonic magic," Noah added.

"Shut up, Noah! You aren't helping." I glared at him and turned back to William. "I joined you because I thought we were both fighting for the same thing, but you hate anyone who's different. It's people like you that are holding the world back from peace. It's people like you that make the innocent suffer and afraid to be themselves. Look at what you did to your own girlfriend. Maybe God can forgive your unspeakable acts, but that doesn't fix anything."

"Don't you dare pretend to know better than the Lord! I was keeping the world safe from the evil inside her by locking her away, but now I see there's no breaking the hold that Hell has on her. If you won't fight then make it easy for me and die so I can end Emily's misery in that twisted form."

"Are you nuts? You're going to kill the girl you love? She's the same person! She still loves you."

"Liar! The monster inside her will say anything to trick me into letting my guard down. It ran at first opportunity to go prey on good, normal people and spread its evil. Fight me, or don't. It doesn't matter. Soon the rest of the Brotherhood will be here. You can't run from us all, not forever. Did you think nobody would notice you terrorizing the city?"

"Most of that wasn't me. I was fighting to survive and trying to draw harm away from others. I know you're not going to listen, but there are good and bad of my kind, just like yours."

"That's not my concern. I slay the monsters at God's command, He sorts them out."

"All right, I've had enough of this waste of time." Noah, who had been remarkably silent, marched up to William.

"Don't hurt him, Noah!" I warned. "It'll only make him right about us. Remember what you said about there being no honor in killing the weak."

"Unlike you, I don't care about being called a monster," he retorted and smacked the sword from William's hands. "Not so tough without your sparkly trinket, are ya?" I heard him say under his breath. Noah pulled William's hood off and put him in an arm-lock. His fangs punctured the skin of William's neck as he began feeding. William struggled for a moment, reaching back to grab at Noah, but was quickly eased by the bite.

I separated Noah from William with a telekinetic shot to the forehead. Noah zoomed behind me now, infuriated that I intervened.

"I told you not to touch him!" I shouted and floated to face him eye-to-eye.

"I don't take orders from you!" Noah yelled back. "I'm *hungry*! What do you want me to do? I wasn't gonna kill him, I just wanted to knock him out so we can move on already! You know it doesn't hurt."

"We've already got enough problems. Why do you need to make everything more complicated?" I wasn't about to back down until I heard William screaming behind me.

"No! I will never be one of you!" he wailed. "My soul is meant for God, not the Devil!"

"Relax!" Noah barked at him. "That's not how you turn undead, you idiot. I wouldn't want to be linked to you in the first place."

"I can feel it inside me!" William carried on, dropping to his knees and pulling at his hair. "The corruption will stain my soul black!"

"William, chill out. It's gonna be okay," I coaxed. "There's nothing inside you. He didn't do anything to turn you." I approached carefully to try and calm him, but I had a bad feeling in the pit of my stomach. He was already so far gone I didn't know what he would do. He was clutching his rosary and praying frantically until he stopped suddenly and threw his head back.

"God, forgive me!" he shouted to the sky. In one movement, he grabbed a dagger from his belt and dragged it across his neck.

"Don't!" I tried to stop him, but the blade was already more than halfway through. Blood gurgled up from his mouth and sprayed me from the slice in his neck.

"Noah, help me! Give him some of your blood!" I tore a long piece from the bottom of my shirt to apply pressure to the wound, but it was soaked through almost instantly.

"I'm sure he'd want that," Noah quipped. "He freaked out from a two-second bite. What's he going to do with 'evil blood' in his veins?"

"Just do something!" I pleaded. There was no stop to the bleeding. William's eyes were filled with tears and going dark as his life faded.

"I don't have any blood to give in the first place. Put him out of his misery if you really want to help him. He's suffering a slow, painful death."

"I can't ... I can't do that." I wanted to cry myself. How could something so good turn into this?

"Why do you care so much? He's just another worthless human whose name you're not even going to remember. They die all the time. This one chose the coward's way out."

"People aren't worthless! We had different beliefs, but I never wanted it to end like this." My hands were dripping with William's blood and I didn't know what else to do but shout at Noah. "I never want to turn into the empty person you are."

"You're only upset because you think if you pretend to care you won't be labeled a monster. I didn't know the guy was gonna do that, okay? We'll get you another one later. We've got a plane to catch. I know I'm fast, but —"

"ENOUGH!" I screamed. I didn't mean to, but I let loose a shockwave the split the earth around us and leveled the trees, snapping the thickest oaks like twigs and leaving a small barren crater.

A gunshot followed the sound of crashing trees. More of William's blood splattered my face and clothes as his body went limp. I checked the now-clear area and saw Owen and Micah.

"Someone had to," Micah said and holstered his gun.

"I didn't do it," I told them. I was still holding on to William's now-dead body. I closed his eyes and stood to face the brothers.

"Doesn't matter. What's done is done." Owen shrugged.

"It matters to me," I said. "It didn't have to come to this. It never does."

Owen came to look the body over. "He killed a couple in town he claimed were demons when we got here. They weren't."

"He's gone bonkers. It's not your fault he had a screw loose." Micah sighed and searched William's pockets. "Bloody hell, that'll be a bitch of a cover up to pull off. Right out in the open. Witnesses and all. At least this we can blame on a sinkhole. Media loves those." He indicated the crater around us.

"Guess he couldn't handle the suit after all," Owen said to him and picked up William's body.

"What do you mean couldn't handle the suit?" I asked. Noah, who had been far too quiet, had vanished at some point.

"They're made of demon hide," Micah explained. "Hellhound to be exact. Easy-to-kill low-level mutts from Hell. The leather is bulletproof and immune to fire, and trying to cut it is like slicing through chainmail with a butter knife, but it weighs as little as cloth. We gave him the old set. Fashion was never his thing. I don't think he noticed how ridiculous he looked."

"Yeah ... he wasn't big on clothes," I remembered out loud, feeling even sadder now. "I always thought it looked silly."

"The armor will drive even the sanest person mad and turn the most pure heart dark if worn too long," Owen continued. "We thought out of all of us, Willy would be the most resistant to it. There's a finer line between sinner and saint than we expected, I guess."

"Did he know what the suit was made from?"

"We never told him, but I had a feeling he knew by the end," Micah claimed. "He would have never put the bloody thing on in the first place if we told him."

"Aren't you worried the same thing will happen to you?"

"Oh please," Owen said. I followed them to a parked car. Owen loaded William's body into the trunk. "He wanted power more than the rest of us. Not everybody gets to fly around tearing up the landscape for fun with their mind."

"There's no part of this that's fun," I defended myself.

"Then you're doing it wrong, mate." Micah jumped in the driver's seat.

"Where'd you get those sets of armor?" I asked before they left.

"Willy's was passed down from the original Blackbourne Brotherhood. We got ours off the black market, you could say. Costly, but nothing a spot of insider trading and extortion couldn't make up for." Micah grinned and revved the engine. "We've got a party to attend. Cheers, kiddo!"

It was still dark out when the Blackbournes drove off, and Noah was nowhere in sight. I found a patch of trees away from the road and curled up. The sight of William's face as he died haunted me.

Something nearby smelled like it was burning and I could hear voices — possibly a search party investigating the crater I had left.

"What are you talking about?" one of the voices asked. The sound of a girl crying cut through the night air. They must have found William's blood. "You never told me your father worked in New York."

I was so tired, but more afraid than ever to fall asleep. I had to move somewhere else so I wouldn't be disturbed.

"Dorian." The voice called out to me and I froze. "What is going on? First you go overboard killing that thing, now you think we're in Boston? You're losing it, man."

Not this. Not again. When are these episodes going to stop?

"Leave me alone!" I flew up above the trees and screamed.

"What do you want me to do, Dorian? Kill a little kid?" the voice yelled back. It was Lyle's voice. This whole scene had played out once before back in the hospital we rescued Emilia from three years ago. My humanity was quickly slipping away as rage and revenge fueled my bloodlust against the Carpathians who took my family from me. Emilia was infected with the same parasite my parents and I had been, and for a moment I found it hard to differentiate her from the monsters. If Lyle hadn't been there to protect her ... I don't want to think of what may have happened.

"I didn't want anyone to die! I'M NOT A MONSTER!" I lost control again and rocked the ground, creating another sinkhole — this one even larger than the last. I was drained after that and couldn't keep myself afloat. I sunk into the darkness below for what seemed like miles. I opened my eyes. I was sitting under the tree again.

"You still mad?" Noah was standing in the crater in front of me. "I really didn't know he was going to do something that stupid."

The burning smell I'd sensed earlier was coming from beside me. I realized I wasn't smelling burning at all. The source of the smell was a big white pizza box with an entire large pizza inside. Next to the box was a neatly folded pair of jeans and a sweatshirt.

"Did you get this stuff?" I asked.

"No, I ordered fucking take-out and told them to leave it in the woods next to the annoying little shit."

"And the clothes?"

"They were having a special."

"Thanks," I said. The pizza smelled great and was still warm. I hadn't eaten real food in a while, but I just wasn't hungry. "I miss Japan. Things were simple there. Whenever I'm around people I'm always worried what's going to happen and what they're going to think. What if they're right?"

"I thought I was a good person and bad things just happen around me, but that amulet of William's ... it reacted to me when I went back to their place. Maybe I'm the one causing the bad things to happen. Maybe they aren't mistakes. What if I can't stop myself from becoming what the Strigoi intended?"

"You're not turning evil," Noah sighed. "I don't believe some piece of jewelry can tell if a person is good or not. I knew that was the first place you'd go, so I fed you my blood on the plane to Germany when you dozed off. The rock was reacting to my blood inside you and as long as it was then you couldn't use it against me."

Hearing that he had pulled a trick like that didn't surprise me. I should have been angry, but I couldn't help feeling relieved that my fate wasn't sealed. From anyone else the meager peace offering of clean clothes and pizza wouldn't even begin to cut it, but from him it was a monumental step.

"You better eat that whole thing. You're always cranky when you're hungry and I don't want you blowing anything up when we leave for Japan." He attempted to steer the conversation in another direction before I could respond. "And don't ruin those clothes by tonight either, since it's too late to go now." Noah disappeared just in time as the first few rays of dawn breached the horizon, leaving me to my pizza and my thoughts.

Chapter Fourteen

"Dorian, why do you sleep out here?" Gianluca's smooth Italian accent welcomed me back to the world. "Where is your home? I can take you there."

The sun was at its peak when I opened my eyes, but it only provided meager warmth on the chilly December day. I hadn't expected to see Gianluca again so soon. Judging by his concerned expression, it didn't seem there were any bad feelings between us after Noah's rude dismissal.

"I don't have a home."

"You have a family, no?" Gianluca's concern deepened as he glanced at the half-empty pizza box and bloodstained rags I had changed out of.

"No." I really didn't want to talk about them. "They're dead."

"Oh ... I am sorry. I think maybe you are so young, maybe you have a family ... to go there." He sounded sincere, but I was more apprehensive than ever about opening up to new people after the ordeal with William. It seemed like the better that things started, the worse they ended.

"I am young. I didn't outlive them naturally, if that's what you mean. They were murdered."

"Come." Gianluca held out his hand to help me to my feet, but I backed away reflexively. "I will take you someplace nice."

"I'm fine. Don't worry about it. I can take care of myself."

"You do not trust me." He frowned. "This is not a place for someone like you to sleep."

"What do you mean, 'someone like me'?" I shot back a bit defensively.

"It is for the animals, not for a beautiful young man." He could have come back with anything and it would have sounded just as good in his voice. I failed at staving off a smile.

"I'll be fine," I restated in a more convincing tone. "Noah will be looking for me once the sun goes down, so I don't want to go anywhere."

"Your friend?"

"I don't know if I'd call him a friend exactly."

Gianluca looked puzzled, but I knew it wasn't the language barrier. My relationship to Noah was just as confusing to me.

"He is your master?" It was an odd question — odd for this time period. I had to remember to whom I was speaking. Gianluca didn't dress like he was stuck in his era, which made me wonder what inspired him to be so modern.

"Oh, no! He tries to act like it sometimes. He was more of a mentor, a teacher, but not as much lately."

"What does he teach to you? He is like, hm, Eastern warrior, no? He wear the armor, the bottom part, and the writing on the skin." Gianluca laughed at himself. "It is ka‑ra‑te? I do not know the word."

"I think you mean ninja." I joined in with his laughter. Noah would have been so pissed if he'd heard us, which only made it better. "He knows it all, but we haven't gotten up to that stuff yet."

"But the sword is not for you. You have a passion for the architecture. Why do you not do this?"

"I use my powers, not a sword, but I can't be an architect. I'm not human. I'm not *normal*. I was going to study architecture in school, but everything changed. Now I can't go one day without being attacked by somebody, so I have to learn how to defend myself."

"In Roma, all the boys learn to use a sword when they are very young. When they are a man many are a soldier, but some are a farmer, some architect, many things. There is always a battle, but not all free men fight. That is the soldiers' passion."

"This isn't the Roman Empire and we're not human."

"We are men. The world is very different, but very similar. I see many wars, but always beauty. The world needs the architect to build the city after the soldier fight the war, and the farmer to feed them."

"It doesn't work like that, Gianluca. If I was human, yes."

"Why does this matter?" He was starting to get agitated. "Who tells you this? Your teacher?"

"Yeah, but not only him. I see it for myself. When I get involved with people, bad things happen. You saw it at the museum. How can I be an architect when I always have to watch my back?"

"At *Aquae Sulis* a soldier came to protect you. Why does your teacher not? He is the ninja."

"He does, but I can't expect others to fight for me when that's what my powers are for." This was becoming depressing. As much as I enjoyed Gianluca's company, all I wanted to do was sleep and avoid discussing my future. Everything always led back to this topic.

"What is your gift? I see you fly." He took a seat on the grass next to me and flashed a coy smile. "Like the baby chicken."

"Funny, but chickens don't fly, Gianluca." He took the opportunity during our brief moment of laughter to brush his hand against mine. His touch only lasted for a second, but that second was equal parts electric and terrifying. I couldn't let myself become enamored with emotions that would never last. "I break and destroy things. It's a curse. I don't have a gift for anything other than fighting."

I fiddled with pebbles in the grass to avoid making eye contact.

"When the soldiers protect the empire they carry very, very heavy supply. Weapon, armor, food, these things. We walk for many days and it is very slow. It is not easy to walk on the hills and with the trees, so you know what they do?"

"Ride horses?"

"Hm, yes. Smart, but no. There is not horses for all the soldiers and Roma had many. Then you walk different speed and it is bad if not all have the horse. The horse is for the leaders and different kind of soldier." Gianluca took the pebble I was playing with from me and left his hand in mine. I watched as he intertwined his fingers with mine. His hand was so much bigger. "We build the road."

He used his free hand to draw a line in the dirt with a stick and placed the pebbles on his line as an example. "It is very easy to walk on this and the enemy cannot see the footprint of how many soldier when it is on the stone. From Roma you can go anywhere very easy now ... Well, now it is different, but you know."

"What does that have to do with my powers?" To him, it all seemed so casual, but my heart was racing. I was nervous and wanted to pull away without being too obvious, even though there was no one around to see.

"You must break the stone and make the clear path to build a road, yes? First you must destroy to make new. You cannot make the architecture without both." I could feel him looking right at me. I kept my eyes down as though I was concentrating on his example. "This is the passion in you. Why you not use your gift for this?"

"It's a great idea, but I can't use my power like that. Lifting things, yeah. I can't control how I break things." I slid my hand free casually to give my own example. Picking up one of the pebbles, I floated it out in front of me and blasted it to pieces. "There. I created smaller pebbles."

My control over my power had improved significantly since I started using it on a regular basis. A long time ago Noah told me my power was like any muscle in the body and would grow stronger with practice, but I doubted him. Fine manipulation and focus was still too difficult and I never saw much need for them. I could hammer nails and turn screws with my power, but the concentration it would take defeated the purpose. I could remove trees and lift heavy materials, but then I would have the nasty problem of exposing myself to humans.

"Break only the small piece. Like this." Gianluca retrieved a larger, baseball-sized rock. He closed his left hand to grip something and forged an obsidian sword from the shadows. I thought he was going to whittle the stone down when he pressed the blade to it, but one quick movement smoothed the edges of the rock. A few more strokes, and he had an almost perfect block. The sword was gone, sent back to where it had come from in a puff of wispy black smoke. He handed me the stone block to inspect. "When I first meet you, you react badly to the darkness. It can be used for this too. We are very similar, this is why I want to know you. And you are very beautiful."

"Thank you. So are you." He caught me looking at him that time and we exchanged smiles.

"I think what you ask that first time. I do not know anyone like me. Maybe it does not matter, but the world is much more brighter when you have a friend. Do you think so?"

"It depends on the friend, I guess." Noah had made the world seem so much more scary and violent than the way Gianluca saw it.

"Try this." He held out a rock about the same shape and size as the one he had turned into a block.

"It's not going to work," I protested. But there was no harm in giving it a shot. I took the rock and cracked it in three pieces. Admittedly, I'd made some improvement, but nobody would be building a house with what I'd made.

"This is very good!" Gianluca exclaimed. He was far too optimistic about a pile of broken rocks. "I will help. Now try again."

He selected yet another stone and nearly covered it with pitch-black shadow. The dark substance nullified my power, limiting me to interacting only with what was exposed. We repeated the process, each time moving the aperture to another side.

"Perfect! You see? This is the work of passion." Gianluca removed the shadow cloak and presented me with a perfect cube made of stone.

"It's something all right, but they knew how to make cut stone thousands of years ago. Not exactly an accomplishment."

"You must feel pride in your work." He threw his arm around me and gave me a squeeze.

"This is one step. Think of the many things you can build."

He waved his hand over the shadows under the tree and erected a miniature Colosseum out of the darkness. "Next you can make the diorama. Look only at what you need. Do not let your eyes be your enemy."

Gianluca dissolved the Colosseum back into the shadows and stacked our blocks in its place.

"You are trembling." He rubbed my arm and held me closer to warm me up, but it only made things worse. I was shaking from anxiety, not cold. It didn't help that he was extremely attractive and his personality matched that outward appearance.

"No, I'm not," I denied, embarrassed. I squirmed away.

"Come with me. Please." He held out his hand again. "I will take you somewhere warm. Not far. I can return you by night for your teacher."

I hesitated and thought of Noah's warning. *This is how it starts. He seems nice now, but what happens when I'm lured in?* Noah wasn't right as often as he wanted me to believe though. And if the spirits regrouped and came after me before night fell, at least I know Gianluca could handle them.

"I do not like to see you like this," he insisted.

"Where are you taking me?"

"Hotel. In the city. You will be safe, I promise."

"You have a room?" I was surprised he knew what a hotel was. Did they have those in Ancient Rome?

"I borrow it." He smiled and took my hand. In an instant we were inside a lavish hotel room overlooking Bath. *That was faster than traveling with Noah and a lot less jarring*, I thought. "See? For you. For a short time," he added with a laugh.

I sat on the bed and he chose a chair, helping himself to some grapes that had been left as a gift for guests. I pictured him dressed like a Roman, eating grapes from the vine and sipping wine at the baths.

"Your clothes ... You dress very, modern, for someone your age." The Archios were always in style too, but except for Aurelia, the ones I'd met were much younger than Gianluca.

"You like them? I make it myself." He demonstrated by dissolving the cuff of his sleeve and changing the opacity. "I see in the store what the people are wearing so I copy. It had color, but I can only make black and a little lighter. I think it is nice."

"Yeah, I like it a lot. If it's made of shadows why doesn't it disappear in the light?"

"Because my dark is very, very strong. Natural light does not make a problem."

I figured light would be his Achilles' heel, since lightning, wind, and steel did nothing to him and neither did my powers. If he did turn on us we'd be in big trouble. Maybe it was better to appease him, but I couldn't see him becoming that diabolical.

Then again, I had to keep reminding myself that William had been a saint when we met. So had Aurelia. *How twisted am I that the first issue I think about is how easy it would be to kill someone?*

"Why does your armor look like a knight's and not a Roman soldier's?" I asked. "You sound like you're still in love with the Empire. I would have thought you'd be wearing their armor."

"Yes, there is much love in my heart for Roma. When I wake one time I see the steel men walking the castles. I think, 'This men are *invictus*, they cannot fall'." Gianluca produced an instant example from the shadows in the form of a tiny knight. The armor was bulkier than his armor, and his put more emphasis on the chest and abdominal muscles, like the molded armor of ancient times. From what I remembered, Gianluca's armor was also quite intricately detailed. It was much more of a work of art than the traditional steel plating. "Their armor is much heavier than Roman, this is true strength. I watch them protect the people and I think I want to be like this. They have the bravery and honor like the Roman soldier. This is what we call *virtus*. It is what makes you a man."

The knight took a bow and disappeared. I laughed, probably louder than I should have. "You like protecting things, huh?"

"Yes, this is what I love. It is important for me. For many, many years I see so much bad things happen. I was once part of this and it hurts my heart. Now I feel most strong when I protect something beautiful. Not just the beautiful person like you, but the art, or the city. How can the architecture survive if there is no soldier?"

"That's very noble of you."

"I will not lie to you. When I wake up this time, short time ago, because I feel you, I was thinking, 'Is this my enemy?' I look for you because I do not know if you will be hurting the innocent people or doing the bad things."

"Not on purpose. I don't want to fight at all if I don't have to."

"I see this now. It is in your eyes. You have a good heart." Gianluca leaned forward in his chair and reached out to take my hand in his. My 'good heart' was racing again. I wanted to make a joke to change the mood, but I couldn't get the words out.

"You're so tan," I blurted, noting the sharp contrast in our skin tones. Not the smoothest thing I could have said. I was already cursing myself for saying it. He just smiled politely and interlaced our fingers.

"You are very shy," he said after a few seconds of letting me stew in my own awkwardness. "I like this, but I do not make you uncomfortable?"

"No, I'm not uncomfortable. I'm not really used to anyone acting this way." It was a nice change from being berated by Noah. To me, Gianluca was also far more attractive, even if he lacked the supernatural allure of the Archios.

"You do not like it?"

"I do! It's just new for me. That's all." I was worried that I had given him the wrong impression.

"Why is this? I think many people would like to, no?" Gianluca looked off to the side, breaking his focus on me for the first time since we had met.

"Not that I've met."

"I have to go," he said without even looking at me, and took his hand back. My heart sunk. I had just blew the first small stroke of luck I'd had in forever by sending mixed messages.

"Okay," I sighed quietly.

"Stay here. You will be safe." He vanished from the room without so much as a goodbye. I waited a few minutes, hoping he would pop back in with a smile and laugh that he was teasing me again, but it didn't happen. The best I could do was clean up before heading back out to the spot where I'd wait for Noah.

After a hasty shower, I took advantage of such precious rare amenities as toothpaste and hair products. I flipped on the TV to kill time. I was a bit worried that housekeeping would come through, but I'd dealt with worse. The problem was that the windows didn't open this high up in most hotels, so an aerial escape wouldn't be an easy option. I turned to the local news in time for the humans' account of last night's events.

"The effects of a small earthquake were felt across Bath last night when geothermal pressure from the famous hot springs forced rushing water to overflow the sewer system and open sinkholes just outside the city. The damage was compounded by a passing thunderstorm, causing chaos in the flooded streets. Fortunately, the natural disaster only lasted a few minutes and no severe injuries were reported."

"Natural." *Yeah, right. People are so quick to believe anything when they don't have an answer.* It worked in my favor, so I shouldn't complain. That veil of ignorance was the only thing keeping the hounds from my door, so to speak.

The light in the room dimmed momentarily and Gianluca stepped out of the shadows. I jumped up from my spot on the bed with an audible gasp, thinking he was one of the spirits at first.

"You know, that is kind of terrifying, Gianluca."

"Oh, I am sorry. I was not thinking." His smile was back. That was a good sign. "Who do you talk to when I was away? I hear the voices."

"Huh? Oh ... I must have been talking to myself when I was watching TV. I do that sometimes, I guess. I get lonely a lot." Why had I said that? Could I make myself any more of an idiot around him? I was never this bad around Noah, though he would probably disagree. "Where did you go?"

"Eh, first I have a question." His smile changed to a more pensive expression. "These people, at *Aquae Sulis*, why do they hurt you? The truth, please."

I was taken aback by the question, and then the fact that he thought I might try to lie to him. "Noah tried to steal a sword from their temple when we were in Japan for training. One of them came after us when we returned to New York and Noah had me take the sword from them. I didn't know Noah had started it at the time, I swear. The man was hurting people, so I took his weapon away. Since then it keeps getting worse every time they regroup. That's the truth."

"I believe you." I was relieved to see his smile return again. "Why the man brings the sword to you if he does not want it removed from the temple?"

"That's ... a really good point. I hadn't thought of that." Despite the language barrier it hadn't taken Gianluca long to find an inconsistency in the story. I would have thought Vance the one to recognize it, but he was too caught up in wanting to study the sword.

"I leave because I sense these people. I cannot understand their words, but they attack the ones like your teacher in the cities here. I think they come for you, so I stop them."

"They're back already?" I was a bit flustered. If Gianluca hadn't been here I would've been screwed. "They're attacking the undead during the day? Why? It's Noah and me they wanted."

"You say they do this in New York too, no? It is not you. They look to kill many people. Why do they bring the sword, then kill people you do not know? This does not make sense."

"I thought they were trying to lure us out in New York, but they've never had problems finding us since then now that I think of it. I thought they stopped hunting the other undead once they tracked us down. Noah can understand them, but he's not one for talking things out."

"I can understand this. I have trouble with the English. If Latin or Italiano, okay, but I do not think they speak this."

"I think you speak English really well. I haven't had a problem understanding you. When did you learn?"

"Hm, maybe ... two years? I do not know. I hear many people speak it, so I listen and watch from the shadow, but I do not practice much. It is good we meet because you will teach me."

"I'll try." I felt my face turning red and the flirtatious glint in his eyes told me he noticed. "I'm so impressed you learned a language on your own in just two years."

"You think so? Maybe then I will be a master when I watch your lips." He casually closed the gap between us by standing against the wall next to me. He was just close enough that I had to tilt my head slightly to make eye contact, which I got the feeling he liked.

"Ah, so anyway, I was thinking ..." I took a seat on the bed behind me to give me some room, but that just made it worse by putting his crotch in my direct line of sight. "What if those spirits weren't guarding the sword? What if they were waiting to be released?"

I jumped up from the bed before I continued and tried to play it cool, but Gianluca still smiled in amusement at my flailing. "I hear the sword has an aura, like it's alive, and when I was cut by it I saw visions of Hell."

"It is *daemonium*. A devil, no?"

"Then that would most likely mean the spirits are under its control. The sword drinks blood, like a sacrifice. The undead are easy targets, especially the innocent ones. They aren't going to draw attention to themselves to get help. This is really bad."

"Do not be afraid, Dorian. I will protect you."

"I can't ask you to do that."

"You did not ask. It is what I want. I am a soldier without the empire, but I am still a man with a heart filled with passion." Gianluca came over to me and placed his hand on my cheek. The warmth of his touch filled me with a comforting sense of security. I closed my eyes, and for a second considered that this was another trick my mind was playing on me. "We can both have what we want. I will find you the safe place to build and I will fight the devils."

"Noah's not going to like that."

"Then I will speak to him as men." Gianluca's chivalry was like a dream, but I had to remind myself that dreams weren't real.

"Thank you, Gianluca, but I don't need to hide while someone fights for me. I don't like to fight, but I'll do it if it's to help people."

"You are a stubborn little one." He smiled down at me and moved his hand from my cheek to my shoulder.

"I'm not little and I'm not helpless." I locked eyes with him in defiance.

"Helpless, no, I know this. You are very strong, but still the little one." He chuckled at my disdain. "Do not be mad, I like this."

"If you say so." I was quick to put to rest the reminder that I wasn't, and never would be, the strapping Adonis that Gianluca was. "You say you can travel anywhere through the shadows? Do you think you can take me somewhere?"

"Yes, where?"

"It's in Germany. I'm not sure exactly, but I think around Munich. I know that doesn't help, but I could show you on a map maybe."

"I can go fast to the place if I have a memory, or I need to travel from shadow to shadow until I find it. You will need to come to my world to travel."

"Sure." I wasn't sure at all. I had never been so unsure in my life. My one encounter with another dimension had left me with permanent mental scars. But it was too late to turn back now. Our shadows darkened beneath us as we sunk into the blackness below.

Chapter Fifteen

Gianluca's description of the dark world was not enough to prepare me for what came next. Once the shadows fully consumed us I choked and gasped for air — he had forgotten to mention there wouldn't be any. I grew frantic floating in the lightless vacuum until my immortality finally helped me overcome my body's natural instinct for breath. The world, if you could call it that, was just an endless expanse of darkness; no stars, no creatures, no atmosphere or landscape. It was an entire dimension devoid of any defining characteristics.

"It is the first time I take someone here with me." I could see and hear Gianluca perfectly in front of me. Without any source of air or light it was a mystery how either was possible. He stood poised with perfect posture, or pretended to stand, since there was nothing below him. I had trouble orienting myself and kept drifting away. Not surprisingly, my powers didn't work here, as they had no effect on Gianluca either. Without them I was unable to fly or control my trajectory.

"I think this is where you want." Gianluca opened a one-way window back to Earth. I was too far away to get a good look and kept drifting further.

"Uh, Gianluca?" I tried to physically swim through the darkness over to him, but there was nothing to propel myself through. I felt ridiculous, but Gianluca was too preoccupied navigating the shadows to take notice.

"Yes, little one?" He looked over and grinned at the sight of my struggle. With one hand out he beckoned the darkness to carry me along an invisible current toward him. I grabbed him to keep myself from floating away into the abyss. He held me close so that my head rested on the triangle of his bare chest exposed by the undone buttons of his shirt. For someone so invincible his skin felt perfectly normal. I was entirely too distracted to concentrate on the more important matters at hand. I could feel the unlimited strength in his arms, but for all his power, he was equally gentle. His robust heartbeat was soothing, as if in some way it was telling me that everything would be okay. I had tried not to be too forward with him before, but felt unnatural keeping my hands down at my sides.

"Thanks," I said as I wrapped an arm around him. "And I'm not little, by the way."

He responded with a laugh and kissed the top of my head. It was a good thing he couldn't see my face because I turned red instantly.

"This is Germania." He pointed to the hazy clearing in the darkness.

It didn't hit me until now that his clothes, those models of the Roman soldier and the chick, and even his weapon were made of the same stuff we were floating in. The buttons on his shirt felt like plastic, and the cloth was as soft as any cotton. The material came from nothing, and yet he was able to will it into whatever form he desired with a tremendous level of precision in texture. He was the catalyst that changed something inherently scary into a work of practical beauty.

"Dorian?" He embraced me a bit tighter. "This is okay?"

"Yes, sorry. I don't mind."

"I am meaning Germania." He gave a sort of half-laugh. "This is where you want, yes?"

"Yeah. That's what I meant," I lied to cover up where my mind had wandered. We were looking through the shadow between two clock towers. This was Munich all right. We were at the *Frauenkirche* to be exact, one of the cathedrals there. I knew this from studying the late Gothic era in preparation for a semester that never came to fruition. "We're looking for the Strigoi, if that helps. It's going to be outside the city, underground. There'll be trees and probably a broken building above."

We zipped through the shadows at the speed of light — or dark, to be more accurate. It was like watching a movie snaking over, through, and around buildings in an invisible bullet train.

"It is the day. Would they not be asleep?" Gianluca asked as we entered a familiar clearing in the woods.

"Then I'll wake them up. But I doubt it. They hide underground so nothing interrupts their studies." I pointed to a spot in the clearing filled with debris. "There."

"You are right. I can hear their voices." As he said that the echoes of Vance and the other Strigoi's conversations whispered through the darkness. Gianluca moved us inside the laboratory until we found the source.

"You should stay here," I told him. "This is, um, personal."

"If you need my help, call in the shadow and I will come."

I floated out through the shadows behind Vance as Gianluca darkened the room.

"Oh that is so cool," I said out loud as Vance leapt from his chair and spun around. No wonder Noah loved dropping in like that. "Hi, Vance."

"How did you get in here? This place is warded beyond your capabilities." Vance and the other Strigoi surrounded me in the small concrete room of books, clockwork gadgets, and questionable liquids in beakers.

"Don't worry about it." *Finally I get to be the mysterious one*, I thought happily.

"I am quite worried and with good reason. It would take a being of immense power to bypass our defenses and I know of no such being."

"I made a new friend. Can we talk in private?"

Vance dismissed the other skittish members of their book club and inspected me head to toe. "You are dealing with a dangerous power — more dangerous than the brute you choose to follow around."

"How do you even know? Just because someone can walk through the shadows they're dangerous?" I wasn't sure how much I wanted to share with Vance about Gianluca, but playing devil's advocate with him might get me some useful information.

"The shadows? Is that it?" he asked. "Shadows alone cannot do what you did. Who is this friend?"

"His name is ... actually, never mind. It doesn't matter. He's friendly. That's all you need to know."

"A powerful dark being capable of breaching our wards is something of serious concern. What have you become involved in? Did you not heed the necromancer's warning? Theoretically a high-tier demon would be capable of this. You know their appetite for destruction, which is the very reason you were made."

"Vance, relax." I had to put an end to this, otherwise he'd never let it go and I wouldn't get anywhere. "He's not a demon. He used to be undead, but now he's changed back after living in this other dimension. It's like the Rift, but full of darkness."

"A dark dimension? The Nether Realm?"

"He didn't give it a name."

"There were stories of an offshoot coven of yore that delved deep into the depths of a bottomless void to gain power. When they returned they became something more than mere undead — something darker and more sinister, with powers to match. They called themselves the Nether Lords and named the source of their power the Nether Realm, although some who don't believe the tale refer to it more simply as the Dark Depths, or the Shadelands.

"Humans have an interesting conception of it. They call it 'dark matter' and 'dark energy,' or 'dark fluid.' It is an entirely different form of omnipresent matter in the universe, with such interesting characteristics as hyper-density and anti-luminescence. It defies many human notions of reality like gravity, being that it is both nowhere and everywhere at the same time. This is mere conjecture, though, as I am no scholar in human science and they are very often wrong about the simplest of things."

"Yeah, it's probably real. He's pretty invincible, so super-dense armor and infused skin would make sense. My powers don't even affect him or his creations."

"That is because telekinesis only affects physical matter. Those manifestations may appear solid, but are neither truly tangible or intangible."

"The Nether Lords sound like the people that turned him in the first place, but he killed them."

"I doubt that. If the legend was even partially true, the Nether Lords were a blend of all the strongest and most defining traits of the existing covens. Manipulative as the Archios, brilliant and magically adept as the Strigoi, and driven by an overt bloodlust like the Carpathians. They are said to have vanished, swallowed by the land they drew their power from. Minerva had told me of them in passing some centuries ago; however, most dismiss the story as a fable to scare the young undead from venturing into other worlds. Needless to say, the Carpathians did not heed that warning with their recent interest in the Rift, nor did Minerva with hers in Hell."

"My friend says he was turned by a group that controlled the darkness. He killed them all because they were evil. He said he had been sleeping and woke up when he felt my power."

"This is a problem. If any of this is true, he is probably one of them. They could have slept undeterred for centuries to lie in wait like the demons for a time to reclaim their lost glory on Earth. My word, what have we done to wake such a beast? I should have never taken pity and saved you from the parasite. What havoc will be wrought upon the world now?"

"Thanks, Vance, really. He's not the havoc type and he's not the reason why I came here."

"He is deceiving you, as any Archios or comparably vile demon would."

"Vance. Drop it. I'm here about something else. Can you erase memories?"

"Not you, too. What is it you could possibly want to forget at your age?"

"A lot." I couldn't take the hallucinations and night terrors anymore. I wanted to forget it all, or at least enough of it to function again. I wanted to have some semblance of a normal life and normal relationships. "What do you mean, me too? Who else came here? Did Noah ask you?"

"That's not what I said."

"Tell me, Vance. What did he want to forget?"

"He will kill me if I tell anyone." His eyes darted about the room nervously.

"I'll kill you now if you don't. We've been through this before."

"No you won't. You're too concerned about the line between good and evil."

"Vance, you're the cause of, or involved in, most of the things I want to forget. Don't push me."

"Yes, he came back after you left the other day. Two or three years ago he came to me when the Carpathians were defeated. I assumed Aurelia had finally sent him to finish me off. He wanted to know what your chances were against her if you were to reach your full potential, but I had no way of knowing without more data."

"His plan was to train you under the pretense that Aurelia would accept you as a replacement so he could be free, but he knew she would never hold up her end of the bargain. When you were powerful enough, if all went according to plan, you would turn on her once you found out she hadn't perished. Her defeat would ensure freedom for all three of us."

"Why didn't he just ask me to help? Why lie to me? I mentioned taking her down a long time ago."

"Because you two are too similar." He stated this like it was common fact, but I had never heard anything so absurd.

"I'm nothing like him."

"You think so, but both of you are constantly running in circles, chasing your tail, leaping headfirst into danger and then away when trouble finds you. If you knew about the plan you wouldn't have trusted him to train you knowing her power over him. You would have inevitably charged recklessly into battle against her to meet a swift demise and doom us all. But, if the plan worked, there is nothing in the known world that could stop the one capable of ending the Archios queen's reign."

"Then what happened? Why erase his memories now? Wouldn't she have known what he was planning the entire time if she could read his mind?"

"Noah has conditioned himself to repress his thoughts and desires, making it more difficult for mind readers. He forces himself to believe the lies he lives. Being halfway across the world helped somewhat too, and Aurelia is too arrogant to think there are any real threats from her own children so she rarely bothers to probe their minds.

"I assume he had a change of heart, although I don't have the foggiest idea why. Sentiment is not exactly his strong suit, but emotions are often unpredictable even to one as resolute as him. Once he found that cursed sword he may have believed he could do her in on his own. Returning with that weapon would surely draw her suspicions, so he went to an old enemy of hers, Castile, to erase his thoughts of using you to kill her. That failed, since the cursed spirits followed him there and interrupted before he could strike a deal. He came to me instead to erase the memories."

"That's why he had no memory of what happened at Castile's mansion. Why didn't he go to you in the first place?"

"Castile is many times more powerful and would jump at the chance to ruin Aurelia. I had never erased the memories of another immortal and a mistake could have left him lobotomized. Fortunately, or unfortunately, it was a success."

"So in the end he was using me to help us both. That also must be what he meant when he said the *katana* was all he had and why he won't give it back even if it means his death. Why does everything have to be so complicated? I can still help him."

"Correct. That cursed blade is his only key to freedom. It can sap the strength of even the most powerful undead, turning a tyrant into a toddler. You aren't strong enough and he is too impatient and prideful to accept your help if you simply offer it."

"He's been enslaved for over a hundred years. I can understand his impatience."

"Worry only about yourself. He will bring you nothing but trouble. Aurelia won't come after you herself; if you can defeat him you'll have one less problem to bother you."

"I really don't want to kill him after hearing all this. He's been looking after me this whole time in his own weird way. The whole time he was telling me to not worry and trust him he was telling the truth."

"I can attempt to make you forget your past, but it isn't guaranteed that I won't fully lobotomize you on accident. His compassion and sincerity are as transient as he is. It won't be long until he turns on you."

"Funny, he says the same thing about anyone who's nice to me. No thanks on the memory wipe though. I don't want to risk becoming a vegetable."

"There is no greater truth than deception. I would consider this when dealing with your new companion, too. It is probably in your best interest to leave your mind intact. Erasing your past only leaves you ill prepared for the future. Whatever you choose, do not seek me out. I will be leaving this place. We have had far too many hazardous visits as of late and I fear the awakened darkness to be the most perilous threat, despite your baseless reassurance."

I left to rejoin Gianluca among the trees, far enough away that Vance couldn't spy on us. Gianluca didn't appear immediately, which gave me just enough time to start mulling over all the doubts about him that had been planted in my mind.

"Ciao, *bello*." Gianluca spoke into my ear. It was going to take some getting used to another person sneaking up on me, but at least this one didn't try to maim me. "I think I see now why you do not want my company inside. You do not want me to meet your father."

"Huh? I told you my parents are dead."

"Yes, the man you speak to inside, the dead one. Your father, no? You have the same eyes." Gianluca was smirking at me like he had caught me in a lie, but it couldn't have been further from the truth. Or could it? I hadn't paid attention before, but we did have the same eyes. Was Vance one of the genetic donors used to create me? "I think you are nervous to make us meet."

"Were you listening in on my conversation in there? He's not my father. My parents are real dead, not undead."

"No, no I only check to see if you are safe, then I leave. I am sorry. The eyes are very similar, so I think this, but I see yours are much more nice."

"Right." I wasn't too happy being compared to someone like Vance. That was worse than Vance comparing me to Noah. The fact that there might be some truth to it compounded my contempt. "Until I use my powers. Then I'm the monster."

"No, little one, this is wrong. It is the real you, another piece. The more I learn of you the more I like. The eyes are beautiful, you are beautiful."

Gianluca's words didn't make me blush this time. They made me sad. What was I really going to get out of this? Even if he did turn out to be everything he said he was, how was he going to feel when I couldn't even lie next to him at night without having an episode? *Sure, he isn't affected by my powers, but how long is he willing to put up with me destroying our surroundings because I can't control my own thoughts?* Maybe it was best to be honest and get this over with before it spiraled out of control. I'd learned my lesson with William.

"Gianluca, the monster isn't just the eyes. It's what's in my own head. Any time I close my eyes I see the people I've lost, or the things I've done wrong, and I lose control. I try and I try, but I can't make the thoughts go away."

"This is like me." He put his hands on my shoulders and looked down at me. "It is why I leave to sleep in the dark for so long."

"I can't sleep. We're not the same."

"I could not sleep for many years. You must honor the memory of the people you lose. Do not try to forget or it will haunt you. You cannot control it because the thoughts want to get out and you hold them in. It is not good for you."

Noah had told me years ago to mourn and get it over with when I lost my parents. I pushed away my pain until I started falling apart. Then more people left me. I thought fighting back would bury the feelings, but I was just ignoring them, not dealing with them.

"I don't want to cry or be sad. It isn't productive. It's weak."

"You have a power, but you are still a man and a man has the emotions. That is real strength." Gianluca put his arms around me to comfort me, but his touch pushed me even closer to coming unglued.

"Get away from me," I warned him as I felt the tears well up in my eyes. I thought of all my failures as we sunk into the shadows to return to his world.

"You cannot hurt anything here," he told me as we floated in the sea of darkness. "Release the bad feelings to make the room for the new good ones. Let yourself go of the emotions so you can build a new future. From the destruction comes the creation. It is always this way in history. When it is most bad is when life has the chance to become stronger."

I couldn't hold back anymore. I wanted him to shut up, to leave me alone and send me back to Earth so I wouldn't have to face my inner demons. But he wouldn't let go. The more I pulled away and hit him, trying to get him to release me from his embrace, the more futile my actions felt. I started to cry, and then I couldn't stop. More strongly than ever, I felt the sorrow of those I had lost or wronged, the fear of those who sought to destroy me, the anger at myself for when I had failed. It all came rushing to the surface. It was more than I could deal with at once. I thought I would explode, and I did.

I screamed out loud, overwhelmed by my confusing emotions, and a surge of power followed. Gianluca held on tighter as the flood of energy radiating from me persisted. The infinite darkness around us swayed and churned like the ocean in a storm until I finally had nothing left in me. I was barely conscious afterward, but I felt good. I felt more than a weight off my shoulders — my soul had been cleansed. I wouldn't try to bottle up my pain anymore. I owed the fallen, like my parents, more than that. I couldn't live in fear of those who might seek to hurt me, or despair for those who tried. I saw now that my time training in Japan was only peaceful because, subconsciously or not, I had been waiting for someone to cross my path on whom I could take out my anger. I'd wanted to prove to myself how much stronger I was. Once that confidence was shaken by the spirits, I had nothing. It was a false sense of strength and not true happiness. There would always be someone stronger out there, someone looking to bring me down in some way, but the secret wasn't in preparing to deal with those people. What mattered most was living my life for myself.

"You are okay," Gianluca reassured me. His voice was just barely loud enough to hear as I slipped into a deep sleep.

Chapter Sixteen

It was dark out when I woke up. I knew I was in a room because I could feel a bed beneath me.

"Gianluca?" I whispered as I searched for a light on the nightstand. I was in another hotel room, different than the last. I called to Gianluca again after a few minutes, but there was still no response.

"Please do not be angry, but I have to say this." His voice preceded him as he stepped into the room from a corner where the lamplight didn't reach. "I think you cannot fight these Eastern warrior. While you sleep I hear their voices in Hispania. They fight the dead there so I go to help, but many are killed. This happens when you speak to the man with your eyes in Germania too."

"Then of course I have to fight them. This isn't a personal grudge. They're committing random acts of genocide."

"Er, I am sorry, I do not understand your words, but this is a war. I have seen many people and places hurt by it in the past. You are the only one like me I know. We just meet, but I feel I would still like to know more of you. I enjoy our time very much. You are kind and brave and very beautiful. I do not want to see you hurt, so I feel I must protect you from the battle."

"That's nice of you, but we talked about this. I can't die and don't say there are things worse than death because I've already been through enough of them. Hiding isn't the answer, right? I don't like to fight, but I will if there's a good reason. And I know you're the soldier, but you can't do this on your own either."

"I will find a way. Something brings the warriors back to fight, so I will find the source to stop it."

"You can't stop me from helping — well, maybe you can, but don't. I want to do this."

"This is not the time to be stubborn, little one. You need your rest. You are too weak to fight right now. I cannot let you."

"I don't need to rest. I feel fine, better than I have in years. Noah is probably already looking for me."

"I will bring you to him. Promise me you will not go after these warriors. They are too dangerous."

"I can't promise that and I don't want to lie to you." The thought had crossed my mind. "Why don't we fight together?"

"No. I will go with your teacher if he wish, but you have work. I want you practice your building."

"I can do that after! There are more important things right now."

"No. It is not for you." Gianluca was incredibly stubborn for someone who accused me of acting the same way. Arguing was pointless, but it was nice to feel that someone cared.

"Okay, okay. Can you take me to Noah?" I had no intention of sitting this out. I just needed to get to Noah before he ran into me with Gianluca.

We were returned to the wooded area outside Bath just as the sun set due to the difference in time zones. Gianluca kissed me goodbye on the forehead before he left. It was a sweet gesture that I would have loved to enjoy, but I was on high alert waiting for Noah to drop in at any moment.

I sat alone for half an hour, whistling and scrounging around in the dirt for rocks to break into shapes. Wouldn't it be amazing if I could sculpt columns with the exquisite Corinthian capitals that the Romans and Greeks used? *Right now all I have is a pile of smashed pebbles that vaguely resemble shapes, but maybe someday ...*

"What the hell are you doing?" Noah dropped down in front of me and kicked my pebbles away.

"Nothing now." I had to swallow what I wanted to say next and remember there was a nice side to him. "Let's get going to Japan."

"First, why don't you tell me what's up with your aura?"

"I can't see auras. You know that." I didn't feel any different, but Noah's squint was unnerving. He grabbed my arm and pricked me with the tip of his sword.

"Ow, what the —" I sucked my finger to stop the bleeding. "Still bleeding?" He crossed his arms over his chest.

"Yes. Wait, yes. Why am I bleeding?" Panic struck. I could still use my powers, but couldn't heal.

"I don't know. Does it have to do with you smelling clean for once, or your new obnoxiously cheerful mood? Or maybe the Italian you were kissing?"

"We were not!" Damn. Noah was watching the whole time.

"I told you to stay away from him, dipshit. He tricked you. That took, what? A day?"

Gianluca wouldn't trick me, would he? He was adamant about seeing me again and protecting me. Did it have to do with releasing so much energy into the Nether Realm?

"I'm sure I'll be fine. I think. Let's just go to Japan. I can still use my powers. I'm probably just tired." *Am I still immortal? Did Gianluca do this on purpose so that I'd have to rely on him and would stay out of the battle?*

"We're going to France first. I have to pick up new side swords, since you're more useless than ever."

Wonderful, just the place I wanted to go.

We made it to Aurelia's oversized seventeenth-century chateau with little incident other than Noah constantly poking me to see if I'd regenerate. This place was nothing but nightmares. I kept watch out his window to be sure no one was coming from the main house while he selected a pair of *wakizashi* from his wall to replace the broken ones. Nothing had changed in his room since I had been there last except for a humble shrine displaying a rose-engraved *katana*. I went over to check it out, but Noah glared at me out of the corner of his eye with a look that said "I'll cut your hand off if you touch it." Candles and an urn were neatly arranged next to the sword in a way that I couldn't picture Noah doing.

"Ready," he announced as he swapped out a sheath from a full-length *katana* to use for the Muramasa. I was going to make a sarcastic comment that I wasn't the one with the super speed while I waited for his usual grab-and-go approach, but he held the side of his head in agony and grimaced with fangs bared. "Stay here. *She's* calling me."

Very rarely had I ever seen Noah react to pain and it was usually in catastrophic situations. This was a bad omen.

I stayed at my post by the window, looking out at the monstrous chateau looming in the near distance. Many of the lights were on, a mix of steady electricity and flickering candles. It felt like the building itself was staring back at me. She was in there somewhere. If there was ever a metaphor for exterior beauty disguising a rotten heart, it was her house. No amount of fine art, gilded halls, masterfully crafted furniture, and elegant demonstrations of luxury could mask the rancidness festering in those walls.

Almost an hour went by and the knot in my stomach tightened with every tick of the clock. The tiny pokes left by Noah had healed over. This was the only positive I had to cling to.

Gianluca did say I was weak and needed rest, so maybe that's all it was.

A thud in the open doorway broke my concentration. Noah was leaned against the doorframe, then staggered into the room. Every inch of his body was covered in deep slices that dripped blood. It was hard to look at and even harder to watch him try to walk. Any mortal would have died from those injuries.

"Are you all right?!" I exclaimed, even though the answer was very obvious.

"Yeah, why wouldn't I be?" He barely finished his remark before falling face-first onto the floor, leaving a trail of blood on the way down. I didn't know what to do. I was scared to go near him, expecting him to lash out at me if I tried to help. A good fifteen seconds passed and there was no sign of movement, so I slowly made my way to his side.

His injuries were beyond disfiguring, but he was still alive since he hadn't turned to ash. I rolled him over on his back, which was confirmation enough that he wasn't getting up. He hated to be touched and so much as brushing up against him usually resulted in violence.

"Noah?" I tried calling to wake him up. I knew he needed blood, but I didn't know what it would do to me if I gave him mine while I was so weak. There was a mini-fridge disguised as a nightstand with wine bottles full of blood that I remembered him using in the past.

Only one half-empty bottle was left, but it would have to do. I popped the cork and sat next to him, unsure what to do next. I just knew the second I touched his face to open his mouth he would leap up and beat me to a pulp.

"This is for your own good," I prefaced my actions. "I'm trying to help, so don't hurt me."

I cringed as I lifted his head and put the bottle to his lips. This was like bottle-feeding a wounded tiger — a very angry tiger with a long history of mauling people. There wasn't much blood, but it was enough for him to open his eyes a bit.

"Uh, any better?" I asked, but there was no response. His eyes were gazing off in the distance vacantly. "I'll be right back. I'm going to look for more."

I put a pillow under his head and left the room. The building we were in was a smaller chateau reserved for guests. Its main inhabitant was Noah, who I supposed was considered the help. Still, it was tremendous enough to host several large weddings without any parties ever running into each other. A map and a compass would have been a nice handout at the door.

I checked every cabinet, closet, and cupboard, until I finally found a single unopened bottle. I opened it to make sure it was blood and not the only bottle in the house that contained actual wine, but I was in luck. I flew back to Noah as fast as I could, bar a few wrong turns down the marble corridors, and fed him the whole bottle.

He recovered enough to sit up on his own and mumbled something.

"What?" I asked, unsure if he was addressing me or just issuing a general exclamation.

"You fucking heard me," he groaned and sat against the bed.

"No, I didn't, but whatever. What happened?"

"I said thanks," he growled with anger in his voice. It seemed more painful for him to thank me than to endure whatever had inflicted his wounds.

"Don't mention it. Actually, I'm surprised you did at all, but what happened?"

"She needed blood for her stupid dinner guests." Noah winced in anguish. Even sitting against the bed was painful with his back all cut up.

"So?" I wasn't getting it. Did she make him go hunt something like a werewolf?

"So she fucking took it, what do you think?"

"Aurelia did this?" She hated getting her hands dirty and the wounds looked like they came from a weapon, which I also couldn't see her bothering to use.

"Not personally. She ordered someone to. Now drop it."

"Noah ..." My heart ached for him. She made him kill his own lovers out of spite, deceived him into becoming undead in the first place and leaving his family behind, enslaved him to do her bidding, and now tortured him for the pleasure of her guests to top it off. "Has this happened before?"

"All the time. Now *drop it*. Go get me more blood if you want to help. There has to be more around here somewhere."

"Why couldn't she have used any of that blood? Why did it have to be yours?" I was stuck on this. It was traumatizing looking at him. I couldn't imagine how he felt. This was another situation that nothing I had been told could have prepared me for. I had learned about war crimes in school, and heard about heinous acts of abuse in the news, but to see it staring me in the face was another level.

"Because mine is better quality. I'm the child of an Ancient. If you aren't gonna help then just leave me alone."

"I'll get blood." I ran through the house, frantically searching, until a noise outside sent a chill down my spine. It was a very distinct sound I had heard once before. It was the sound of glass shattering, followed by wicked shrieks of laughter.

That was none other than Rozalin's signature laugh. *We defeated her. She should be sealed away somewhere. What, or who, released her? And better yet, why?*

I tore rooms apart for blood like an addict looking for a fix. There had to be a bottle here somewhere. I'd take anything I could get so we could leave. There was no telling what Rozalin would do and I didn't want to stick around to find out.

"Oh thank God!" The irony of my praise in this situation wasn't lost on me. A glass-fronted cabinet containing wine bottles of blood was waiting for me in the basement. I broke the glass to get past the lock and collected as many bottles as I could hold. In my hurry I nicked myself on the broken glass. Regeneration wasn't fully back yet. Great.

Thunder boomed and lightning struck amidst more fits of raucous laughter outside from Rozalin. I reached Noah's room just in time. Noah was on his feet steadying himself against the bedpost and snarling in Korean at the wind spirit, who was over by Vivi's shrine. The man picked up the rose-engraved sword in its sheath, carelessly knocking the urn of ashes and some of the candles onto the floor. Noah tensed up and with an enraged roar tackled the wind spirit through a wall.

I couldn't let Noah fight in his condition. Without blood he was more powerless than I was. I threw the bottles on the bed and pulled the two apart before the wind spirit could snap Noah's ankle in a leg lock. Getting people to attack me was a talent that finally came in handy. I goaded the spirit into fighting me with a shockwave to the face. He retaliated with a gust of wind that sent me through the window. Sharp pains and the warm trickle of blood down my extremities quickly reminded me of my reacquired mortality.

"What fun! Another twisted soul joins the party!" Rozalin cackled at me from overhead. She soared through the air with her gown of woven shadows billowing in the breeze like her hair. "I will be there soon, my dear!"

She was engaged in battle with the other two spirits, but she seemed to be enjoying every second of it. Black lightning crackled from her fingertips as she traded blows with the long-haired man, who summoned his own storm of bolts. I didn't know who I should be rooting for. No matter who won, it was still a loss for me.

"Isn't this so delightful? I was beginning to think I would never see you again!" She continued to mock me from the sky while she conjured pillars of black flame. I rolled out of the way at the last moment and redirected the wind spirit into the fire as he attempted to pounce on me. The unholy flames seared him and kept on burning until he transformed into air to put them out.

Even among all the mayhem I could still feel Aurelia's authoritative presence as she watched silently from the chateau steps. Around her neck was the amethyst pendant used to seal Rozalin away. *I guess that answers who released her, but I thought they hated each other.*

The geisha from our encounter in Bath called upon the water below the stone fountain to put out the flames around her.

"Fool! You cannot squelch the fires of the Underworld with mundane elements!" Rozalin jeered. "I will teach you what the power of a billion burning souls can do."

The winds began to churn around me, but it wasn't Rozalin. The spirit had recouped from being tossed in the fire and created a vortex of slicing wind to surround me. I had been through this before. I couldn't fly up and I couldn't stay on the ground. I had learned something since then, and calmed my mind to the point of the serenity I felt in the Nether Realm with Gianluca. A psionic force flooded outward, silencing the storm. The very earth beneath me disintegrated in a perfect circle and the wind spirit fell from the sky with a thud. Neither of us could move. I was too exhausted after that to fight, but it was worth it if I bought Noah enough time to recover. I lay there semi-conscious as the battle continued without me. Both spirits engaged with Rozalin weren't making much progress against her. She seemed completely satisfied to drag things out by alternating between her own otherworldly elements to torment them.

The long-haired man's lightning was overpowered every time by Rozalin's dark version. He pulled out a spear strapped to his back. A strange choice against an incorporeal phantom, but I soon saw his strategy. When Rozalin unleashed her streams of black electricity, he blocked them with the metal tip of the spear. He aimed and threw the spear — charged with her energy — through the pillars of flame, setting the wood portion alight. The weapon passed through her as expected, but her dark powers turned against her on impact. This was the same method we had used to defeat her years ago; only something from the Underworld can harm a being from there.

She vanished in a puff of black smoke like one of Gianluca's creations. *I wish he was here, but calling for him would only prove he was right — that I can't handle the war.*

"You cannot stop death!" Rozalin screamed upon reappearing in a roiling mass of shadow. "*I AM DEATH!*"

She let loose the wail of a banshee. Her cry shattered the remaining windows of the chateau and rocked the ground. My ears bled and I went deaf for a moment. The remaining spirits were equally as jarred, holding their ears and dropping to their knees. The geisha attempted to hide behind her barrier, but it too shattered like glass as soon as she erected it.

"End this." Aurelia spoke for the first time. Her voice was stoic and quiet, but there was never a problem hearing her no matter the circumstances. "I grow bored and have other matters to attend to tonight."

"Your guests have all been slain. What matters could be of such importance?" Rozalin balked. "I am just beginning the real festivities."

Rozalin opened a portal to the other side and released a swarm of spectral reapers clad in black robes and wielding scythes to assail the spirits. The water woman was the first to fall, overwhelmed by the dark forces and Rozalin's unholy fire and lightning. The spear-equipped warrior shifted his focus to Aurelia. Bad move.

She had just turned to go back inside when the man called a bolt of lightning from the sky to block her path. She sidestepped the bolt effortlessly and ignored the attack. Again the man called more lightning for her to walk around. A minor annoyance at most for Aurelia, until a bolt came too close and clipped the tail end of her purple ball gown.

"Are we having fun yet, sister?" Rozalin laughed.

Aurelia looked over her shoulder with murder in her eyes. She faced the spirit toe to toe and grabbed him in her dainty porcelain hands. In one motion she ripped him in two at the torso and crushed his skull under her heel on her casual stroll back to the chateau.

The wind spirit next to me got to his feet. Part of me wanted to call for help, but I knew I wouldn't get it and I still couldn't move. He bent down and said something in Korean that sounded angry. He reached out to grab me by the hair, but his arm fell off at the elbow, followed by his head. Noah appeared behind him looking healthy again and dropkicked the body as it faded away.

"Too bad for him the wind only looks in one direction at a time or he would've seen that coming." Noah picked me up by the back of the shirt and flung me over his shoulder. "You're a pain in my ass, you know that? Why would you use a move like that if it leaves you incapacitated? You could've died."

"I was trying to buy you time while you got your beauty rest."

"Ahh!" He dropped me back on the grass and then fell to his knees, clutching his head. Aurelia was standing before us.

"Why don't you leave him alone, you —"
Noah stopped me from finishing that sentence with
a hand over my mouth.

"Clean this mess," she commanded him.
"Then —"

"Dorian!" Gianluca appeared. It was more of
a relief to see him at that moment than had he
shown up during the battle.

"I told you he would come, sister!" Rozalin
returned next and circled us. "The Senatus
Tenebris' own herald returns to our world! I kneel to
you in worship, my lord."

"How unbecoming." Aurelia addressed her
sister's flamboyant outcry. "You mentioned
darkness, but you did not mention the handsome
form it would take." She placed a hand over her
mouth to hide a coy smile aimed at Gianluca.

"Eh, I am sorry, do I know you?" he asked
Rozalin.

"My lord, we have not yet met, but there is
time for that." She floated around him, putting her
ghostly hands all over him. "I have waited oh so
long for the Herald of Shadow to reclaim the lands
rightfully yours. The world has grown *tolerant* of
darkness, I fear, and must be reeducated to cower
under your might."

"I … do not understand." Gianluca brushed
her hands away. He could actually touch her as if
she were a solid object like any other person. "I am
not here for this."

Rozalin stared at him, then laughed
flirtatiously. "Oh, you tease me, my lord!"

"Gianluca, what is she talking about?" I asked.

"I do not know. I have not met this woman." He seemed more nervous than confused. I couldn't imagine him being scared of Rozalin and she was practically dropping to her knees for him. "She has the wrong man, I think, no?"

"No ... no. I make no mistake." She smiled. "The legendary Dreadlord himself stands before me, devourer of the innocent and conqueror of the pure. I have been a fan of your work for centuries! The way you cut a swath of death across the Earth. The Underworld has much to thank you for, and I, as its humble representative, wish to show that appreciation in *any* way you desire."

"Come, Dorian. We go now." Gianluca held out his hand to me.

"Oh, I see now," Rozalin continued. "You have taken an apprentice. This makes perfect sense! I would agree wholeheartedly with your choice. The creature does have potential, but so do *I*. We can all work together! Darkness and destruction welcomes allies with open arms!"

"Come now, sister. The so-called Nether Lords rejected you enough in the past to remember your hideous face. Why do you think it would be any different now?" Aurelia mocked, but kept her eyes on Gianluca with a sultry look. Rozalin spoke in Latin to Gianluca, who grew increasingly uncomfortable with the conversation.

"What is going on?!" I shouted. I looked to Noah who shrugged.

"I don't speak Latin."

"You haven't told the boy, have you?" Rozalin provoked further feelings of anxiety from Gianluca. "How dastardly! I am impressed. You still have not lost your brutal sense of fun after all!"

"Told me what?" I had a really bad feeling that everything Vance and Noah had warned me about was about to come true.

"The man before you is none other than the glorious harbinger of darkness so many of us have awaited. Had I known he would choose you as a disciple I would not have tried to reap your soul!" She giggled. "Maybe."

"You *are* the ancient evil?" I yelled at him.

"I told you so," Noah mumbled. Aurelia shot him a cold look that stopped him. Gianluca wasn't answering. If it wasn't true he would deny it.

"There is no mistake! The Dark Senate makes no mistakes. Isn't that right, Gaius Belisarius?"

"Who the hell is that? Gianluca, what is going on?" He wouldn't answer me. His face was frozen in shock.

"Gianluca? Is that what you go by now?" Rozalin questioned. "Why cast off such a noteworthy reputation? A challenge perhaps? To start anew and outdo yourself?"

"My name is Gianluca Belisardi," he stated, but he didn't sound too sure. "I am my own master. The ones you call Dark Senate are dead. I kill them many years ago."

"Fascinating! A *coup*!" Rozalin cheered. "Your malevolence outshines even my own! This explains your rise in power. Tell me, what did their souls taste like? How loud did they scream? Did they beg for mercy like all the other innocents you gutted like pigs?"

Gianluca took my hand. "We must go. It is not good for us here."

"No! Mutilating innocent people? I'm not going anywhere with you." I didn't know where else *to* go, but far away from all of them was a start.

"You are always welcomed here, 'Gianluca,' " Aurelia offered with a meek and humble smile. With that, we fell through the shadows and into his world. Fighting back was hopeless, I knew that. We didn't stay in the shadow realm. He brought us to an open field in a place with a much warmer climate.

"It is not me," he said.

"Don't lie to me. She knew who you were. I saw your face when she said your real name."

"It was me, yes. It is not me today."

"Just tell me what she meant!"

"You are very stubborn ... so much like him." Gianluca's voice drifted with his thoughts.

"Like who? What are you talking about?" Nothing he said was helping me put any of this together. It was a puzzle with more and more pieces and no end in sight.

"You will not like me if I tell you."

"I won't like you if you lie, either."

"Then I am in trouble both times." He turned away from me with a half-hearted smile and shook his head.

"How bad were these 'bad things' you said you did when we met? You were a soldier. I figured you killed people. How many could you have killed to make someone like Rozalin worship you?" Grilling him wasn't getting me anything but frustration. I wasn't about to give up if he was going to take me captive.

"Many ... many people." I stood there waiting in silence for him to continue. There was nothing else I could do to make him talk. "Please. No more. I do not want to talk."

"Then I guess we have nothing else to say to each other," I told him. I started to walk away. It was only symbolic; I knew he could pull me into the darkness.

"Wait," he called back. "You will leave no matter what I do, so I will tell you. I owe you this."

"Let me make that decision. I just want the truth." Suddenly, the ball was in my court again. It was like he wanted to tell me.

"I was a soldier, you know this. In the army I meet a boy like you: very, very stubborn. But, he was not, ah, *vir*, the free man, like me. He was a slave, but I love him. I teach him the sword and I protect him. He sleeps in my arms each night even when many other soldier want him because he was very beautiful, like you too. Because he is a slave he cannot say no to the other free man for the pleasure, so I keep him with me to be safe because we are in love."

271

"Wait, all these soldiers slept with other guys? What kind of army was this?"

"Yes, why does this matter? There is no woman in the army. But, you do not have to be the soldier to like a man. Even the *Caesar* or the scholar can. This is the same, no?"

"Uh, we'll get to that another time. How does this boy make you a bad enough person to get that kind of reputation?"

"He does not. He makes me the man I am now. Before I only want the *gloria,* the glory of the battle, but when I love him my heart fills with passion to protect. As a free man I only have to serve the army for short time, then I may choose another life. But he is a slave and cannot choose, so I stay to be with him.

"The other soldiers, my brothers, know I love him so after some years they do not try to take him from my arms. One night I return from the battle and cannot find him so I am scared he is hurt. My friends, they tell me the *centurion* has him in his —" Gianluca made a box shape with his fingers to try and describe what he was saying, then created it from the shadows.

"Oh, a tent?"

"Yes. The centurion takes him there for his pleasure. He is a cruel man, but many like this because he is strong in the battles. I knew I should not stop it because the centurion is my leader, but I am angry and my heart is hurting. When I go there I see my love with no clothes and holding the sword in the centurion's body. He is crying because he know that he is a slave and rape is only the crime against free citizen. When the guards come I say to spare him because I am the one who killed the centurion, if I do not he will be executed. I know I will be killed too, but it does not matter."

"You two really loved each other to make that sacrifice." This was making me feel sick. Somehow I could sympathize with the futility both of them must have felt, but my own negative experiences seemed more insignificant by comparison. I had been through great physical pain, but always recovered without a scratch. I had lost people, but sooner or later, everyone dies in the mortal world and I would have had to come to terms with it. Being enslaved, raped, tortured – I had never experienced these things that even mortals suffer through every day. *I can understand now why Gianluca is so passionate about protecting what he likes.*

"Yes. He is in my heart today too." Gianluca looked so sullen, but a smile appeared on his face as he recalled another memory. "After the battles he would cry 'Gaius! Gaius! You are hurt!' and come to clean me, but he is always the more hurt one. He was very stubborn and would not let me help him first. I think when I am hurt he has the strength of all Roma. I tell him, 'Do not worry, my little love. Every battle I come back to see your face I grow stronger. One day I promise I will be so strong I will not bleed.'

"I worry because the slave, they do not fight with the other soldier. Many wear the light armor, or no armor sometimes, and they are the first in the battle to fight. Sometimes they do not get food and are weak, so I save mine to give him."

"What was his name?" I asked.

"I do not speak it. He is resting in the heavens now." Gianluca took a moment and closed his eyes briefly before continuing.

"So, what happened when the guards found you two in the centurion's tent?"

"I was put in the jail and beaten while the senate decide to kill me or not. My brothers in the army try to say I did no wrong, but the guards beat me so I cannot speak and change my mind. The centurion was very much liked so I know I have no chance to live, but I was happy that my love would be safe.

"At night before I die, five of the senate come to me. They say they know the truth and they believe the soldiers that I am innocent, but if I admit this I know what it means for my love. They make an offer because they say I am brave and strong to stand against the face of my death. If I say yes, they will release me as a secret and I will work for them to protect the people of Roma by killing the men like the centurion. When I agree is when they drink my blood and give me the dark power.

"They did not tell me what I was, but only I can work at night. They say I cannot just kill the bad men, but I must make others fear the crimes so it will not happen again. I will use the darkness to scare the people around the men I am told to kill. Then I am told to go to check my love because he is in danger. When I find his body ... it was burn all over and his eyes and tongue cut out. The Senatus tell me the soldiers do this because he is traitor and they know he killed the centurion. I cannot control myself and I kill the soldier, my old friends, in their sleep. My heart knows only anger and because I am dead I cannot cry.

"The Senatus give me more and more men, then group of men, soon entire village and cities across the empire. I even destroy the temples to give them no hope. I was to show them no god could excuse their crimes. For the glory of Roma I think. I am the devil that punish the wicked. But it is not true. I am just the monster. I kill the women and the children, the innocent and the old. I break their bodies and drown their souls. The Senatus poison my mind so I cannot think. They tell me these people are touched by evil and must be taught the lesson, but soon I do not care and kill for no reason. I cannot count the faces of all the victim, there is too many. I see them all when I close my eyes, I hear their screams in the darkness they were swallowed by. My beautiful Roma I once loved now fear me.

"When the Senatus say to darken the sun, kill the humans so only we will live and start a new empire, I find strength to say no, it is too much. The sun should fear no man, but I was no man anymore. I did not deserve this world, but I could not die. This is why I hide in the darkness for many years. I was a coward, but there I could not hurt the people."

"You didn't have a choice, but you stopped the ones making you evil. You're a different man now."

"It does not make me the good person. You know who I am now and you do not like it."

"I like the Gianluca I know today. You can't bring back the people you killed, but you can help save others. Hiding and sleeping won't make up for it."

"I try this, but you do not let me. I want to protect you. My heart feels the passion again when I look at you. I feel I can do anything, I can save the innocent people from the Eastern ones."

"I understand why you don't want me in battle, but I'm not *him*, Gianluca. If you're really different now, we should work *together* and do good."

"Yes, this is what I want."

"Then let's get Noah and go to Japan. He has something that can stop them." *I would ask Gianluca to help free Noah, but I know Noah would never accept. I can't just ask Gianluca to kill Aurelia for me either. Not only is that overstepping our friendship, but I'm not even sure he could kill her and I wouldn't want to endanger him too.* The sisters were enamored with him, but I knew it was his power they wanted, as per the usual in this world. He could bargain for Noah's freedom peacefully, but Aurelia would keep her mental hold on Noah. It looked like the only way Noah was to win his freedom was by the end of a sword, the Muramasa to be exact. I wouldn't give up on him.

"No, you are hurt." Gianluca rolled up my shredded sleeves and inspected the cuts from the glass.

"I'm fine," I lied. It hurt more now that the adrenaline was gone. I tried not to wince when he touched me even though he was being extra careful. My regeneration had totally stopped after releasing so much of my energy.

"This is not good. You are too stubborn." He used his thumb to wipe away a droplet of blood from my face that I didn't even know was there. "First, I take you to a place for healing. Then we go to your friend."

"You aren't going to let me say no, are you?"

"No." He smiled.

"No hospitals. I have bad experiences with them."

Chapter Seventeen

"I can do it," I said. Gianluca had brought us to yet another hotel and fetched a first aid kit while I showered. He insisted on wrapping my wounds for me after they had been cleaned since they still weren't healing, but I wouldn't let him. It just felt odd having someone dote over me.

"Stubborn." Gianluca surrendered the bandages. "Always the little ones are very, very stubborn."

"My parents were doctors. They taught me some basic things like how to properly dress a wound, set a splint. That kind of stuff."

"They would be proud."

"I don't know about that." I saw stars when applying the alcohol swab to sterilize each cut. They were deeper and more numerous than I had thought before I cleaned away the blood. Not the most attractive sight, and Gianluca was sitting right up against me on the bed. My regeneration needed to come back fast, even if only for the purpose of my vanity. In all seriousness, its loss was a major problem for the battles ahead. "I don't think this is the life they wanted for me."

"Why do you say this? You know so much. The battle, the medicine, the architecture. And you are so young. I would be very proud."

"I'm not that young. Compared to you, yeah. But, I'm twenty-three, twenty-four soon, and I haven't done anything except barely survive. And right now I can't even heal."

"Twenty-three? You are just a baby!" He laughed heartily and rubbed my back.

"No, I'm not. In your Rome twenty-three was middle-aged. How old did you think I was?"

"I do not know. Two hundred? You are very strong and wise. In Roma I was not like you at this many years. It was fight, fight, fight. I did not think much about the life after."

"How old *are* you exactly?"

"Hm, the empire was new. I start becoming the soldier some years before."

"Wow. You're older than the Colosseum. So you were already undead when it was built?"

"Yes. I like the sports and I always want to fight there. I go to see many times. The lion is my favorite. I cheer for it, not the gladiator sometime." Gianluca was smooth. As we talked, he finished bandaging me while I got lost in the sound of his voice and thoughts of what it must have been like back then. I couldn't help stealing glances at him and smiled when he noticed and our eyes met. He smiled back warmly and moved so I was sitting between his legs with my back to him. We were in a hotel room, at night, and I was shirtless on the bed. This was going one way and I wasn't sure I was ready for it.

"We should, um, go get Noah and head to Japan." It wasn't that I didn't want anything to happen between us, but I was nervous. I wasn't about to open my heart to someone who could disappear as quickly as a fleeting shadow. I was also entirely too inexperienced in affairs of the heart, both romantic and carnal. It wasn't an opportunity that presented itself often in my current lifestyle. In the past I had tried to conceal my orientation for fear of what people might say.

"Tomorrow. You need rest." He spoke quietly into my ear and then tickled my side.

"Hey! Not fair! Stop it!" I squirmed and let out an uncontrollable laugh.

Gianluca held my hands in his and hugged me tight. His nose grazed my ear on its way down to my neck. My heart began to pound. "You smell very nice. I like it."

Well, that's something I don't hear too often. Thank you generic hotel soap. I couldn't respond. I tried not to make any noise because I knew whatever I'd come out with would be embarrassing.

"I make sure you have the room all tonight and go check your friend is safe." I felt his lips hover just above my neck and his warm breath against my bare skin. The tip of his nose travelled back up my neck to my cheek, where he kissed softly. "Have sweet dreams, little one."

He disappeared, taking the light along with him. I lay on the bed feeling a bit guilty that I couldn't sway my thoughts from Gianluca and focus on the war. Was love really a weakness I should avoid? Not that I was in love. I didn't even know what being in love felt like. But, what if by some crazy chance it happened? If I was fighting to make the world a better, safer place, didn't I deserve to enjoy it and live with passion?

I wished I had somewhere to call home again, something that was mine — anything. I had nothing to my name, not even the rags I wore. It wasn't the acquisition of material goods I cared about. I wanted to stop relying on others. Sure, I could continue surviving out in the wild alone, scavenging for bare necessities, even sleeping off a decade or two to pass the time. But I didn't see Aurelia out there in the mud worrying over her next meal. Why should I? Even a modest place I'd earned by myself would mean the world to me. I could practice my gift, maybe even create something of worth to be proud of. *What will Gianluca do now that he's awake from his centuries-long torpor?* I wondered.

"*Buon Giorno!*" An unfamiliar man's voice woke me.

"*Silenzio, per cortesia,*" Gianluca whispered somewhere in the room. His voice was followed by the squeaky sound of a cart rolling. "*Grazie.*"

"Wha–?" I asked in a daze as I rubbed the sleep from my eyes.

"Oh, never mind! He is awake," I heard Gianluca say in a cheerful tone. I noticed I was tucked in under the covers. Gianluca opened the curtains to let the morning sunlight stream in. My eyes adjusted as a member of the hotel staff finished setting a table with many plates of food from a serving cart.

"What is all this?" I asked once the man left.

"A breakfast. I do not know what is your favorite, so I take them all."

"We can't eat this! We have no way to pay. This is a lot more than just sleeping on the bed for a few hours." I got up to look at all the food when I realized where we were from the scene out the window. "Oh my god, that's the Colosseum ... We're in Rome!"

"Do not worry so much, little one. I pay with the money." Gianluca wrapped his arms around me from behind as I stared out the window in awe. The stubble on his face tickled as his lips found their way to my neck again. I put my hand back to touch his cheek and felt his smile grow as he made me squirm.

"Can we go there?" I asked, still gazing fondly at the Colosseum. "Hm, I do not think so, little one. I am sorry."

"Oh," I sighed in disappointment. The Colosseum was *so* close and it had been a dream of mine to see it. But I had all the time in the world to visit it on another trip. At least there was a warm meal.

"I think the Colosseum is the most beautiful thing in Roma until I bring you here. It would be jealous of you." He cracked a smile and waited for me to laugh. "It is just a joke! Of course we will go."

"Very funny."

"Come, eat. Then we will visit the Colosseum." He pulled a chair out for me and started filling my plate. "Your favorite. It is like the dessert." He added a croissant filled with jelly. There were all sorts of breakfast pastries, fresh fruit, and best of all, coffee.

Gianluca rested his arm across the back of my chair while we ate and looked out at the wondrous landscape.

"You are quiet," he said after a few minutes of silence. "I think you need more sleep, no? The Colosseum will be here for you later."

"No, I'm sorry. I slept really well." For once I wasn't conflicted about whether or not someone had ulterior motives. I felt in my heart that Gianluca was genuine despite his past. Or maybe I just wanted him to be more than anyone else I'd met. Either way, at the moment I was nervous about normal things like what to say, what he thought of me, what the future would hold. Unlike the other supernaturals, I coveted normalcy more than power, but now that I had a taste of it I didn't know what the heck to do. Was this like an actual date? *Do people like me get to do that stuff? I mean, without pretending we're something we're not.*

"What did you dream?" he asked as I got lost in my own thoughts again.

"I didn't. I usually have bad dreams, so I was happy to make it through the night without one." That sounded like more of a downer than I wanted. I didn't want to tell him that I had been thinking about him before I fell asleep. That would be awkward. But what would I say instead?

"You have a good dream sometime, no?"

"I daydream a lot. I was thinking how I want to practice more of what you taught me."

"You are very talented. I want to be with you when you do this."

"Definitely." I smiled at him and finished off my coffee. "What was it like staying in the shadow world for so long? Wasn't it lonely? Or were you asleep the whole time?"

"Hm, I will be honest. I do not think this when I am there, but when I see Roma, my home, I miss it very much. I would like this again. Now I feel only lost."

"Me too. It's only been a couple of years, but I miss having a home and people I care about." It was amazing how much I had in common with someone from a completely different time period. He was older than most present-day countries, but sometimes when we talked it was like we had grown up in the same world.

"Why you do not have this?"

"After my parents died I moved in with a friend. He wasn't like us, though. I thought he didn't understand me and I would get him in danger, so I left. Since then I've just traveled with Noah, trying to stay out of trouble, but we haven't been doing a very good job." For the first time I considered that Gianluca and I were the same. It was always the undead, with me as some side-note abomination without a label. Then there were the Blackbournes: still just another place I didn't actually fit in. With Gianluca, I felt like I belonged. It was a group of two and that was more than enough.

"You will be safe, little one," he reassured me. "I will help find you the place to have a home. Then you will make beautiful work and I will watch."

"Thanks, Gianluca. That's really sweet, but I didn't mean I wanted you to do that for me."

"It is no problem. I know what you feel because I want this too. When the soldier leave the army in Roma he is thought to make a family. I do not think of this until I come back here because of what happen in my life. Now I have no empire to serve and no loved one to protect. When I have a dream it is to do this. I like the 'sweet' things." Gianluca selected a strawberry from the bowl of assorted fruit and offered it to me. "Do you like it?"

"Yes, I do." I went to take it from him, but he pulled away. He got such a kick out of teasing me. None of the undead I met had any sense of humor or playfulness left in them. Maybe the undead condition also gave them an aversion to fun along with sunlight. Gianluca wasn't one of them anymore.

"With your mouth." He insisted I let him feed me the strawberry by putting it near my lips and watching them with an eager smile.

"Really?" I laughed through the tension.

"Yes, why not? You say you like it," he coaxed. After some hesitation I bit into the fruit. I couldn't believe I was doing this. It was making me laugh even as I finished chewing. It seemed so corny when I saw other people do it, but actually experiencing it was kind of romantic in a way I couldn't explain.

He placed his hand on my cheek and by the look in his eyes I knew what was coming next. My stomach clenched. I felt hot all over and the hairs on the back of my neck stood on end as his face drew near to mine. He brought me closer to meet him halfway until there wasn't enough room to slide a piece of paper between us.

"Gianluca, wait." When I spoke I could feel my lips brush against his. "I can't do this."

I turned my head away and blocked his kiss with my other cheek, not knowing what I was feeling. Was it nerves? Shame? Embarrassment? He sat back in his chair, but I couldn't look up at him.

"I know. You do not like what I have done in my past," he said in a forlorn tone. "I do not blame you. It is wrong to try make you to forget."

"No, it isn't that. I like you a lot. I'm just ... I don't know, not very good at this stuff. I'm not used to it and I've never really done it before. Well, once, but he was nothing like you and that was years ago."

"Oh?" Gianluca brightened up slightly. "I know you are very shy. I think after I tell you of me, you do not look at me the same, but I must try."

"I guess I am shy. I'm sorry."

"Do not be sorry. This is who you are." He moved in again and gave me a hug with one arm. "The future has many years when you cannot die. It is good I am a very patient man."

"Do you ever want to go back?" I asked. "To your time, I mean."

"Yes, but this is my time now. We can change where we are and who we are with, but not when. I am so lucky to found you because you make me feel welcome."

"Good." I smiled up at him. "You make me feel the same way. I don't always feel like I belong in this world."

Gianluca finished his coffee and stood at the window looking out. He was every bit as statuesque as the aesthetically flawless city beyond. I could see him posing for a sculptor in Ancient Rome to be immortalized in marble.

"Come, we go to see the beauty of Roma now," he said. I grabbed my sweatshirt and tore the sleeves off to get rid of the bloodstains. With my forearms and hands wrapped up I felt like I was preparing for a fight in the ring. Fitting for a trip to the Colosseum.

The shadows sucked me in and together we were pulled to the dark recess under an archway of the Colosseum. Gianluca was taking a lot of risks by using his powers. We bumped up against a tour group where there was no room for a person to have snuck by. Some of them looked at us, puzzled. I could tell they were trying to figure out where we had come from, but turned back around after failing to come up with an explanation.

Gianluca and I had stars in our eyes as we took in the ancient architectural masterpiece. Just being there fulfilled a long-forgotten dream. I had to touch everything in reach within respectful limits. I wanted to experience it all in every way possible with as many senses. These stones had survived thousands of years and stood against the test of time. This monumental piece of art had withstood regime changes, uprisings, wars, and natural disasters. *What better icon of enduring splendor in the face of destruction is there than work like this? And who better to be here with than an actual Roman?*

Parts of the walkways were sectioned off to prevent visitors from accessing them during restoration. This didn't deter Gianluca. He stepped right through the shadows of the chain-link gate to the other side.

"Come back! We can't go there!" I wanted to stop him before anyone saw us and we got in trouble.

"Why?" he asked with curious innocence.

"They're doing work here. See the sign?" I pointed to the big colorful "Restricted Access" sign that listed its notice in a multitude of languages.

"That is not for us." He gave it a quick once-over and pulled me through to him. His carefree nature made me made me laugh. As much as I enjoyed him hugging me again it was making me even more nervous. "You are so happy, it is very cute."

"Don't change the subject. We're going to get in trouble!" It was funny hearing a former Roman soldier say "cute." I could picture him hearing it used for the first time and deciding to add it to his vocabulary.

"When do they bring the lion?"

"I don't think they do that anymore. There are laws against that kind of thing." I tugged on his arm, trying to get him to leave, but I had a better chance of moving the Colosseum itself.

"I know. It is a joke. I see here many times when it changed. Now the men fight in the small metal cage."

"You mean MMA? Yeah, I guess that is like a modern version of the gladiator battles. That's something else we have in common."

He shrugged in disappointment. "The fight, no men die. It is just a practice."

"You can't kill someone for entertainment. That's cruel. Most of the gladiators were slaves that didn't have a choice."

"Yes, this is true. I think they are not the slaves today though, no? It is their choice, their passion. It is entertainment for the people to watch, but if it is the passion for the one who fights then he should put his life in it. To die for the passion is the greatest glory. This makes the good life filled with honor."

"Gianluca, the guards are coming. I don't want to be thrown out of my childhood dream on my first visit here."

At last he listened and returned us to the walkways teeming with tourists.

"They do not put the water in anymore?" Gianluca held my hand as he listened in on a tour guide's speech. "Not many people die in the sea battle. I think they could make the show still, no?"

"Um, I don't know." I pulled my hand free before anyone noticed, but he put his arm over my shoulder instead. "Didn't that only last a short time?"

A group of tourists passing by glared at us. I couldn't understand what they were saying to each other, but from their expression it wasn't nice. I brushed Gianluca's hand away and walked ahead a few steps. With a single look from a group of strangers my joy turned to anxiety.

"This is much more better than the diorama, no?" Gianluca came up behind me again and wrapped his arms around me.

"Yeah." I wasn't even enjoying the Colosseum anymore, or Gianluca's advances. My eyes were on everyone's disgusted faces. There was nowhere I could look that wasn't met with probing stares. "Gianluca, stop touching me."

"You are such a tease." He leaned over and kissed my cheek, then snuck in a quick tickle to my side. "I do not see the sign this time."

I choked back the natural urge to laugh and tried to push him off. "I'm serious, get off of me."

I wanted to leave, but didn't know where the exit was. I was all turned around and my head was spinning from nerves after being demonized for doing nothing wrong.

"Why? I do this many time before and you like it."

"Not in public." I shoved my way through the crowd, growing more frantic every second.

"What is wrong?" he asked as he followed after me.

"You can't act like that with people around," I told him as soon as we got past the initial group of people.

"Why? I do not understand." He went to touch my arm, but I moved back.

"I just want to leave." I kept looking for an exit until Gianluca made one for us through the shadows. I'm sure that freaked out some spectators.

"What did I do? You are so cold now." We were back in the hotel room and I finally felt like I could breathe again.

"I don't know what it was like back in your Rome, but the world is different now. You can't be like that with me when other are people around." I stood at the opposite side of the room. This was the furthest apart we'd been physically in the same space since we met.

"Why? You are embarrassed of me?" He looked completely lost, like he was waiting for me to say I was joking. I was angry with him at first for putting me in that situation and not understanding, but it wasn't his fault.

"No, it's not you, it's what you're doing. People don't do that."

"This does not make sense. I see the romance all the time."

"Not between guys." I sat on the bed and ran my hands through my hair, frustrated that I couldn't explain myself, and even more so that I had to. "People now days don't want men to be together. It's men with women only."

"But, I like you, a man. Why does this matter what the people want? They are jealous?"

"It's got nothing to do with jealous. They hate us because they think it isn't normal.

We're different, just like why we can't use our powers around them."

"I use the powers all the time."

"Maybe that was a bad example. You can't use your powers either, because people will get scared. When people are scared they get violent."

"I think you are worried to be hurt, but this will not happen with me. I will not allow it."

"You can't fight millions — billions — of people."

"Yes, if they try to hurt you, then why not? I am strong and they are weak. In my Rome as you call it, it does not matter if you love the man or the woman. If you want the baby and family, then yes you look for the woman and love her. But, if you love the man this is not bad. I like you very, very much, but how can I show you this if you say to hide?"

"I like you too, but we can't let other people know. Something changed after your Rome so that now people don't accept love as anything but man and woman. They think it's evil and gross for two men or two women to love each other."

"This cannot be serious? Love is never evil. I hide in the shadows for enough years, I do not want to do this anymore. I am happy to be back here and be with you. If the people want to hate a good feeling then maybe they are the evil one, no?"

"Maybe some of them. I think most are just confused or believe what they're told by the evil ones. Like how you were tricked."

"Then we will find the ones who tell these lies and stop them." Gianluca's expression shifted from befuddlement to anger. I might have made a mistake bringing up his former masters.

"That's impossible, even for you. There are so many and there's no way to tell who's misinformed and who's spreading the hate on purpose. The Catholic Church is always preaching it, but I don't think they're evil. I think they're just scared because of what they read in the Bible. they think God only wants men and women to be in love."

"Oh, oh ..." Gianluca's face changed again to an expression I had seen once before, when Rozalin outed his true identity. "This is still here? The Church?"

"Of course it's still here, what do you mean?"

"Er ... maybe you will be mad."

"What? What else could possibly trump mass genocide?"

"The Senatus, when they make me kill the people, I hear their plan. They say to the emperor we will need the soldiers, soldiers for Roma. We must make the citizen have the babies to replace the evil I killed. They want me to destroy the temples of the old gods to show there is no hope for the old evil ways. They say the old gods allow too much bad to happen, they are weak, but they have a new god. The emperor and the new church tell the people, only with man and woman in the bed. Then they write this. But, this is just for now, to make more citizens. I do not think this still happens? There is no empire and there are very many more people today."

My stomach and heart sank further than ever before. I was dating, if you wanted to call it that, one of the men responsible for the persecution of our own kind.

"Gianluca, what you did didn't stop there. Your actions and those of your masters sent ripples through history that turned into a tidal wave of hate against people who just wanted to be in love."

"I did not know this. I only hear a piece of it and I think I do not understand it. It sound to me like a celebration for love. It make sense then, there needs to be children to keep the empire alive. It was a warning not a crime. When I wake up to kill the Senatus later, in the time with the knights, I still see the Church. I think when I kill them it stops, but the building just stay like the Colosseum."

"No, people still believe that. That warning turned into a crime and then a war against love that's lasted centuries."

"I will fix this. I will find the way to make it right."

"I told you, you can't. There's no way one person can stop it no matter how strong you are, unless you plan on killing everyone again and starting over."

"Then I will not use strength, I will use my head and my heart until it is better."

"I've heard the Catholic or Christian God was around much longer than that. He's the one that cursed the undead to not walk in the sunlight to protect humans from them during the day. The Senatus couldn't have made Him up."

"No, I do not think this. They pretend to be one of His men after the empire. They trick the people to fear him like they fear me when I leave, so they can be the ruler. If the people does not do what they say, then the God will punish them."

"Hopefully God is getting his revenge on the Dark Senatus for using his name for evil."

"If He is the one to make the undead like this, then maybe he is the one to take it away when I sleep? I wish all the time to be a good man again, but there was no old gods to pray to when I destroy their temple and their people."

"You can't pray to become good. You have to make a choice and do it, which you did by escaping and stopping the Senatus."

"Yes, maybe this is true." Gianluca sat on the bed beside me, not touching me. "I will make it okay. Do not worry. Even if you do not like me, I will not let the people hurt you."

"I *do* like you. It's just hard to express it."

He placed his hand on my leg cautiously. "Is it okay?"

"Yes." I nodded in agreement. He was trying so hard. This was confusing enough for me; I couldn't imagine what was going through his head. He had been used as a pawn, a common concept even for someone as powerful as himself. It wasn't his fault, but now I felt bad he was assuming the weight on his shoulders alone to fix it. I hugged him first for the first time.

"Is this why you are so shy?" he asked as he embraced me.

"I wasn't always. I had a good childhood and was a happy kid. When I grew up and found out what made me different I started having to hide pretty much everything about myself. Friends left me. I was scared I would disappoint my parents. The only guy I ever dated used me as a dirty secret."

"You are a good person, you should not have to hide. When you are scared you can stay here in my arms where it is safe." He kissed the top of my head. Again, Gianluca had a strong yet soothing way of making everything all right.

He picked me up like I weighed nothing and sat me on his lap. He carefully started to unwrap my bandages to check whether I had healed.

"I can do it," I argued, and pulled away to finish myself.

"So stubborn. I think you are not the chick, you are the bull with the horns. The small one though."

"I'll take that. It's better than a chick." I held one of the bandages in my teeth while I worked on the next. He tugged on it like he was playing tug-of-war with a dog, so I growled at him and made him laugh.

"I think maybe you are both. The chick with the horns." He was very amused with himself. He rested his chin on my shoulder while I worked and I kind of liked it. "Why do you laugh?"

"Your stubble is tickling me."

"What is a stubble?" He knew because he made it worse by scratching my neck with it even more.

"This, your scruff." I ran my hand along it and tickled him back under his chin making him scrunch his nose.

He was such an amazing guy. I was glad to have gotten everything off my chest, but hoped it didn't put the entire burden on him now. I was lucky to be around him at all and he made me feel hopeful for the future. *If there is some great big cycle and history is bound to repeat itself, then maybe love will be unshackled from hate and judgment once again*, I thought.

"You are looking much better." He traced his fingers along my forearm, giving me the chills. The cuts and scrapes had all healed. Only the deepest puncture wounds had a bit left to go. "This feels good?"

"Yes." Now I was blushing again. I could feel it. When would that stop? I was annoyed that my body had a mind of its own. I wasn't the type of person to like being tickled either. I hated not being in control, but with him it felt okay.

"I would like to show you more of Roma, but I think I need a rest. While you sleep I search for the Easterners' home and I check for your friend to be safe too, so I do not get the rest."

"You slept for centuries! You don't get any more rest," I joked.

"You are too cruel to me, baby chick." He flashed me a sad puppy-dog look. "There is no time in the shadows. To me it was only one night, maybe two. I can only tell what happen when I look out and listen to the world."

I had a hard time paying attention. Our lips were dangerously close again and I kept looking away and then back. I thought my head would fall off. I had one arm over his shoulder and was in a compromised position on his lap that I couldn't easily escape from.

"Will you like to sleep with me?"

"Um, what?" I stared into his eyes, shocked by this new level of assertiveness from him.

"Here in the bed. To sleep. You will be tired in the night if you are awake now, no?" I had a feeling from his devilish grin that he knew exactly what I thought he meant. It was already afternoon, so it was a good idea to get some additional rest.

"Okay, but you better keep your clothes on."

Chapter Eighteen

"Gianluca?" I called into the shadows. I had half expected him to break his word. I thought I would wake up to him semi-nude and gazing at me with bedroom eyes, but he wasn't even in the room. The clock on the nightstand said it was already 2 AM. I had overslept in a bad way and was worried that Gianluca had gone on his own to stop the invaders from the East.

I wasn't used to oversleeping, or sleeping much at all. Even after the events at the Colosseum I still had no trouble falling asleep and staying that way without night terrors. I didn't think I'd be able to fall asleep next to someone, either. I had never done it before, unless you count camping with my parents, and felt uneasy about the connotations it held with a stranger.

Gianluca was so much more forward than I was used to, not that I had been on very many dates to begin with. Aside from the architecture I knew very little about Ancient Rome, but I could imagine people hadn't gone through much of a courting process when they were interested in someone. Between disease, war, and generally lower life expectancies, most couples probably got right to the point. It was hard to picture him back then. He seemed to have caught up so quickly.

I removed my bandages and called to Gianluca once more. I was fully healed and ready for battle. The shadows converged around me as I finished looking myself over and pulled me into the darkness. It was getting less frightening each time, thankfully.

"I think maybe you will not wake up for the many years too. You look very peaceful," Gianluca greeted me as we exited the shadows. We were in the aisle of a huge library, still in Italy judging by the book titles.

"Sorry about that. I'm glad you didn't leave for Japan without me." He didn't appear to be his usual happy self as he flipped thoughtfully through a book. "What are you reading?"

"I come to read the book on what I miss. I see the many different building and clothes and this does not bother me. When I learn the automobile and the human *tecnologia*, I think this is nice. It is the new magic."

"Yeah, that's a good way of putting it. I was just thinking how you've been fitting in well for someone gone for so long." I thought my praise would change his mood, but he seemed rather distressed.

"Thank you. I think this too. These are just things, the clothes, the new building, but the people are very different. I think people do not change, but I am wrong."

"Is this because of what happened at the Colosseum?" I asked. Some people entered the aisle, one replacing books on the shelf next to us.

"Yes, I want to learn the people, why this happens. I do not care so much for the others, but I do not want to make you mad with me. I want to live here now and know the new things, but there is many." He showed me the book he was reading, but it made no sense to me in Italian. "It is the laws and some history."

"Oh, Gianluca, you don't have to do that, not for me. I guess this is harder on you than I thought. You just seemed to fit in so well, I assumed you understood most of what was going on. But it isn't just the way people dress and talk that has changed."

"I close my eyes to sleep and when I open them it is a new world. It is like a dream. Then I do it one more, and another new world today. I think I am maybe not the man good for you. I do not understand the things I need to be here."

My heart hurt hearing that. I was poisoning him with my own self-consciousness. I only had myself to blame for pushing him away.

"That isn't true. You've helped me so much. In only a few days of knowing you, you solved a problem I've had for years." It was now or never. I could talk until the end of time and hope I got through to him, but only action would really change anything. I reached out and held his hand, fighting the butterflies in my stomach and the disorienting anxiety in my head. I didn't want my courage to falter. I kept my eyes on him so I wouldn't see the faces of the people around us.

"This is okay?" he asked as always, but this time with noticeable surprise on his face.

"Yeah. We're the strong ones, right? The world doesn't change when people hide. It's up to us to set the example." I checked to see if anyone was watching through the corner of my eye. Nobody seemed to care. Even if they did, what could they possibly do to us? I wouldn't let fear and hate prohibit me from happiness. Not everyone out there is an unaccepting asshole. There were still the "Lyles" of the world out there.

"This makes me very happy, but I do not want you uncomfortable for me."

"You're worth it." I smiled and squeezed his hand tighter. "And it will only make me stronger."

"We will be strong together." He gave me a much-welcomed hug. "Hm, I think I would like this book to learn more still ... maybe this too." He selected another from a stack he had made.

"You need a library card to borrow it," I started to explain, but the two books disappeared from his hand like a magician's vanishing act. "You can't do that!"

"Shh, I only borrow it for the short time." He put his finger to my lips and with a grin we also vanished into the shadows. *We definitely just caused some hysteria among a whole bunch of people ... again.*

"What happened to you?" I asked in shock as Gianluca and I arrived in Noah's room to find him slumped over against the wall and covered in blood. There was so much of it I couldn't even see where it was coming from.

"The Eastern ones have come back?" Gianluca asked.

"Yeah," Noah groaned after a few seconds without raising his head.

"I think we cannot take him with us like this." Gianluca turned to me. "I will go alone. Stay to watch your friend. The enemies can come back here for him."

"I don't think it was them that did this ..." I looked at the Muramasa lying on Noah's bed. The spirits wouldn't have left the sword behind with him unable to stop them. "I'll go get him blood. Can you stay with him?"

Noah was remarkably compliant, only grunting in disapproval. That was a bad sign. For once I wanted a snarky quip.

"I am most honored you have decided to return to us, Gianluca." Aurelia's voice entered the room ahead of her along with the sweet smell of flowers before I could leave. "To what do I owe the pleasure of this visit?"

She looked almost heavenly, with her ankle-long brunette hair let down behind her and adorned with a wreath of lilacs atop her head. Her white embroidered lace gown hovered somewhere between the purity of a maiden and the promiscuity of a French courtesan, most notably in the corset area.

"We come for Noah," Gianluca replied. "I think he has the information to stop our enemy?"

"We're taking him with us," I added. "Far, far away from here."

"I wish only to help in *any* way I can, but I believe my loyal guard to be indisposed at the moment." She was a good actress, I had to give her that. *I would almost believe she cared if I didn't know her reputation.*

"Gee, I wonder how that happened." My glare was ignored by all but Noah, who shot me his own look to be silent from under his matted hair.

"Then you will join us?" Gianluca's question surprised me. It surprised me even more when he took her by the hand and stared into her eyes longingly.

"I am no brave warrior like yourself." Aurelia tilted her head away shyly. "There must be some other way I can be of assistance. I would gladly lend you my guard's sword-arm were he capable, but alas —"

Her hand had just touched his bare chest when the amethyst pendant around her neck fluttered to life.

"*I* am quite capable, dear sister." Rozalin burst forth from the jewel, forcing Aurelia and

Gianluca apart. It gave me a moment of relief until she took her turn running her spectral fingers along Gianluca's torso. "And I would be *most* willing to aid you, my lord."

"Uh, Gianluca, can I talk to you for a minute? Alone." I tried pulling him away from the wicked sisters, but it was no use.

"Then who would be left to protect me, should those fearsome miscreants return?" Aurelia covered her mouth with a gasp, playing afraid.

"Oh come on. You ripped one of them in two." My ploy to call her out failed as the three started jabbering amongst themselves in Latin like they had all been best friends for years. Gianluca delicately removed the necklace from Aurelia's possession. His face leaned in close enough to warm her cold dead flesh with his breath. I was trying not to let their intimacy get to me, but I couldn't help the feelings of jealousy building up.

"What is going on?!" I shouted in frustration.

"I don't speak Latin, but it sounds to me like you're losing the game, kid." Noah spoke from the floor for the first time so far. "Told you he'd turn on us."

The three stopped chatting abruptly.

"Then it is finish," Gianluca announced. "I will take Noah and the lovely Rozalin with me as the guide, my soldier will watch for the beautiful Aurelia to be safe." He constructed two imposing knights from living darkness that kneeled before her and then melted into her shadow to stay guard.

"How is Noah supposed to go anywhere like this?" I asked.

"Why, there is fresh blood in the chateau, he knows that!" Aurelia exclaimed cheerfully on her way out.

"Oh yeah, I never thought of that," Noah mumbled under his breath. "Guess I better start crawling."

"This is a horrible idea," I said out loud to no one in particular.

"That's kinda ironic coming from you, don't you think?" Noah tried to laugh at his own remark, but was in too much pain. I actually had the chance to kick him for his sarcastic comments for once, but had to refrain.

Gianluca brought us to the chateau. Rozalin appeared on her own after us.

"How delightful this will be!" Rozalin mused as she floated around the main hall. "I am starved for the chance to see what darkness we will bring ... *together!* Let us make our enemies tremble at our feet. The Strigoi's prodigal child gone astray would do well to learn from a true master of destruction!"

"Gianluca, can I please talk to you alone?" I looked down at the pendant in his hand to indicate he should leave it behind. He brought us to the dark dimension where I didn't know what to say first.

"What troubles you, little one?" He smiled his usual welcoming smile.

"Those sisters are evil!"

"Yes, I know this."

"Then why are we working with them?"

"We have the common enemy. They want to help, I let them. Do not worry little one, I will keep you safe."

"How can I even be sure it's you talking and they're not in your head right now? I know their games."

"You are the only one in my head, in the good way." He floated up close to me. "I know these games. It is a dance. They think I do not know them because we do not meet, but I see many like this before."

"I don't want to dance anything with them." I pushed away from him until I realized I couldn't stop myself in the vastness of empty space. "Noah is Aurelia's slave and she's hurting him. That wasn't the Easterners."

"I know this too." Gianluca pulled me back in. "I did not hear the warrior voices so I know it was not them. This is why I make a deal to take him with us. But if he is her property I cannot keep him forever."

"Slavery was over a long time ago, Gianluca. She can't keep him like that. She has no right."

"In the human life, yes, but this is not that. There will be the other way. Trust me, okay? I promise to help."

"I do trust you. I just don't want to see him suffer any more than he already has." It felt good discussing Noah's situation as equals. It was nice to be included in the plan for once; Noah had always left me out of the loop.

"You will stay close to me, okay? I do not know what can happen where we go, but it is more safe with me and not alone."

"I can fight. I know how to take care of myself."

"Yes, I know this. You are the very stubborn chick." He sounded so grave when he said it this time, like it was cause for concern. He brought us back to the chateau, where Noah was able to stand on his own again, although he still didn't look too good.

"You can fight?" Gianluca asked him and reclaimed Rozalin's pendant.

"Uh-huh," he answered without looking at either of us. "Just keep the kid from blowing his load in one shot again so it's one less thing to deal with."

"I do not understand?"

"Nothing, Gianluca. I know what I'm doing. I learn from my experiences." I quoted Noah's own line from the other day back to him. "Why don't you tell us what Vance gave you to stop the invasions, since we're all one big team now?"

"When we get there you'll know," Noah said and stretched, tossing another empty bottle of blood so that it shattered on the marble floor.

We watched the world fly by like a giant movie screen against a backdrop of an infinite void. Places Gianluca hadn't been or wasn't familiar with were darkened over until we passed through them. It made my stomach churn at points when the window to Earth would suddenly zoom out to miles above the ground and then back in to a single shadow below as he got his bearings. He utilized every bit of shade available to travel, from an individual person, to a bird, plane, or building. This twisting and turning rollercoaster ride across the world certainly wasn't for the faint of heart, but it soon ended with our arrival in Japan.

With Noah's guidance, Gianluca was able to track down the mountainside Kyoto temple where this had all started. It was morning when we reached our destination. Sunlight filtered through the foliage where we hid. The temple grounds comprised several buildings and each was a sight to behold. It was a completely different aesthetic from anything I had studied so far. Some structures were made with very bold coloring, yet their wooden designs were delicate. It was a striking contrast to the Roman artisans' use of heavy stonework. The domes, rounded arches, and intricate geometric embellishments of the Roman style were also absent here. Instead, smooth, simple lines were present in everything from walls to roofs and wove together to form a more beautiful bigger picture.

A vibrant red pagoda was striking against the bleak winter sky. Not even the light dusting of snow could contain its brilliance. Was it magic or sheer genius in craftsmanship that allowed this place to remain standing for so long when it had been made entirely with decorated woods?

"There." Noah pointed to the three-story pagoda I had been looking at. "Around there is a cave a few hundred feet underground. It was sealed off after the Muramasa was put down there, but I was able to get in traveling as mist through cracks in the rock."

"You can stay here, my friend," Gianluca offered Noah. "You are not in good shape to fight."

"I'm not your friend."

Gianluca was visibly displeased by Noah's rude retort, but opted to let it go and search instead for a way to the shrine below. It seemed a shame that we were here to bring war to such a place. I knew how highly Noah respected the culture despite his disregard for most other things. He would only have stolen from this place out of absolute frenetic desperation. I myself would rather not spread violence, especially to somewhere so peaceful. But I knew there was no going back. There was no possibility of a truce or forgiveness. What the spirits continued to do to the innocent on our side of the world, even when they had reclaimed the sword for a time, was inexcusable.

"We are here." Gianluca brought us to complete darkness. The only way I knew we were no longer in the Dark Depths was because there was a floor beneath us now. Finally I had a reason to use my psionic sonar. The cave felt no bigger than a small garage and there was some sort of podium in the middle of it, which must have been the shrine where the Muramasa had rested. I could tell the podium wasn't just a rock by its clean, symmetrical edges. Aside from the podium there was nothing else in the cave but stale damp air.

"Now what?" I asked.

The pendant in Gianluca's hand glowed as Rozalin flew out, giving the cave an eerie illumination.

"When does the killing begin?" she hissed. Someone grabbed my arm and I felt a sharp prick. It wasn't Rozalin, since she was the only one I could see, and Gianluca was never that rough with me.

"To stop the spirits we need to go to their world and seal them there from the inside," Noah said. "To do that I got this handy pre-made spell on a scroll. Just add blood, burn it at the location of the curse, and we're there."

Noah struck a match and lit the ensorcelled parchment on fire.

"What about Gianluca? He can't bleed, his skin will break the blade before it's cut." I didn't care that Rozalin didn't even *have* blood to add. Leaving her behind would be good news.

"Looks like he's out of luck." Noah smirked at him. "Thanks for the ride."

When the paper finished burning, Noah and I disappeared before the matter could be discussed any further. It felt like I was being turned to liquid and sucked down a very long drainpipe.

"I think I'm going to throw up," I said as I got to my feet after being violently spit out into yet another new world.

"Good. You were starting to put on some weight." Noah was up ahead of me, deciding whether to wield his dual *wakizashi* or the Muramasa.

"We're screwed without Gianluca. I know you kept that quiet on purpose, but we can't do this alone."

"We've gotten through worse without him. That guy's a douche. I told you not to get involved with him and now he's cozied up with both sisters."

"Why are they even working together?" I asked. "I thought Aurelia and Rozalin hated each other. Did you know about this too?"

"Nope. They're both using each other for something. Whatever it is, it probably isn't braiding each others' hair and talking about boys."

I hadn't taken much notice of this new world yet, mostly because of the lack of horrifying alien beings or immeasurable darkness. It was actually rather tame and bland. I was standing by a rundown wooden gate to a village and I had no idea if it was dusk, dawn, or midday. The sky was so overcast there was no sun and a wall of fog behind me obscured whatever was beyond. Only a river of yellowish water could be seen running along the edge of the dense fog.

"What is this place?" I asked. A better question may have been *when*. From the looks of it we were in a feudal Japanese village. There was nothing supernatural here at all. The village was bustling, but I wouldn't exactly call it lively. Everything here was so gray and drab. The villagers were downtrodden and shuffling through their daily chores. An old woman chasing two chickens into a pen in front of her thatch-roofed house was the most action this place had going on.

"Yomi or Huángquán. It's the Eastern Underworld." Noah squinted into the distance to scan the area.

"They get to have their own?"

"Yeah, Yomi is the Shinto land of the dead. Believe in anything long enough and it just may become true."

"That's dangerous. All religions can be right at the same time?" Gianluca had mentioned the "old gods" of Rome, but I figured he had been referring to a symbolic transition of faith. I didn't think he meant there were actually other deities out there besides *the* God.

"I guess." He shrugged. "People create religions, religions don't create people. They all start to blend together based on people's collective beliefs. Some die off. Maybe we're just imagined, too. Who knows."

"People *do* think supernaturals are just a dream on Earth, yet they're willing to accept that those things exist on other planes."

"Humans don't like to deal with reality until they absolutely have to." Noah began walking down the dirt road that ran through the middle of the peasant village. "Anyway, we have to find the shrine here in Yomi to place this seal Vance gave me. Show some respect and don't bother anyone here or break anything. These are the souls of people at rest."

"I was expecting something more grandiose for a final reward." It didn't seem to me that any of them were aware they were dead. They still went about the same mundane lives they must have led back on Earth. I guess they just stuck with what they knew and kept repeating it for eternity.

"You get what you give."

There was some inconsistency in space and time in this world. We had been walking for a while and passed several streets of meager shacks and their residents, but when I looked back the entrance to the village was only a dozen yards away. I counted the paper lanterns hanging outside the homes as a guide. Four lanterns between me and the gate. We passed two more lanterns, so I checked behind me. Still four lanterns.

"Uh, Noah? Are we trapped here?" I had the feeling that if I ran for the exit I would never reach it.

"Quiet." Noah shushed me as two samurai approached from the opposite direction. In the distance, a single mountain peak reached above the thick clouds. Maybe that was their Mount Olympus.

The samurai walked right past us like we weren't there. I would have thought we stood out enough to cause some alarm with the guards, but no one here seemed to realize our presence.

This must be a first for Noah.

"Why don't you super-speed around to find where we need to go?"

"Because it won't matter. Most of my speed comes from warping time around me, but there's no time here to manipulate."

I flew up into the clouds to try and get an aerial view, but no matter how high I went, when I looked down I was only a few feet off the ground.

"Stop trying to take the easy way out," Noah called up to me.

"You're the one who taught me to fly in the first place."

Our bickering was quieted by the sound of someone singing nearby.

Chapter Nineteen

"What's that song?" I flew next to Noah and looked around for the source.

"Who cares? Just keep moving."

"I'm going to find out. It's kind of strange someone is singing a lively tune in a place like this."

"Don't wander off, dipshit."

I headed toward the singing anyway. The voice was a girl's, tiny and unassuming, yet the song was bewitching. I couldn't understand a word of it, yet the more I heard the more I wanted to hear. It was happy, at least I thought it was. She could have been singing about mass suicide for all I knew, but it drew me in.

Near some broken-down merchant stalls was what I guess you could call a tavern. It was the size of a closet, and that was being generous. That was where the singing came from. I peeked in to see three men sitting at one of the few tables in the building, ogling a Japanese girl on a stage. She was no more than fifteen or sixteen, a pixieish little thing. She was barefoot and in dirty rags and had her hands folded in front of her. When she sang she kept her eyes down, only occasionally looking up nervously. Her song never seemed to stop, but I wasn't anticipating an end either. She shifted uneasily on the dusty wooden stage. She looked like she was close to tears the whole time she sang. Her demeanor didn't really fit her upbeat rhythm.

Some patrons shuffled in past me to watch the show. Nobody was eating or drinking, but maybe that was beyond their mockery of life. I found myself mouthing the words even though I hadn't a clue how to speak the language in the first place. The people that had just entered were doing the same thing. Their eyes glazed over and they smiled as they swayed back and forth mimicking the girl's nervous movements on stage.

"You idiot." Noah's voice startled me as he grabbed my shoulder. When I turned to him I noticed there was a throng of villagers piling up to get a look at the girl singing. It was an endless sea of lost souls lumbering toward the tavern. They weren't hostile, but it was still a bit worrisome.

"Stop listening to that shit!" Noah barked. "She's leeching out the energy of everyone that hears her sing, including *you*. I can see it in their auras."

She started singing a little louder to overcome Noah's interruption. Her voice was shaky and unsure, but no one clapped or cheered her on for reassurance. The crowd just stared and swayed in a unified trance.

Noah dragged me out and kept walking. I waited for a lecture or some form of chastising, but none followed.

"Get your game face on." He unsheathed his *wakizashi* in favor of the Muramasa on his back. Up ahead, two of the three spirits blocked our path.

"Where's the geisha?"

"Keep an eye out for her and leave these two to me," Noah instructed.

"Are you sure that's a good idea?" I asked, but Noah had already stepped up to engage them.

"Just trust me," he shouted back. I flew up to the roof of a shack so I could keep an eye on the area. The men circled Noah, but it wasn't long until the three collided. If Noah was going for the element of surprise, it certainly worked. Instead of his usual aggression he took a defensive stance and deflected the spirits' attacks with parrying. Now I knew why he'd chosen his *wakizashi* over the Muramasa; with two short blades he could cover his front and back with greater dexterity. He didn't strike back once, but managed to get the long-haired lightning spirit to stab his wind counterpart through the chest by turning to mist at just the right moment. Noah even got the wind spirit to punch his fist into the lightning spirit's electrified *katana*, which had been slowly chipping away at Noah's health each time it shocked him on a parry.

The two backed away to compose themselves after seeing that humiliating Noah through skill wasn't an option this time. I felt a sense of pride watching him best them at their own game. It was bothering me that the last member of their group had yet to show her face, but our goal wasn't to fight them head on.

Noah took cover as a slew of lightning bolts struck from the sky. A tornado ripped through the street, exposing his hiding spot. The wind spirit was unaffected by his buddy's electricity as incorporeal air, but when he turned back to physical form to strike Noah he could be hit. Noah used this by purposely getting sucked into the vortex as mist, then baiting the wind spirit to attack him by changing back. He threw a *wakizashi* into the wind with enough force to throw the spirit out of the tornado. The sword stuck in the wind spirit attracted the lightning, which fried him.

A rumbling in the distance didn't stop the fight. My question about the geisha's whereabouts was answered. The river at the edge of town overflowed and flooded the streets, toppling everything in its path. The geisha herself was nowhere in sight, but I was sure it was her influence over water causing this. I levitated Noah over the water with me as the rapids tore apart the village.

We had nowhere to go and our luck was getting worse. The spirit of lightning called down more bolts that electrified the rushing waters and threatened to zap us out of the sky. I lost my telekinetic grip on Noah as he turned to mist to avoid being electrocuted. The wind spirit was nowhere to be found now, but a powerful gust sent soaked wreckage at me to try and knock me out of the air. There was no one I could attack to stop the chaos. The only one around was the lightning spirit, but he would zip across the water using pieces of debris before I could get him.

The combination of wind and lightning was too much at once. I tried to fly away, but was struck by lightning and caught in another twister that threw me into the water. I struggled helplessly against the electrified current, which slammed me against every stone and jagged piece of wood along the way. The nightmare ended with a tremendous pain in my chest as a splintered wooden plank got me right in the heart.

The water turned red from my blood as I kept trying to heal. It was too painful and disorienting to free myself from the fierce winds above and the electrified rapids battering me from below. Noah appeared and tried to help dislodge me, but he was fighting against the tide and his muscles seized up from the constant shocks of lightning. He endured everything he could to unsheathe the Muramasa and sliced through the wood. Once freed, he grabbed hold of me and the two of us sailed downstream.

"You have to throw us out of the water!" he yelled. I launched us up and out, trying to aim for anywhere dry. We fell through the roof of a house that hadn't been submerged yet. Neither of us moved.

"I don't think we can do this." I wasn't just being doubtful. There was no way we could combat these spirits, especially on their own territory.

"We have to get ... to the shrine." Noah barely managed to get up. "Then hope ... the seal ... Vance gave me still works ... when wet."

He gave me his hand to help me out of the rubble just as the waves came crashing through and destroyed the house. We were sent reeling again as lightning surged through our bodies and razor-sharp wind cut us any chance we got to lift our heads above water.

"Give me the seal and stay in mist form," I shouted. "I can't die. I'll get it there eventually."

Noah didn't answer. He looked like he was about to go unconscious, but fighting it. I held on to him, more for his sake than mine.

"I can do this," he argued. "I only need to eliminate one of them and this will be easy." I tried to fly us out again, but was shot out of the sky by more lightning. The glimpse I got of the town made it seem as though we hadn't traveled anywhere at all. We were in a perpetual loop without a clue of how to escape. I actually welcomed the tornado that skimmed the surface of the water and hurled us hundreds of feet into the air. At least it was something different for a few seconds, a new type of excruciating pain. Had Noah not toughened me up over the years I would never have taken such perverse optimism in a situation like this, but that was what kept me going.

Noah didn't let go as we whipped around the swirling vortex. I expected him to turn to mist; he was still conscious and could have. As everything went dark, I wondered if these were our last moments together. *As much trouble as he's put me through, it's still hard to swallow.*

I opened my eyes to see the water gone and Noah on his back beside me. All three spirits were present in the remains of the village. They had been joined by the peasant girl from the tavern.

"What happened?" I asked. "I didn't feel us land."

"I don't fucking know," he groaned. "But I lost the Muramasa and Vance's seal was destroyed by all the water."

Soot-black clouds gathered around a central point in the sky. None of the spirits were responsible; they were watching just as I was, and the girl had stopped singing. Her skin was luminescent when she was near the other spirits and together all four of them shone like beacons in the encroaching darkness. She had been one of them all along, stealing the last of these poor souls' life energy with her song as they tried to rest in peace. Our Eastern enemies' acts of malevolence weren't limited to outsiders after all.

Rozalin's laughter ripped through the air as she descended on the ruins, accompanied by crackling plumes of unholy fire and lightning. If she had made it here then maybe Gianluca could, too. In the meantime, Rozalin could provide the perfect distraction, allowing Noah and me to regroup.

"Fools! You challenge death herself to battle in the Underworld? I will claim this land and all its souls as my own." Rozalin's mad ranting wasn't getting through, but it was enough for Noah and I to make our escape. I could hear the peasant girl's song over the sound of Rozalin's shrieks and the elements clashing in a trial of magic. It grew louder by the second as she belted out the same tune as earlier. The song drowned out Rozalin's banshee wail as she fought to remain the star attraction. Soon the land itself pulsed to the songstress's beat, creating background music with claps of thunder and trembling earth.

"That little bitch is drawing energy from the whole Underworld and infusing her buddies with it." Noah was digging through the wreckage for the Muramasa, only stopping to glance up at the fight once.

That mousey barefoot girl wasn't so timid anymore. She had a big smile on her face as she raised her hands to the sky. Fire sparked from her fingertips, then traveled down her arms like a fuse. The girl burst into flames on a high note and was transformed into sentient fire.

"Why did it have to be fire?" I asked myself out loud as I helped Noah search. "It's always fire."

The other three spirits followed suit and transformed into living humanoid versions of their corresponding elements. Rozalin's dark magic didn't work against their new forms and her aggravation was clearly visible. She flew up and turned her attention to the souls that remained in the untouched portion of the village. By conjuring a miasma of corruption, she turned the inhabitants into reapers similar to those she had used against the spirits before.

"What a wonderful thing the soul is! Such unlimited potential and so readily available. To think the demons waste souls as meals. All it takes is a creative enough mind and a little magic to mold them to your will." Rozalin stayed out of range as she mused to herself and observed her thralls fight. "How I will writhe in sweet bliss at the joy of claiming this untapped land for my own! What would you simple constructs of aether have a need for in such a lovely place as this? Or was it them that created you with their prayers for salvation?"

"It isn't here." Noah slammed his fist through a fallen wooden support beam. "All of this is for nothing without that sword."

We were both running out of gas and the situation was hopeless enough to begin with. It was no consolation that Rozalin was our best and only line of defense, seeing as she would turn on us in a heartbeat. *If we defeat the spirits, Rozalin will take over Yomi and most likely become more powerful than we could hope to deal with. If the spirits win, we have no way to stop their rampage*, I thought.

"Noah, we have to leave. We're going to die here if we don't. We can come back with help we trust." I tried to pull him away and still be gentle about it. I knew how he must have felt with his plan crumbling around him.

"Then go, but I'm not leaving here without it."

"I'm not leaving you here."

"We'll get out of here and go back to Vance once I get the sword." He looked up at me with an expression I had never seen on him before. He appeared thankful that I wouldn't leave him behind.

"There it is!" I spotted the Muramasa sticking out of the debris. Of course it was in the worst possible location, right at the spirits' feet. They were busy fighting with Rozalin, but there was no way they wouldn't see us take it.

"Get ready to run," I told Noah, and willed the sword to me. Before it reached us the wind spirit took notice and used his gale-force winds to assault us with large chunks of debris, which the fire spirit then ignited.

"You're playing catch with the wrong person," I shouted at them. I suspended the flaming wreckage in midair and sent it back at them rolled into a giant ball. I knew it wasn't enough to do any actual damage, but it bought us a few seconds as they dispersed, along with the girl's singing. Noah grabbed me and the sword and raced for the exit. It felt like we were moving at his usual breakneck speed, but when I checked we weren't making any better progress than a lazy stroll.

"Where do you think you're going?" Rozalin laughed. She tried hitting us with dark lightning, but Noah evaded it just in time. "No one leaves. Your souls are mine, like all the rest."

The spirits joined in the pursuit and it seemed like we were the only ones bound by the strange time warp. They had no trouble catching up.

"We have to split up." Noah put me down. "I'll lure them away so you can get to the exit."

"No! We leave together," I insisted. He maintained his position on the subject and threw me out of the way before running off in the other direction. The spirits chased him and no matter how fast I went I couldn't keep up. I saw their attacks ahead as they tried to thwart Noah's escape. I knew he was already in bad shape and my heart stopped every time I saw another attack go off, sure it would be the one to do him in.

"Don't run." Rozalin rose from the shadows to block my way. "I'm sure we can work something out. I owe you for reuniting me with my dear sister, you know. I can travel anywhere in the Underworld, but on Earth —"

A cluster of loud explosions went off and Noah's body was thrown into the air. He was struck from the sky by lightning and disappeared in the black smoke of another explosion.

"NO!" *I won't lose someone else. I can't.*

I flew right through Rozalin and headed toward the spirits in a rage.

"Gaius isn't here to help you. He has abandoned you to prove yourself to him!" she screamed. "Prove yourself to the darkness! And when they are done with your body, your soul will be *mine!*"

I tore the land up from under us, meeting them head-on with a tsunami of earth. I looked everywhere for Noah's body, not wanting to admit to myself that I should probably be searching for ashes instead. The spirits burst through the ground and converged on me. Their immaterial bodies weren't directly affected by my powers, and neither was Rozalin, who watched from a safe distance. I would have to be more creative.

I raised two slabs of earth beside the fire spirit and smashed her between them. The other three leaped into action, but I was no stranger to pain. The earthen coffin began to melt around the intense heat, but with enough pressure ...

My body endured the wind and lightning, and even when the water focused into a narrow laser and cut into my skin I didn't give up. I was stronger than I had ever thought. The slabs of earth had turned to molten rock, coating the fire spirit and hardening with her trapped inside as I applied more pressure.

They didn't expect me to roll out of the way in time for the beam of water to hit super-heated rock. I had been getting them used to attacking me without thinking about a moving target. Trick them into learning your pattern and then switch it up unexpectedly, just like Noah had done that night at Castile's.

The water let off an incredible amount of steam as it cooled the pressurized liquid rock. The spirit inside was trapped, fused to the core in what was now a tangible statue of herself. I smashed it to pieces in the blanket of steam. That was one down, at least for now.

The other three spirits reverted to their normal forms, unable to remain pure energy without their fourth companion. I knew I had to take care of the geisha next before she disappeared and summoned the same flood. She hid behind the prismatic shield that I had yet to be able to break on my own. *What's built can be destroyed.*

J. Armand

Rozalin decided now was her chance to be helpful again and began riddling the area with her power. The flames of her dark pyre hit me more than once. I knew our uneasy alliance was over. This fire burned differently and once it touched my skin it wouldn't extinguish. There was no way to put the flames out and it felt like I was burning from the inside.

The sky darkened as Rozalin defeated the lightning spirit. Soon the whole village was shaded by an unsettling eclipse. Something even darker than the blackness above was descending rapidly upon us. Rozalin cackled in glee and the flames on my arm went out.

The black mass caused a seismic quake when it landed on top of me, but it didn't hurt. I couldn't see anything, and then I felt the cool sensation of metal against my skin as I was cradled by someone's arms in the dark.

"Gianluca?"

"Yes, little one. I am here now." His voice had an unusual echo to it. Still unable to see, I felt around in the dark and could make out the shape of the helm he was talking through. "Are you hurt?"

"No, I'll manage, but Noah ..." I didn't want to finish that thought. "Rozalin turned on us."

"I know. I hear everything when I come to find you." The shadows cleared around us so I could get a good look at him. I wished I could see his face. There wasn't an inch of skin showing anywhere. His armor was imposing and nothing like him as a person. There were no horns, or skulls, or anything demonic about it, but it made him look even larger

331

and the way the shadows bent and swirled around him was unnerving. The armor looked impossibly heavy to move in, and from the cracks in the ground he left it was amazing he could move at all. But the design was sleek and contoured to his muscles in all the right places. There was even a chainmail underlay of matching obsidian texture and a short waistcloth that moved like real fabric.

The last two spirits turned on him after he set me down and walked up to face them. His footsteps shook the ground as he advanced.

"Gaius! You are just in time! Break their bodies and let us claim this land in the name of the new Nether Lords!" Rozalin cheered.

"Surrender to the dark." Gianluca held out his hand and opened a tear in space that began sucking everything in around it, including light itself. The spirits' attacks were repelled by his armor without effort until they were dragged away by the vacuum. I felt my shadow anchor me as Gianluca maintained the black hole. Yomi began collapsing in on itself and soon Rozalin's laughter turned to screams for him to stop as she struggled to get away.

As more debris cleared I saw the glint of a blade. It was the Muramasa, and next to it Noah's scorched body was stuck against the foundation of a building.

"Gianluca! Stop!" I shouted. He didn't hear over the noise of the world imploding and I couldn't move from my shadow. I reached out and summoned Noah to me, along with the sword. It was hundreds of times more difficult with the pull of the vacuum working against me, but Gianluca stopped as soon as he noticed.

"And to think I was almost starting to believe you had gone soft, Gaius." Rozalin flew back in to join us.

"That is not my name and this was not our deal." Gianluca spoke from behind the mask of his helm. Her pendant appeared in his hand. He crushed it to dust with his grip and bound her in abyssal chains that dragged her down through the shadows. "She will not bother us again."

"I told you she was evil." I opened Noah's mouth and cut my wrist on his fangs to let the blood run down his throat.

"I know this. I only need her to find this place. I plan to come alone, but this does not happen." His armor dissolved back into his normal clothes and he took a seat beside me.

Noah moaned and opened his eyes. I realized his bite didn't have the same pleasing sensation when he was unconscious. He dislodged his fangs from my arm and climbed to his feet.

"Thanks, Blood Bag," he said. "Didn't think you cared."

"Of course I care, you big idiot! You're the one who says we're not friends."

"Because we're not." His skin and broken bones healed up slowly as he smirked at himself in the reflection of the Muramasa's blade.

"I swear ... I still hate you so much sometimes."

Four shining balls of light streaked across the sky from the direction of the mountain and landed around us. The lights turned into the spirits in their full elemental forms.

"They came from the temple. That must be where it is," Noah said.

"Go." Gianluca stood and donned his armor. "I will hold them here."

"Are you sure?" I asked as Noah dragged me off. Gianluca formed a sword and shield to combat the spirits, but his blade passed right through them. Their powers were just as ineffective against him, however. He walked right through the explosions and storms without pause like he was on a scenic trip through the park. It must be terrifying to be the enemy of someone so immune. I could only hope these spirits were capable of feeling fear.

Chapter Twenty

"It looks just like the temple back on Earth, except for all the stone samurai patrolling it." I stood at the gates to the temple next to Noah after we had finally reached it.

"Vance said certain places overlap in other worlds. I didn't think it'd be this literal." Noah parkoured his way to the top of the red pagoda. "The actual temple is that big building over there. We just have to get through about a hundred guards."

"Only a hundred? Today is a good day." I flew up to sit with Noah. "Now might be a good time to share your plan."

"Don't have one. I've been winging it since we got here."

"That doesn't surprise me. It's been going so well so far, too. How are we going to seal them without a seal?"

"I still have the paper the seal was on. Most of the writing is gone, but I can write it again." He retrieved the paper from his pocket. It was burnt, crumpled, torn, and water-damaged from battle. The paper itself was a strip no bigger than a small index card. It would be a miracle if whatever magic it possessed still worked.

"Look at that." I pointed to the mountain; we were at its base now. A tremendous serpentine Asian-style dragon had been carved out of the mountainside, coiling all the way up to the clouds. The fins along its back made a staircase to whatever was at the peak.

"Come on." Noah dropped down as close to the temple stairs as he could get with me close behind. We instantly drew the attention of every animated samurai statue on the grounds.

"Ignore them and get this door open," he growled, straining as hard as he could against the giant golden doors of the temple, but they wouldn't budge. I put everything I could into opening them while trying to ignore the encroaching army. Even with both of us using all our strength we weren't getting anywhere.

"We're going to have to fight," I said, and waved my hand, shattering the first row of statues to rubble. That was much easier than I'd thought it would be, but their threat was in numbers, not individual power. "I'll take care of it. I don't think swords are going to do much against them."

Not to be outdone, Noah got one of the statues in a headlock and constricted his muscles until its head came off. The stone samurai didn't stop once decapitated, however, and swung wildly.

"Why would I expect any differently," Noah remarked, and tore off one of its arms with brute force. This still wasn't much of a challenge, but for that I was thankful. We cleared the courtyard in no time and went back to pushing on the door. Noah even zipped around the building to find an alternate entrance he could mist through, to no avail.

"Spirits only, I guess." I tried knocking down a wall as Noah stared at me, eyebrow raised.

"Behind you." He indicated the broken statues quivering on the ground. The pieces pooled in five locations and began to combine into larger statues with three heads and six arms, equipped with a stone *katana* or polearm in each hand. They were nimble for being over ten feet tall and made of solid rock. The amalgamated statues closed in fast, but were no more difficult to destroy than their singular counterparts.

"Stop doing that," Noah demanded from a perch on the roof. Two of the statues I smashed merged to form one gigantic one double the size of the last. Interestingly, none of them would approach the temple doors. *Not very effective guards if they won't go near what they're supposed to protect.*

"What's the point of —" I started to ask, when the golden doors creaked open. A ball of azure light flew out above us as we ran in. Gianluca must have defeated the long-haired lightning spirit on accident, allowing it to revive from inside the temple. He was only supposed to hold their attention, but this was the only way we'd be getting in.

"This isn't how it is on Earth," Noah said as we took a look around. It was dimly lit. Only some braziers and hanging lanterns lit our way in the two-story rotunda. A replica of the dragon coiled around the mountain outside was in the middle of the room. It felt like the statue was watching us, but no part of it moved upon closer inspection.

"What exactly are we looking for?" I asked. The temple interior was stunning. The architecture was minimalistic, using simple interlacing boards, but all the embellishments made this place extraordinary. From each side of the four corridors around us hung silk banners, each a different color: blue, red, black, white. *Just like the lights of the spirits.*

"I'll know it when I see it."

The banners all followed the same pattern. On the left of the archway was a banner depicting an animal; on the right was a banner with Japanese writing on it. The animals I could make out were a bird, a turtle, a tiger, and a dragon. The tiger on the white banner was exactly like the wind spirit's body tattoo.

"What do the banners say?"

"North, south, east, west," Noah answered, eyeing the dragon statue skeptically. "I knew I should've coerced Vance to come …"

"You mean bullied him." There was a breeze coming from the tiger hallway, causing the banner to flutter, except that this place was airtight. Otherwise, Noah would have been able to mist himself in. "I think we have company."

"I hate that guy," Noah said after taking note of the tiger banner.

"Because he's better than you."

"You wanna say that to my face?" Noah appeared in front of me, fangs bared, eyes narrowed, and muscles tensed to look intimidating. "Because we still haven't tested whether your head grows back after being cut from your body."

"Save it for the next time I'm nursing you back to life with my blood." I pushed him away with a smile and proceeded down the windy corridor.

One foot past the archway and the faint sound of singing froze me in my tracks. The same song from the peasant girl was coming out of the bird hallway.

"Split up. I'll take the guy, you go catfight with her," Noah ordered.

"No way. I can handle him. You take the little girl." I didn't want to admit my reluctance to be immolated again. Our arguing was interrupted as the rest of the temple came alive with the sound of running water and the Japanese string instrument, the *koto*. Then came the whinnying of horses from the dragon's hall.

"I get the turtle being water, but why are there horses with a dragon?" I asked. "I'm assuming that's the lightning guy."

"I don't know, just take the West Gate since you're not gonna listen anyway."

"Uh, which one is that?"

"The tiger. Now move your ass before they get the chance to team up."

I ran down the tall corridor of wood columns and paper lanterns to a glaring white light at the end. After passing through to the other side, I ended up on a windy mountain. A steep cliff replaced the hall from where I had just come. This wasn't the mountain outside; it might not even be Yomi, or Japan. I was on a grassy plateau by a large encampment that looked suspiciously similar to the abandoned Buddhist one I had stayed at with Noah. The only difference here was that it was far from abandoned.

The sun had just finished setting and the bald monks in their red robes closed the gates to the settlement. Whatever power was working to create this illusion wasn't trying to fool me into believing I was actually there. I could tell from the hazy, mystical atmosphere that this was more like a projection by someone trying to show me something.

I walked around, unnoticed by the inhabitants as they filed into their homes to retire for the night. After some time a man crept from the shadows and along the perimeter wall. I watched as he opened the gate a crack and snuck out, leaving the gate open behind him. I followed for lack of anything else exciting to witness, but wasn't too impressed when I tracked him all the way down the mountain to a small town where he stopped at a tavern to drink. It was a bit odd seeing a monk get hammered, but not odd enough to deserve a fabricated dream sequence.

In the candlelight at the bar I got a closer look at the monk; it was the wind spirit. He wasn't nearly as buff and his head was shaved, but it was definitely him. Time sped forward while he finished one drink after another, until he was facedown on the bar. It was almost sunrise when he staggered back to the settlement.

I trailed the spirit back as he stumbled along the mountain path. I could see another bright light coming from the encampment. As we drew closer, I realized it was coming from a roaring inferno that had engulfed the peaceful monks' home. Raiders on horseback finished off any survivors and pillaged their food and meager possessions. Unarmed, the spirit rushed in to stave off an attack on a helpless elder as best he could, but both met a swift end by the sword.

The horrible vision ended and I was returned to the temple. The room I was in was filled with rows of repeating banners hanging from the ceiling. In the middle was an enormous tiger statue lined at the base with candles and half-burned incense.

Those spirits were regular people once? Like the undead? Like me?

There was nothing else in the room and it seemed a shame and unnecessary to destroy the statue, so I went back to the rotunda with the breeze at my back. Noah was just leaving the bird's corridor when I arrived.

"What did you see?" I asked.

"Nothing useful." He was more frustrated than apathetic by the tone of his voice.

"Didn't you get a vision?"

"Yeah, big deal. I don't care about their life story. I want to trap them here forever so they'll leave me alone."

"Are these spirits actually undead of some kind?"

"No. They don't have an aura, so no soul."

"Rozalin called them 'constructs of aether.' What does that mean?"

"I have no idea," he snapped as he looked over the dragon statue again. "It sounds like magic crap Vance would know about. I need to find some central shrine. They're being summoned by something and I need to know what if I'm going to use this seal."

"They're being summoned by the Muramasa, aren't they?" I asked. "The vision I saw of the wind guy showed him as a human monk. He snuck out and left the gate to his camp open, letting in raiders that killed everyone. If that sword is evil or linked to Hell somehow, maybe these spirits are people who have sinned and were turned into these forms to serve whatever is in the sword."

"They're being summoned by the temple itself. There has to be some shrine or something here that connects the four of them for me to use the seal on. This is the temple of Seiryu, Azure Dragon of the East, also called Qing Long or Meng Zhang, depending on when and where in Asia you hear the legend. It has nothing to do with Hell and the sword isn't as old as the spirits."

"Then maybe the answer is in that hallway." I pointed to the dragon hallway. It was likely the lightning spirit's room if the turtle meant water and was related to the geisha.

"I'll take the dragon. You head to the North Gate with the turtle so we can cover both."

"We have to hurry. I'm worried about Gianluca." Time was different in this world, but it still had been a while since we separated. I knew he was strong, but no one could go on forever.

"The more they wear each other down the better it is for us in the end," Noah said as he walked off. "He's next on the list."

"You're not hurting him! He's helping us and ... I like him." It felt weird saying it out loud, especially to Noah.

"Like him?" he scoffed. "The guy commits genocide and that turns you on? You're about as fucked up as Aurelia at a fraction of the age. And I know I've told you about exposing your weaknesses by forming relationships."

"He didn't have a choice. He was manipulated and enslaved. I'd think you would know what that's like, Noah. He's doing everything he can to make it right and I believe him."

"We'll see."

"I never told you this out of respect, but before Vivi died she admitted to me she wanted to be with you." This might get my limbs cut off, but maybe it was just what he needed to hear. "She loved you and she didn't think it was a weakness. Vivi didn't want to see you suffering alone. She wanted you to be happy, and blamed herself that you weren't. I know you cared for her too, but you aren't doing a damned thing to honor her by going around saying love and friendships are weak and unnecessary. You can still be strong on your own when you're standing beside someone else."

I was poised and ready for him to come up behind me and cut something off, but he just walked down the hall without a word. I waited a minute, wondering if I had done the right thing by telling him. I wanted him to be happy. I felt that he, like Gianluca, was a good person on the inside, regardless of past actions that were out of his control. Vivi may have been the only one ever capable of getting through to him, but hopefully happiness wasn't forever lost for him.

Water rose up to my ankles as I walked down the turtle hallway. I was getting too tired to fly above it, so I sloshed my way through to the sound of the *koto* playing beyond a black cloud. On the other side of the dark fog was a gorgeous sunny day. I was standing in the middle of a pond where koi and turtles brushed against my feet. A woman sat beside the pond playing the instrument I had heard. She was easily eight or nine months pregnant and practically radiant.

The scene appeared to be on the grounds of a large Japanese estate, maybe owned by a feudal lord. Past the paper sliding doors behind the woman was a tatami room where an unfriendly looking man in heavily decorated samurai armor, sans helmet, watched her. I couldn't distinguish if this woman was the geisha we had fought. Her robes were grey and tan with longer sleeves and she wasn't wearing the white face paint or any makeup at all. She was a bit older than I had thought, maybe in her mid-to-late thirties, but her age only added to her dignified appearance.

Time sped forward until it was night. The woman was going into labor in the tatami room, assisted by a midwife and a much younger handmaiden. I looked the other way. Childbirth and anything connected to the medical realm still made me uneasy, despite all the gore I witnessed daily on the battlefield.

The samurai stood by the koi pond in the moonlight, waiting for what must have been his child's birth. There was no sound as the midwife finished her work. The only crying was from the woman in labor. The midwife wrapped up a bundle of wet blankets and carried them out, shaking her head. The handmaiden approached the samurai, but had second thoughts and scurried away. He went in to comfort his wife with a hand on her shoulder, then drew his sword. I knew it wouldn't change anything, but I yelled for him to stop as he plunged the sword between her breasts.

The man showed no emotion as he cleaned his blade in the pond water until he let out a scream at what he saw in his reflection. His wife's face stared back up at him with the same blank expression he had worn when killing her in cold blood. The samurai couldn't control his panic and grabbed a torch from the wall, lighting the house on fire before fleeing into the night.

The illusion faded and I was in a room lined with black silk banners, featuring a statue of a turtle with a snake wrapped around its shell. This information was interesting and explained who they were, but it still left the question of how they had become malicious spirits.

"What was yours?" I asked Noah back in the rotunda.

"He was one of the Eight Princes of China."

"Who?" Castile had said something about a fallen prince when the lightning spirit attacked that night, but there was too much going on for it to register at the time.

"Read a history book. It doesn't matter, it's not gonna help us."

"What about the door? It has all the animals on it from this side." The golden door we had come in from was plain on the outside, but inside was an elaborate mural of the four beasts in their cardinal directions. The dragon statue in the middle of the room, which I had thought was looking at us, was actually facing the door.

Noah didn't respond, probably feeling stupid that he hadn't figured it out himself. He took out the paper the seal was on and poked my finger with his *wakizashi* to draw blood.

"What the hell? Why me?" I complained. I knew it was out of spite. He wrote out three symbols in kanji, then dabbed wax from one of the candles on the back and stuck it to the middle of the doors.

"That's it? Really?" I asked.

"It should be. This paper was from one of the books that he used to ward his safehold from us. The writing specifies what's to be sealed."

"How are we going to be sure this works?" I had serious doubts that a piece of paper was all it took to stop something as powerful as those four spirits.

"We have to kill them so they revive in here again, but they shouldn't be able to get back out. Unless Vance is fucking us. Then I'm going to break his stupid face."

"Okay, but how do we get back out? Only the spirits can open the doors," I said. Noah looked at me like I was the stupid one and pushed on the doors. They didn't open. "Great plan. Now *we're* trapped."

Noah pounded on the door while I sat and watched. Whenever the spirits came back we were in for a world of pain. We'd be trapped in here with them for eternity. The only other option we had was to hope Gianluca could hear us and bring us out through the shadows. I yelled for him until I started to lose my voice, along with my hope of ever seeing Earth again. Noah, of course, wasn't willing to ask for help. He lay down and stared at the ceiling.

"How were we supposed to get out of here without Gianluca?"

"Don't know. I'm sure if Aurelia wanted me back bad enough she probably would've sent her sister to find a way."

"You were planning on staying here, weren't you?" I had a sinking feeling that I didn't want the answer. "This wasn't about the sword itself. You only wanted it as a bargaining tool to trade it back for sanctuary away from Aurelia."

"I don't need sanctuary. I can handle myself. If they wanted to play nice in exchange for the sword I might be willing to listen, but it's not like I'd go far if they killed me anyway. This *is* an Underworld and I'm already halfway there being undead and all."

"It's the people who say they can handle themselves who really can't. Let me help you."

"Help me with what?" He laughed sarcastically.

"Freedom. You're willing to kill yourself for it, but not accept help."

"I don't need your help. Anything worth doing is meant to be accomplished alone."

"That isn't true, Noah. Vivi may be gone, but you still have a friend that cares about you as much as you try to push him away."

"Maybe he should take the hint."

"Why keep me around, then? Why take the time to teach me and jump in when you think I'm in trouble?"

"So you don't end up like me."

The lights in the rotunda dimmed even further until we sat in total darkness. Something grabbed me by the leg and dragged me across the floor. *Please let this be Gianluca, and let him be all right.*

Chapter Twenty-One

My sight returned along with the noise of battle and the fire spirit's song. I was on my back outside the temple, where Gianluca was fighting off all four spirits and the stone samurai army with army of his own shadow knights. I couldn't see his face behind his armor, but I knew he was running on fumes. His movements were sluggish and his shoulders slumped between swings of his obsidian greatsword.

This was it, the final push. Stopping them here would put an end to our spirit troubles if the seal worked as planned. I rushed in, only to be tackled back to the ground. A wave of fire passed overhead narrowly missing me.

"Th-thanks?" Noah was on top of me, blocking the flames. He turned to mist and dissipated without saying anything back. I flew more cautiously this time to Gianluca and cleared away the statues. By compressing them into stone spheres I was able to prevent them from reforming for a while. I smashed the fire spirit between the spheres to defeat her the same way I had earlier and quiet her singing. With the loss of their fourth, the spirits returned to their more human form. Noah didn't waste time ambushing the gale-force monk with the Muramasa across his throat.

My eyes were glued to the golden door as the Nether knights surrounded the water spirit and ended her with a trip to the shadow realm. Gianluca's blade was parried by the lightning spirit's *katana*. Gianluca overpowered him, cleaving down through the *katana* and then the spirit himself.

"Come on," Noah mumbled under his breath, watching the door with me. The wait was agonizing.

"I hear them. I can feel them in the shadow." Gianluca broke the uneasy silence. "They cannot pass the door."

"It works!" Noah cried in elation. "It fucking works! I'm so happy I could stab Vance for making me doubt him."

"That's it? It's over?" I tried holding back my screams of joy until I was absolutely sure, but for Noah to be celebrating was a good sign.

"Yes, I will make sure," Gianluca said. He removed his helmet. Chains of darkness sprang up from the shadows and covered the temple from every angle. "It is inside too. They cannot take the paper away."

I couldn't describe my happiness. A single piece of paper had just ended a war that had claimed so many lives. Maybe this was what Noah had planned from the start, maybe it wasn't. But now he had the key to his freedom in his hands. Even when the spirits were presented with the peaceful option of taking back the sword, the anger that carried over from their past lives drove them mad with violence.

"Come, little one." Gianluca called up to me, smiling the warm smile I had missed seeing behind the armor. "We go now."

I flew down, still exhilarated from our victory, right into Gianluca's arms. I hovered at eye level, smiling back at him. Before I could let myself hesitate any more I grabbed his armor and pulled him toward me until our lips met. Our embrace gave me a feeling of pure bliss like nothing I had ever felt before. I closed my eyes and held his face in my hands, feeling along the coarse stubble as his soft lips locked with mine. We ran our fingers through each other's hair and continued kissing for countless minutes. It was sweet, tender, and most of all *passionate*.

I had been afraid of nothing this whole time. There wasn't any awkwardness between us; it was fluid and natural. Every subtle move we made anticipated the other's. We flowed together like we had done this a million times and it only got better with practice. Nothing else was important, not where we were or who we were. My senses were all on him and I didn't care otherwise. I felt accepted and safe in his arms, and I never wanted to go back to living in fear of something so good. I would remember this moment forever. It was transcendent.

"This is the best prize," Gianluca whispered to me in his deep sexy accent. He pressed his nose to my cheek before kissing it and squeezing me closer to him. The steel-hard armor softened back into regular clothing so I could feel his skin. I kissed his palm and then his lips before realizing we had forgotten someone.

"Where's Noah?" I asked. Gianluca located him atop the pagoda where he was looking out over the village and brought us to him.

"Sorry," I apologized.

"I ain't even mad, kid." He turned to us, ready to leave, and clutched the Muramasa tightly. "I've got everything I could ever want."

He wasn't smiling, but there was an expression of hope in his eyes I had never seen before.

"Then, to home!" Gianluca announced.

"Gianluca, where are my clothes?" I shouted from the hotel bathroom. I had just finished taking a shower and my clothes had gone missing. "I know you can hear me in there if you can hear me from two worlds away."

I wrapped a towel around my waist and went to see what he was up to in the room. I wasn't really prepared for what I saw. Gianluca was lying on the bed in black underwear he must have seen modeled in a store. The sight of his chiseled body was enough to make anyone lightheaded; every muscle was sculpted with perfect symmetry and definition. It was the first time I had seen him like this and the sight was certainly a welcome surprise. I had guessed he was fit and had the body of a very well-built Roman soldier, but he was more like a Roman god carved from olive-skinned marble.

He looked up from a book he was reading, his grin turning from sheep's to wolf's. "Very nice, but I think it is too much?"

"Funny, but it's not gonna be that easy!" I noticed my clothes sitting on a chair that I hadn't left them on. "What are you eating? Is that ice cream?"

"*Gelato?*" He looked down at the big tub next to him on the bed. It was big enough to be behind an ice-cream counter.

"Where did you get that?" I couldn't hold back from laughing at him as he ate from a giant ice cream tub in his underwear while reading a stolen history book.

"Eh ... I do not understand."

"You stole that, didn't you?"

"Sorry, my English ..." He shrugged and went back to his ice cream. "Maybe in *Italiano?*"

"At least share it with me." I got on the bed and lay next to him. "Hm, if you say it in Italiano, then maybe. Okay? '*Gelato.*' "

"*Gelato,*" I repeated with a frown.

"No, sorry. This is not very good. Maybe you practice sometime and we try again." He was trying to be very serious and took another spoonful.

"Gianni!"

"Oh, I am Gianni now?" He put down his ice cream and book and curled up with me.

"You have enough nicknames for me. I figured you needed one."

"I like it." His lips found their way to mine again and, feeling a little adventurous, I let my hands travel the smooth curves of his abdominals. "I have something you will like more than a *gelato*."

"One step at a time, Gianni, we only had our first kiss yesterday."

He reached into the shadows of the wall behind the bed and pulled out a stack of three white boxes. "For you." He presented them to me. As if things couldn't get any better between us.

"I can't accept that." I was smiling ear-to-ear and dying of curiosity to see what was in the boxes, but too humble to take them from him.

"Yes, you must," he insisted and opened the first box for me. A very expensive-looking white sweater was wrapped in tissue paper, looking like something the Blackbournes would have had.

"Gianni —" I couldn't say more than his name without sounding giddy, so I let my kiss do the thanking instead. It was taking some getting used to expressing and accepting my own emotions, but I was loving the journey. "This was really nice of you, but you can't steal for me."

I checked the price tag and was shocked to see the sweater alone was worth more than my first car.

"Stop, you are so stubborn. It is not stealing. I pay with the money." He opened another box for me with an even more expensive white jacket. "You will not let me make you the clothes, so I must buy them."

"I won't let you make them like yours because I know you can see and feel through them. I don't think I like the idea of you looking under my clothes and touching everything like that just yet."

"Even the normal clothes have the shadow under them for me." He grinned roguishly.

"Gianni!" My protest turned into a fit of laughter as the shadows under the towel I was wearing tickled my leg.

"Okay, I will be good. I will promise to you."

I rubbed the faux-fur hood of the jacket against my face in admiration. "Where do you get the money from? Stealing the money doesn't count."

"Always the stealing. I am not the thief. Gianni is not a bad man." The third box contained a pair of designer jeans and underwear. I imagined him selecting this stuff in the store and had to wonder how he knew my size so well already. "I read this is worth very much money, so I find the place to trade."

He pulled out Ancient Roman coins from the shadows to show me. They were in near-pristine condition, something that no human collector or museum on Earth would have ever seen. A handful of these could be worth hundreds of thousands of dollars. Gianni was as ingenious as he was attractive. It also made me feel a lot better about accepting his gifts.

"Put on the clothes." He kissed my hand. "I want to take you to a place."

"You have good taste for someone who slept through centuries of fashion," I said after changing in the bathroom. "I'm noticing a pattern with all the white. I'm surprised you didn't pick black."

"It is to match your skin. In my Roma the very white skin like you is the most beautiful. Only the very rich person can stay this white because he does not work in the sun like the farmer or soldier. They make the statue in the white stone like a marble, in Latin it is said 'alabaster.'"

"I always just called it pale. Alabaster sounds so much better. Everything sounds better when you say it."

"Come, little chick. We will go to see *our* Roma now." He created his usual clothes and took us through the shadows to the Colosseum. I hadn't thought about going back, but this time would be different. I hoped.

It was a bright sunny day. The air was crisp and clean, and I felt cozy in my new clothes. It wasn't as crowded here as it had been on our previous visit.

Gianluca hooked his pinky around mine playfully and looked away, pretending he wasn't doing anything. I made my move and took his hand.

Like all the other couples around us, we were holding hands.

Thoughts of Gianluca trumped even the Colosseum, which was little more than a backdrop for me. A few curious or unkind looks made my anxiety flare up again, but the strangers' expressions faded from view as quickly as they did. We were all that mattered.

We sat together in the stands, looking out at the ancient amphitheater. Gianluca put his arm around me and nuzzled his face past the fur of my jacket hood to sneak in a kiss on my neck. My stomach still filled with butterflies any time we touched. It was magical. I surprised him again by kissing him back and pulling his arm around me.

Two skinny teenage boys kept looking over their shoulder at us and whispering to each other. I didn't let it get to me. I thought of getting up and moving, but I had every right to be here and express myself the same way as all the couples did.

"I think they are with envy." Gianluca spoke into my ear.

"You always say that." I squirmed, not from embarrassment, but from the feel of his facial hair tickling my earlobe. "It doesn't bother me. Not this time."

I stopped paying attention to the boys until a few minutes later I noticed the two of them fidgeting. Then something amazing happened. One of them finally grabbed the other's hand and held it. They were trying to be discreet by hiding the coupling under their coats, but I watched the whole thing happen. The boys moved closer to each other as inconspicuously as possible until one kissed the other on the cheek with lightning speed that would make Noah envious. They looked around to check if anyone noticed, then smiled back at us with beet-red faces.

Gianluca and I smiled back at them. They talked among themselves nervously, and then came over to us. The one who had initiated holding hands spoke in Italian to us, which Gianni translated for me. The only thing I caught was a "thank you" at the end.

"He say they are being in love two years, but do not show anyone because they never see it until us today. They are very thankful."

I was touched and suddenly felt more powerful than I ever had. And that was saying something coming from someone who could lift a car over his head with his mind. I had judged them as incorrectly as others did me at first. It was the best feeling being proven wrong.

"Be proud of who you are," I told them through Gianni's translation. "Nothing can stop you when you love yourself."

They shook our hands and walked off together with big smiles.

"This is a very strange world," Gianni said after they left. "Why love is a bad thing to some people? I do not understand, but I am happy to help the change."

"Me too." I rested my head on his shoulder as the sun moved across the sky over the Colosseum. A group of Chinese tourists passing by pulled out their phones in unison to listen to a ringtone. At least, I thought it was a ringtone. The tune was eerily familiar and kept going.

I got up to look over their shoulders at their phones. They were all watching a video of someone named Kamiko Yamamoto, "Japan's Hottest Songbird."

The tourists started to sing along. I had no doubt the tune was the fire spirit's song, and she was the one singing on the video. But the song was different, and so was she. The song had been remixed into a techno rave trance beat and her hair was dyed yellow-blond, with the rest of her done up like a modern-day pop star.

Her song pumped throughout the Colosseum, but it wasn't coming from just the cellphones.

"Hey, a live concert!" someone shouted from a lower tier of the stands.

"Gianni!" My heart pounded as I looked down at the roped-off staging area. The fire spirit, Kamiko, was belting out the new version of her hit soul-stealing song with a tremendous captive audience. Everyone, including security staff, had the faraway dreamy stare as they listened to her sing. Hundreds of cellphones played the background music.

Gianluca wasted no time and jumped over the railing to confront her. He donned his full suit of armor on the way down, throwing away the slim possibility of keeping this under wraps. The tourists thought it was all part of the show as she nimbly dodged and danced between Gianni's sword strikes. He tried swallowing her into the dark abyss, but she just reappeared to even louder cheers from the crowd, who thought it was some preplanned illusion act. It wasn't until the sky started to rain fire at her command that they realized this was more than pyrotechnics.

I saw the teenage boys separated in the crowd as people trampled their way to the exits in sheer terror. The oval tiers of the Colosseum were turning into rings of fire, trapping the tourists. I couldn't use my powers here and let people see. I shouted for Gianni to stop so we could flee and take the battle somewhere else, but he was either too focused or too angry to listen.

The intense heat melted the supports of scaffolding fastened above an exit. One of the two boys we met earlier was directly underneath, but no one was paying attention in their rampage. I yelled for people to look out, then tried to get Gianluca's attention again.

"Fuck it," I shouted to myself. I was going to wind up being outed someday anyway and I'd rather it be on my own terms. It wasn't as though I had led a peaceful life up until that moment, anyway. I froze the scaffolding and tons of falling rock in the air before they could crush anyone. For a brief moment I thought maybe no one would notice I had done it, but the guy with the creepy black and grey eyes kind of stood out even in this chaos. I moved the debris to the center where Kamiko was performing, hoping to hit her, but no such luck.

Now people really noticed me. In typical human fashion, the word spread like the plague throughout the Colosseum to people who hadn't even seen me themselves. Some screamed, others ran. I wanted to think their fear was because of the fire, but to be honest it didn't make any difference.

I looked back as I flew down to Gianni. The teenage couple was reunited, openly holding each other in the mosh pit. One stared in horror at the demonic visage floating in the sky, the other in wonderment at the idyllic saint that had rescued them. I wasn't going to win everyone over, but they were safe and I had opened at least one mind.

Kamiko danced about singing to the entrancing beat. Her evasive footwork antagonized Gianluca and I until she decided her show was over and left the scene in a burst of flame. Her taking us both on without her friends and in our world was cause for serious alarm. This siren spirit had been posing as human to use her song on unsuspecting fans. The Muramasa stole blood and she stole souls. It was the perfect combination for evil as their group exacted their vengeance on the world that had wronged them.

"We have to get to Noah," I told Gianni. "They're going to go for the sword." Without another word, Gianluca brought us to the ruins of what had been Noah's residence on the chateau grounds in France. I started to lift away the remains of the building to find him when Gianluca stopped me.

"Here." He pointed to a dark corner where the dust hadn't settled.

"You just missed them. They got the sword and left after three of them trashed the place." Noah's voice spoke from the cloud as he reverted from the mist he camouflaged himself with. He was in a deathly state again. His puncture and slash wounds were covered over by burnt skin. "Aurelia bailed to leave them to me."

"I will go to their lands," Gianluca said to me. "I will not stop until they do not come back. They disrespect Roma, the people, and you."

"I'm coming with you," I told him.

"No, this is more danger than before. I will not allow it," he protested and held my face in his hands. "You are important to me. Stay with your teacher. Help his wounds and build his home. I am the soldier and I will fight."

"I'm not giving you a choice. You can't do everything on your own. Even you aren't that strong. There is more than one soldier in an army. If you don't take me with you I'll find my own way there."

"Just take the brat. I'll deal," Noah said. "He's not gonna do what you tell him to. He never does."

"You're important to me too, Gianluca. I'm just as passionate as you are about fighting for what you care for."

"I will take you." He gave in with a sigh.

In a flash of darkness we were back at the temple in Yomi. The chains Gianluca had used to bind the temple were broken. The village had been rebuilt and the dead roamed the streets again like nothing had happened. It took no time at all for the spirits to be alerted to our presence. Kamiko's song was nearly deafening. The background music bled through the atmosphere itself.

"It's coming from the mountain," I said. "They're luring us into a trap."

"Be close to me. I do not want you hurt." Gianluca brought us to a cliff high up on the mountain where the four spirits waited in human form. Kamiko had ditched the peasant girl act and was in her modern earthly appearance. Her long blond hair was decorated with feathers, and she wore a flowing fire-red sundress.

"I give you a chance to stop this. No more war," Gianluca shouted to them. To make sure they understood he forged his sword from the shadows and threw it on the ground between them. The spirits didn't waste any time and leapt for us while we were unarmed.

Gianluca responded by causing his weapon to detonate in dark energy, taking out all four spirits.

"I have a bad feeling." As he said that, the four lights of the spirits streaked across the sky from the temple and shot past us into the clouds above the mountain. The sword reformed in his hand and his full body armor materialized around him. The mountain itself shook under the effects of a powerful earthquake and I started to have the same bad feeling as he did when the clouds parted.

Chapter Twenty-Two

"Are they trying to drop a meteor on us?" I tried to discern what the giant sand-colored rock was that peeked from the clouds. There were two holes in it like caves, but the closer the rock got the more they looked manmade.

Gianluca covered me in shadow armor, but I reminded him my powers wouldn't work through it and I'd be useless. The meteor, or whatever it was, moved so slowly that we could walk out of its way. The earthquake grew in magnitude as the stone carving of the dragon along the mountain began to break free.

"You've gotta be kidding me." I peered off the edge of the cliff to watch the dragon carving shake the stone from its scales and reveal its natural sandy color. The holes in the "meteor" above weren't caves, but nostrils. Gianluca and I stared up into the face of the titanic dragon, trying to wrap our heads around what we were seeing.

The dragon let out a thundering roar and the cliff beneath us crumbled. I flew off to get a better view of the mythical beast. Its mouth could have fit an apartment building and each fang was the length of a city bus. Its talon-tipped hands, which were tiny by comparison to the rest of its body, were each the size of a small house. Its entire body seemed to stretch on for miles as it uncoiled itself from the mountain.

Gianluca grabbed me through my shadow and gripped me by the arms.

"I will send you to Earth. Wait for me there. It is too dangerous." He spoke firmly, but with concern.

"No! There's no way I'm leaving you to do this alone." Our disagreement was put on hold as the dragon's tail sundered the earth between us, creating an enormous chasm in its wake. Gianluca animated the tail's shadow. Inky chains shot up and ensnared the tail in the now tar-like substance of its shadow.

The dragon roared once more and breathed fire at its own tail to free itself. The breath turned the chasm into a gargantuan pit of flame, but was not effective in burning away the shadow bindings. I didn't know what I could do to even start inflicting damage on something of this scale. Noah had taught me to observe my enemy until I found an opening. That was my only option at the moment.

Gianni bound the rest of dragon's body back to the mountain with its shadow. The fight would be much easier if this giant couldn't move, but things were never that simple. The dragon electrified the length of its entire body, breaking through the shadows. It thrashed its tail free and knocked boulders away like toys. I yelled for Gianni to get away, but it wasn't like he could miss something that size coming toward him. He was struck with the full force of a direct hit from the tail. I tried slowing its impact, but it was just too big.

When the dust settled I saw Gianni standing strong behind his shield. Anyone else would have been liquefied into a fine paste by such a blow. I still didn't know what I could do. All I wanted was to rush in and attack, but just one of this dragon's attacks would have been more than my regeneration could handle.

It flew up and began circling the mountain like a halo. The clouds were sucked in around its body. Thunder and lightning filled the sky, and then came the wind and rain of a catastrophic hurricane. I was sent spinning out of control in the punishing winds and struggled to rejoin Gianni below. He grabbed me out of the air and hid me behind his shield. Whole buildings were uprooted and smashed into us. Bolts of lightning zapped him. Fortunately, the shadows weren't conductive, but the rain pooling at our feet was and the electricity shocked me.

"I want to send you home, please!" Gianni begged.

"Look out!" The dragon's tail came down through the hurricane again. Gianni teleported us through the shadows and left me in a safe clearing. I couldn't see where he went, but the dark clouds above became one solid mass. Enormous black tentacles the size of skyscrapers descended from the darkness and entangled the dragon.

I felt insignificant compared to a toenail of this creature. This whole battle was making me question the importance of a single man. I was so far out of my league it wasn't funny. Gianni's power was humbling and far greater than what I had imagined. I could picture the terror he must have inflicted in his past life. He truly was a walking apocalypse. Maybe it wasn't only the darkness, but his own mental fortitude that had helped him become so powerful.

The dragon broke free of the bindings again as I flew back into the fight. The remaining shadow tentacles turned razor-sharp and whipped back at the dragon, causing it to roar in pain. I could see Gianni riding on its back, plunging his sword between its scales, but something that big wasn't going to take much notice. Darkness spread from his sword and traveled between the scales, but I didn't know what that was supposed to do either.

With yet another ear-splitting roar from the dragon the dark skies opened and rained fire in a much larger version of Kamiko's performance at the Colosseum. The firestorm evaporated the water and mixed with the high winds, creating an enormous vortex of flame and lightning that engulfed the mountain. The dragon wasn't affected by any of the elements and its scales were nearly impenetrable. I saw my opening staring me right in the face, but it would take teamwork.

I called for Gianni in between dodging geysers of stone summoned by our serpentine foe. "I think I can kill it from inside," I yelled over the storm. "But I won't be able to get back out."

"You are crazy!" he shouted back.

"Yup!" I flew headfirst at the dragon and into its mouth as it roared. There was so much space inside the cavernous maw that it almost wasn't as scary as I had thought it would be. A ball of fire building deep in the back of its throat sapped some of my courage, but that was also my light at the end of the tunnel.

I closed my eyes. In the darkness I felt the strength I had in Gianni's world when I left the pain and self-doubt of my past behind me. I channeled that with the empowerment from my experience revisiting the Colosseum and the result was pleasantly cataclysmic. I pushed back the flames and let my heart and mind soar in tandem to fuel the disintegrating shockwave of psionic energy.

My consciousness faded. I gave everything I had in me and could only trust in Gianni now as I fell down the beast's throat in my weakened state. It was quiet until I felt something around me and realized I had already been transported to the shadow world. Gianni came through and was pulling me back out to Yomi with him. He extended one hand and tore the darkness from the mouth of the dragon once I was safely in his arms. The shadows swirled into an orb between us and the dragon as it was pulled apart from the inside.

"There was no darkness inside the beast, so I give it some to take away later." Gianluca must have meant the way he'd spread shadows through the dragon's scales. *These creatures of Yomi don't have blood or darkness in them. Is that why they're so hungry for souls and blood?*

Cracks appeared along the dragon's sandy scales and they began falling off. It roared a final time as the massive body crumbled and went limp and disappeared.

"Please be over," I said and looked around, barely able to stand on my own. The four lights, joined by a fifth yellow light, came down from the sky in front of us. The four spirits we were familiar with showed themselves. Someone new emerged from the fifth light.

It was a woman. Her skin glowed in a shifting array of colors. Every inch of her was covered in strange runic symbols. I couldn't tell if they were painted on or actually part of her body. She had the yellow eyes of a dragon and horns sticking up from her black hair.

"Never before have the living displayed such power, nor have they reached these lands with the intention of leaving." Her voice resonated in my head and every time she spoke I heard the faint tinkling of bells or chimes along with her words.

"You can speak English?" I asked out loud.

"She speaks to me in Latin," Gianni said.

"My natural tongue communes directly to the soul." Her voice and the light sound of bells were projected into my head again. "For I am guardian of these lands both heavenly and not. I go by many names in the mortal world, but you may call this image Kamakura, Empress of the East."

"We want no more war with you," Gianni said.

"You invade our lands and defile our temples for sport and not conquest? A greater insult I have not heard."

"Invade? Defile?" I questioned. "One guy stole *one* sword and you and your friends started murdering tons of innocent people. We came here to stop you."

"Our actions were not purposeless, but to right a wrong. Our eyes opened upon the desecration of our temple. The dead have never walked the lands of the East. Our gods would not allow it. But the West is rife with corpses not yet returned to the earth. They carry on as the living and make mockery of the universal cycle. Death is a transition, not a choice. The soul to the Underworld to be reborn, the body to the Earth to nourish the living."

"It isn't their fault," I argued. "Most of them are tricked into becoming undead and are only trying to live out what was taken from them in peace."

"We do not want a fight, but we will protect the innocent ones," Gianni added.

"That is not my judgment. Our duty is to protect the East, the world beneath, and the heavens above. All manner of threat will be dealt the same fate. Our concern was not with the West until we feared their encroachment on our lands."

"I'm sure there have to be some undead in Asia. It isn't just a Western thing," I said.

"We rid the living of our dead and return their souls to the afterlife."

"If you're so big on protecting the East, then why is she stealing their souls?" I pointed to Kamiko.

"The Vermilion Bird collects the prayers of our people to feed the slumbering Heavenly Ones. There is no harm to their mortal souls. It would be destructive to our cause."

"You're tricking them into worshiping gods that aren't even doing anything for them?" I asked. "That's not much better."

"You are both powerful, but cannot comprehend the work of such beings. It is not for you to know. The soul of the Dark One beside you is stained deep with the blood of his victims. A stronger being of flesh there may not be, but at what great a cost. I am impressed to see one ascend to a power reserved only for deities, but I mourn the loss of what makes you human."

She was making me angry talking to Gianni like that. If I had my power back I'd give her a real reason to mourn.

"I would die a hundred times for every life I take in my past," said Gianni. "I do not want blood. My action was mine, but my thoughts were not. This is why I fight today for the innocent. I will protect what I love."

"Your words are most admirable, Dark One. I can sense sincere truth in them."

"Please, why we can not work together then?" Gianni asked. "We have the same passion to protect the people. These undead, they do not all do bad things. There are many men living who are more evil."

"The world grows ever more faithless. The last decree of the Heavenly Ones before their slumber was not to interfere in mortal affairs. Should their hearts grow colder, their last remaining prayers would cease and cause us to starve. We must be mindful of the delicate balance between life and death if we are to maintain our existence. Only when the greatest darkness, one more than your own, reclaims the land can we hope to start anew."

"Wait ... Apocatastasis? That whole clean slate *tabula rasa* thing? There's really someone in control of more darkness than Gianni who's going to cause it?" I thought we had kind of skated by that when Gianni became good and stopped the Nether Lords.

"It is not a person, but an event, a predetermined cycle. No one person or deity is the cause. It is beyond even my own comprehension, but I sense it drawing near.

"The world is nourished by *chi*, or aether in your tongue. The four before you and myself are beings of aether. We do not possess mortal souls, but are gatherings of this aetheric energy ascended to sentience. Souls emit aether, as does the Earth itself, but it is the souls that wield the power to temper this aether into beings and effects as magic.

"The four guardians before you are not the mortals you saw in the temple below, but their memories imprinted into the aether to give it shape. Those mortals have long since ascended to Heaven, leaving behind the echo of their lives in these manifestations. They were chosen for their conviction to seek retribution in the afterlife: Kamiko Yamamoto, Vermilion Bird of the South; Chouko Minamoto, Black Turtle of the North; Hyun Jeong, White Tiger of the West; and Junjie Liang, Azure Dragon of the East.

"When mortalkind grows faithless the gods weaken without the aether from their prayers and fall to slumber. Without divine protection chaos will reign. The mortals will cry for help in the wake of their destruction and all will fall to darkness as it began. This time is soon. The mortals already forget who we are with each passing day and twist our teachings to abhorrent ends."

"If it helps in the long run, why not reveal yourself to the humans so they'll pray for you?" I asked.

"I am bound by oath as Guardian to the Heavenly Ones."

"You already kind of bent the rules with stealing aether through song. Why not help us stop the world ending when it happens? Wouldn't you benefit more from the immediate praise of billions for saving them instead of starting over when you might not come back?"

"Yes, your logic is sound, but I cannot act without order. However, I do not wish to fade from existence."

"Then we will protect you." Gianni stepped forward boldly. "Leave the undead, please. You did not hurt them before. When it is the time for the battle I will fight to save both our lands.

I change the world once, I can do it one more time. You and your heavens will be strong again and protect these people."

"A reasonable offer, and one with no worse outcome for my kind. You take a great burden so willingly with little reward. Very well. I accept your terms, Dark One. This is a first for a transcended deity as yourself to enter such an alliance."

"I am no god. I am just a man," Gianni answered and hugged me closer. "A man with love in his heart, for his world and his people."

"Return then as men to your lands in peace."

"Wait. I need that sword, the Muramasa," I said, eyeing it in Junjie's hands. "I can't leave without it."

"It must remain in our care," Empress Kamakura refused. "An insatiable demon resides trapped inside. It was these four guardians that set it there to stop its feeding on mortal blood."

"Those four guardians caused more trouble than the sword did in the short time we had it. I need that sword."

"Our duty is to protect," Kamakura insisted. "A demon is the greatest threat to both our lands. We cannot risk its release, especially when we have been weakened in the wake of battle. These lands are in peril now. Should one come to feast on the souls of the dead here we may not have the strength to stave off the attack."

"Then I will stay. I will protect this place until you are strong again in exchange for the sword," Gianni declared.

"A sword for a sword of greater worth is a fair trade, but again you burden yourself on our behest. I accept this trade, but what is the sword to you?"

"It's the key to a friend's freedom," I answered, then whispered to Gianni. "You can't do this. You don't need to. It could take centuries. The world could end before they regain their strength. We already beat them. We could just take the sword."

"It is my honor, little one. I send many to their death when they do not deserve this. It was not these people, but my action here puts them in danger. I will make sure nothing bother them."

"Then I'm staying too. I can help rebuild the place. It's perfect."

The lightning spirit walked up and presented the Muramasa to me with a bow. I kept my eye on him, still hesitant to give my full trust, and levitated it from his hands to my side.

"This is not for you, little one," Gianni continued. "I will be the stubborn one this time. You belong where it is beautiful like you. This place is all death."

"Am I going to see you again?" My happiness, which had persisted through battle, was now decaying.

"Yes." Gianluca removed his armor and spoke with his lips inching closer to mine. "I want to see this beautiful face many times. I am always close as your shadow and will come to be with you when I can."

Our lips finally met as we held each other in bittersweet bliss. It was every bit as magical as the first time. I already knew I was going to miss Gianluca, even though he hadn't left yet. He had opened my eyes, and my heart, to a world I had been numb to.

"Go now. I return you to Earth, but I see you soon." He spoke of leaving, but wouldn't let go either. "Soon" was an ambiguous term for someone who was two thousand years old and who inhabited a place where time didn't exist. My worry was that the years would slip away without him realizing, but I trusted him. For once, I trusted somebody again. "I want to see what you build when I visit. Make it nice for me."

"I will. I promise."

The shadows swallowed me and carried me along a gentle current back to Earth. I felt his hand hold mine one last time in the darkness.

"You look like shit."

"You smell like shit." Noah was right, I did smell bad ... again. My expensive white outfit was ripped up and turned to charcoal, and hung from my body. "What do you want, kid?"

"This is about what you want." He hadn't even turned around from his spot on the floor in the shambles of his room or he might have seen what I was holding. I tossed the Muramasa at the back of his head. He caught it without looking. "I know how much it hurts you to say thank you, and it doesn't look like you can take much more of a beating, so I'll just cut to the chase and tell you you're welcome."

He still didn't speak. While he stared at the sword in his hands I looked behind him. The little urn with Vivi's ashes, which had fallen to the floor during Hyun's attack, was cracked. It was a miracle any of it was left when most of the building around it was gone. There was a pile of ashes that Noah had been trying to gather up to place in another vessel.

He turned back around and sat with the Muramasa on his lap. "How'd you do it?" he asked.

"Gianni ... I mean Gianluca and I made a truce with their leader. We didn't give her much choice, but it worked out for all of us in the end."

"You're a lot stronger now. I almost thought it was someone important walking in here by the aura until I smelled you."

"Funny."

"I taught you well."

"I wouldn't go ahead and take all the credit, but you were — *are* — a good teacher."

"I'm only taking credit for the good things. The rest is your own fault." We stayed in silence for a minute. I didn't know what to say, or actually how to say it.

"Noah ... if you need help — not *help*, but —"

"You've done enough, kid. Now get lost before I get curious just how immortal you are." Typical Noah. That was the best I'd get from him, but I was glad I could help. "Dorian," he called back to me as I went to fly off. "Don't think this makes us even on those sunglasses."

Epilogue

Ah, Manhattan. How do I always wind up getting drawn back here? Maybe it was me, but something about the city that night didn't seem as ... *dark.* Not that Manhattan was ever without its shining skyline, but maybe the real source of light was that I could look people in the face again without fear. Or maybe everything just seemed so much less hopeless after fighting a dragon. Either way, I had a goal in mind. It was a simple goal, but it was mine, and not someone leading me around on a leash telling me what to do and how to think.

I turned on to West 138th Street with the Outsiders' old building in sight. It was condemned now; there were boards across the windows and doors, and a notice marking it for demolition. I was hoping someone would have returned, but was equally interested in something else inside. I went around back to find a less conspicuous spot to break in. There was another notice on the back door that I almost disregarded, but it was written out in colorful crayon.

"*Em O Em's relocated to 500 West 140th Street!*"

"Em O Em's"? *This, I've got to see.* I headed up to the address, not sure what I'd find. A sign above a storefront clearly indicated my destination.

"*Em O Em's Open for Business!*"

It looked like a restaurant or maybe a hotel.

"Hello and welcome!" A girl's jovial voice greeted me at the door.

"Emily?" I wasn't sure if what I was seeing was real. Emily, who was dressed very nicely in a full-length skirt with a blouse and cardigan and a ribbon in her hair, was standing behind the front desk of an inn.

"Oh! Dorian! It's so nice to see you again. Mr. Octavio said you would be visiting." She came out from behind the desk and hugged me as though we had known each other forever. The inn was very well decorated. It wasn't lavish or over the top, but charming and comfortable with a lot of cushions, carpeting, and paintings arranged like a home. Plenty of people were crowded into the building, but I couldn't really tell who were guests and who worked there.

"Octavio's okay? What is this place?" I asked.

"It's a bed and breakfast!" she exclaimed with overwhelming joy. "Isn't it great? We provide cheap housing and food for the local people, and those that don't have any money can stay here by working. No questions asked! We take in all kinds."

"This is amazing, Emily. How did you get the building?"

"Mr. Octavio had tons of money just sitting around in coffee jars. I convinced him we could put it to good use and he said I could have it if he could keep the cans. There are two churches nearby that help out a lot too, and we hold Bible study for them on Thursdays."

"Yeah, that sounds like him." After a closer look I was able to tell who was supernatural and who wasn't. It was so odd to see so many of both kinds working and living together, but it was heartwarming to watch. "Where is he?"

"He could be back at the old apartment. He said he wanted to get some things before they tear the place down, but he should be back soon."

"Do all these people know what you and the Outsiders are?" I whispered. "The humans, I mean."

"I don't know. They never asked. I don't think it matters though, does it?"

"No. I guess not." I smiled.

A face peeked out from one of the rooms down the first hall to our left.

"Hi, Emilia." I waved and breathed a sigh of relief seeing her stand there. That slippery old coot managed to save her life yet again. She gave me a wave back and came to tug on Emily's hand to pull her away.

"Can it be story time now?" she asked Emily. Now I got what the name of the place was for, Emily, Octavio, Emilia. Em O Em also spelled out "mom," which fit the inn's homey appeal.

"Okay, sweetie pie. Go pick out a book and I'll be right in."

I felt like I should tell Emily about William. It wasn't going to be easy. "Emily, it's about, ah, William." I strained to find the right words.

"He's passed on," she said. "I know. I saw it happen."

"You did?" I was a bit anxious about what her perspective would be.

"I wasn't there, but I saw it in my head. It's something Mr. Octavio is teaching me."

"That's cool." I checked to see who was listening. She was being so frank with so many people around. "I did everything I could."

"I know." She didn't seem sad, but also wasn't stoic. She was already at peace with it. "Only the Lord can truly save him. You tried your best and that's what counts. You always do."

"You barely know me, but I'm glad you think that."

"I heard how you saved the city years ago, and again this time. You saved me too. It really opened my eyes. I've learned to be stronger and turn a negative into a positive. The Lord doesn't test us so we'll give up. He tests us to make us better people."

"You're definitely doing a lot of good here. I'm really happy for you. You're a survivor and an inspiration."

"I'm just good at following directions, that's all. You told me what to do."

"It's time to make your own directions. It's your life now, undead or not, so enjoy it. Your choices are what will make you a good person, not what you are."

"Yeah, you're right! Are you going to be staying with us? I hope you will. I'm teaching Emilia how to bake for the guests, but it's a tad difficult to motivate her when we can't taste it ourselves."

"Emmy! Stories!" Emilia screamed from her room.

"Inside voices," Emily replied in a loud whisper.

"Sure, I'd love to stay. And I'm sure I can find some way to help out around here. I think I want to go visit with Octavio while you read."

"That's great news! I'll see you when you get back."

I left the warmth of the bed and breakfast and returned to the Outsiders' old haunt. There was no sign of Octavio inside, but that was no surprise. Knowing him he was probably out scavenging for cans somewhere. I checked his makeshift office, but most everything was already cleared out. On the floor beside his desk was the sepia photo of him as a human. I picked it up and stood there looking at it in the light of a broken window. It was a grim vision into what could have happened to me if I went through with the procedure of erasing my bad memories.

What happened to you, Octavio? What did you want to forget so badly that you were desperate enough to erase those memories and turn yourself into what you are today?

I put the photo on the desk and left to go up to the roof. The night sky was just clear enough that I could see a few stars alongside the moon, so I lay on my back to enjoy the view. And when I closed my eyes, I smiled as I felt my shadow embrace me.